W9-CNL-840

Praise for *The Demoniacs*:

"There is swordplay by moonlight, a veiled portrait of a legendary woman, as well as mystery in this, one of the author's most lively, suspenseful journeys into the past."

—*Saturday Review*

"This is a lively tale, colorfully written and certainly among the most entertaining mysteries of the decade."

—*The Times*

Other John Dickson Carr mysteries available from
Carroll & Graf:

Dark of the Moon
Deadly Hall
The Devil in Velvet
The Emperor's Snuff-Box
Fire, Burn!
In Spite of Thunder
Lost Gallows
Nine Wrong Answers
Most Secret
Panic in Box C
Papa Là-Bas
Scandal at High Chimneys

# John Dickson Carr
## THE DEMONIACS

Carroll & Graf Publishers, Inc.
New York

Copyright © 1962 by John Dickson Carr
All rights reserved

First Carroll & Graf edition 1989

Reprinted by arrangement with Harold Ober Associates, Inc

Carroll & Graf Publishers, Inc
260 Fifth Avenue
New York, NY 10001

ISBN: 0-88184-543-4

Manufactured in the United States of America

*This book is for*
*Renée and William Lindsay Gresham*

I wished to compose pictures on canvas, similar to representations on the stage.

—WILLIAM HOGARTH, *Anecdotes*

They now beheld a little creature sitting by herself in a corner, and crying bitterly. This girl, Mr. Robinson said, was committed because her father-in-law, who was in the Grenadier Guards, had sworn that he was afraid of his life, or of some bodily harm which she would do him, and she could get no sureties for keeping the peace; for which reason Justice Thrasher had committed her to prison.

—HENRY FIELDING, *Amelia*

# CONTENTS

|       |                                              |     |
|-------|----------------------------------------------|-----|
| I.    | *London Bridge Is Falling Down*              | 1   |
| II.   | *Mary, Mary, Quite Contrary*                 | 13  |
| III.  | *The Young Woman, and the Old*               | 24  |
| IV.   | *Swords by Moonlight*                        | 34  |
| V.    | *Dilemma at the Magic Pen*                   | 44  |
| VI.   | *Of Lavinia Cresswell in the Alcove—*        | 56  |
| VII.  | *—And Justice Fielding in the Parlour*       | 67  |
| VIII. | *The Crossroads of Perplexity*               | 77  |
| IX.   | *A Fiddle-Tune at the Waxwork*               | 89  |
| X.    | *The Bagnio in Covent Garden*                | 100 |
| XI.   | *The Way Back to Newgate*                    | 111 |
| XII.  | *Pistols above a Lake*                       | 122 |
| XIII. | *Midnight in St. James's Square*             | 134 |
| XIV.  | *A Challenge from Bow Street*                | 143 |
| XV.   | *The Demoniacs Begin to Assemble*            | 153 |
| XVI.  | *Life-in-Death*                              | 161 |
| XVII. | *Needles and Pins, Needles and Pins*         | 168 |
| XVIII.| *The Walker of the Crooked Mile*             | 179 |
|       | Notes for the Curious                        | 191 |

# I

## London Bridge Is Falling Down

THEY were approaching town from the Southwark side of the river. There was a flighty September wind, smelling of rain. Dusk had almost become night when the two-horse post-chaise from Dover, driven at the usual mad pace of such expensively hired vehicles, went clattering and bouncing along the cobbles of Borough High Street towards London Bridge.

That post-chaise contained two passengers, a fashionably dressed young lady and a fashionably dressed young man sitting in the corners as far as possible from each other; and these passengers bounced too. Carriages were equipped with springs nowadays, but they bounced all the same. The young lady seized at a window-strap to steady herself. In her low, sweet voice she whispered a hearty curse.

Instantly her companion, very haughty-seeming, became a drawling man of the world.

"Pray, madam," he said, "try to moderate your transports of joy."

"Joy!"

"I have paid for this luxury. They'll give me my money's worth if they kill the horses."

The young lady was in a passion and very near weeping.

"I wish *you* would die. I wish you would catch the smallpox. Lord, lord, I don't know *what* I wish. Not content with abducting me—"

"Abducting you, madam? I am taking you home to your uncle, that is all. Have you any notion in what sort of French establishment you were lodged?"

"I am quite well able to look to myself, I thank you. This sudden fear for my virtue—"

"Come, madam. I am not concerned with your virtue or any woman's."

The girl smote her fist against the glass of the window.

"No, you would not be," she said furiously and inconsistently.

"You are of the very sort and kind who would not be. My uncle paid you well for this, I daresay?"

"To be sure he did. Else why should I have risked my life? Yet you were frightened, Peg. Confess it."

"I will *not* confess it. 'Tis a monstrous lie. 'Paid, paid, paid!' Is there anything on earth you would not engage to do for money?"

"Yes, madam. Contrary to the humour of our times and indeed to my own principles, I would not love Peg Ralston for money."

"Oh!" cried the girl addressed as Peg.

And they looked at each other.

Here in Southwark, at a veer of the wind, you could already sniff the City-smoke rising in a palpable black cloud at the other side of the Thames. Here in Southwark, with most men abed at gusty nightfall, you could hear little except the crashing of iron-shod wheels on cobbles as the post-chaise flew towards London Bridge. Only a few fish-oil lamps, one supposed to be set burning at each seventh house but most of them unlighted, threw gleams into kennel-filth and gave them glimpses of each other's faces.

Miss Mary Margaret Ralston, a tall girl and very well shaped, again clutched at the window-strap when she made as if to rise. The tears in her eyes went deeper than mere rage; essentially, under her mannerisms, she was gentle and good-hearted and without guile, though she would have denied this and believed herself to be a past-mistress at all deceits.

Miss Ralston's eyes had irises of the true, rare, jet-black colour, vivid with glistening whites against a rose-leaf complexion and a strikingly pretty face. She sat muffled up in a travelling cloak, its hood back to show the straw hat with the cherry-coloured ribbon. No wig or powder disfigured her sleek light-brown hair; such fripperies were worn only by men in the year 1757. Yet her face was as heavily painted as usual, having a small black beauty-patch on the left cheek-bone. This unmaidenly practice, combined with such manifest bodily charms, had a strong if different effect on every man she met.

There was one reason why Mr. Garrick, a staid character but a shrewd man of business, had offered her the chance she craved at Drury Lane Playhouse. There was another reason why Sir Mortimer Ralston, when he heard of this offer, fell into a choleric fit for which he had to be bled. There was a third (and most understandable) reason for the feelings of young Mr. Jeffrey Wynne, now brooding beside her in the carriage.

'Rot her soul,' Mr. Wynne was thinking.

And yet his heart misgave him.

"Peg—" he began in a very different tone.

"Foh! Get away from me!"

"As you please, madam."

"And as though I had been in the least danger. That establishment at Versailles, into which you broke like a common thief, was none other than the school for the French King's private theatre."

"Your pardon, madam. It was none other than the school for the French King's private brothel. Madame de Pompadour keeps it as shrewdly as any bawd in Leicester Fields."

"Mr. Wynne, you shame me."

"Yes, madam. That is the true reason for these megrims of yours, and all the tears now. When I was surprised and set on by every servant in the cursed place, all ten of 'em, what could I do but throw you over my shoulder and run for it? Was it my fault if your skirts flew above your head and somewhat impaired your dignity at our taking-off?"

"Now 'fore God, Mr. Wynne!"

" 'Fore truth, madam."

"It was no ridiculous figure *you* cut, I suppose? I am as tall as you; don't deny it. I am far more brave than you. Foh! To shrink and run from a parcel of Frenchmen, more than half of them women!"

"I will run, madam, when the odds are even three to one. I will run with right good will, be assured, when the odds are ten to one. Peg, Peg! Pray use good sense."

"Good sense!" cried the romantic-minded Miss Ralston. To do her justice, she scorned good sense for herself as much as she scorned it for others. "At last I apprehend, Mr. Jeffrey Wynne, why you resigned your commission in the Army. Or else they would not have you; they cashiered you. Merciful heaven, should I ever have fancied myself in love with such a caitiff. To shrink and shiver like any silly woman. To flee from the likes of Johnny Crapaud."

Ungallantly Mr. Wynne extended his forefinger and shook it under Miss Ralston's nose.

"Now hark'ee, Peg," he said, with a slight roar in his voice. "It is well enough for all stay-at-homes to sneer at Johnny Crapaud. You don't have to fight him."

"Foh, for shame."

"We are cock-a-hoop today, we idiot English. When a poor devil of an admiral merely defeats a French fleet without destroying it utterly, our lords of the Sea Office must have him shot for cowardice on his own quarterdeck. That was folly, Peg; that many think it a scandal must be small consolation to the kinfolk of Admiral Byng; we may live to repent such heroics."

"Good sir," and she lifted one shoulder, "do spare me your philosophic discourse and your long words. Or keep them for my uncle Mortimer. *I* have no patience."

"None; you are too flighty and too desirable. I do not protest, in general, that so often you think and speak as a jackass might—"

"Oh, give me strength."

"Though you have wits enough, madam, when you care to use them. But I myself will not be transformed into a jackass, which is what you are always contriving. Have done with it."

"Go away," commanded a shivering Miss Ralston. "Your wig is awry; you are most horrid silly, and I hate you. Go away!"

"Peg—"

A lurch of the post-chaise threw them together. Instantly they both drew back into corners. Mr. Wynne folded his arms under his own cloak; Miss Ralston uptilted her pretty nose Each had hurt the other badly; each knew it, and was conscience-stricken. But Jeffrey Wynne would not retract a word; the girl had never learned how to retract. In their passion to behave as they thought they ought to behave, both la-di-da and powerfully stately, Mr. Wynne succeeded better: his long, sardonic face, green-eyed and sharply intelligent, matched his words as well as his thoughts.

And yet he spoiled the effect. He seized at the offending wig, a white bag-wig tied with dark ribbon at the back of the neck, and jammed down his three-cornered hat. Whereupon, catching her eye, with a bang he lowered the window on that side and thrust out his head as though wishing to be decapitated by the oncoming gateway at London Bridge.

That this whole mood changed in an instant was due to something he saw or heard. Coachman and postilion must have seen it too. A long whip cracked. The postilion swore.

"Jeffrey," Miss Ralston twitched round, "what's amiss now? What ails you?"

There was no reply.

Just ahead, where the Borough High Street opened out in a half-circle of shuttered shops and two tavern-signs on the right, loomed the dark mouth of a gateway in a squat tower with battlements. They should have gone thundering under that gate, out across wooden planks bolted together ten inches thick. For well over five hundred years, since the time of King John, the same stone bridge of nineteen stone arches had spanned the Thames from here to the foot of Fish Street Hill on the City bank.

Grown shaky in its old age, often gutted by fire from the City shore and repaired at heavy cost, it was lined on either side with tallish crazy-built houses whose heads almost touched and were shored up with horizontal beams to prevent them from toppling inwards on a crush of wheeled vehicles by day. Flood and ebb tides roared through its narrow arches for a fall of six feet between water-level above-bridge and water-level below it, so that to 'shoot' the arches by wherry became dangerous or impossible. For it stood sixty feet above the rapids, which claimed a score of drowned victims each year.

And now . . .

"Jeffrey dear, what is it? I vow I shall die of curiousness if you don't speak."

Mr. Wynne drew his head in from the window.

"Peg," he answered, "I have heard something I never thought to hear."

"Oh?"

"I have heard silence on London Bridge."

It was not precisely silence. The water still roared beneath the arches, as it had roared five hundred years ago. But he did not mean this, as she well knew. He spoke of the hive, the community, the bustle of folk who had lived and worked and died since King John's time.

"There does not appear," he said, suddenly with so odd a look that Peg Ralston peered at him, "there does not appear to be a living soul on the bridge. Or any light at all, except—"

"Hold, there!" called a voice in their path. "Hold!"

"Whup-ho!" said the coachman's voice. There was a hiss of the brake-shoe; the post-chaise swayed, clattered amid volleying oaths, and ground to a halt.

The tall girl bounced up, her delicate complexion flushed between excitement and alarm, and thrust her head out of the right-hand window as Mr. Wynne was again doing on the left.

At the entrance to the bridge, swinging a lanthorn, loomed a foot-soldier in high pointed grenadier cap with royal insignia. To Peg it meant only another of the swarming military. But the weather-faded red coat and blue braid, no less than buff waistcoat and breeches above high black gaiters, identified him to Jeffrey as being of the 1st Foot Guards, a regiment often quartered at the Tower nearby.

Hesitant, uncertain, yet as stolid as though under fire, the guardsman marched out and addressed Jeffrey.

"Sir," he said, "where d'ye come from?"

"From Dover. What does it matter?"

"Sir, d'ye lodge on London Bridge?"

"In a rat-hole like this? Is it likely? But what does that matter either?"

"Sir, this is Friday night. On Monday they'll begin demolishing all houses on the bridge."

"Demolishing—?" Mr. Wynne stopped short.

"By your leave, sir, I'd best fetch my officer."

It was not necessary to do this. A door opened in the gatehouse wall, emitting light as well as an officer whose single epaulet marked him as a captain. He was a stout young man with drink-pouched eyes but a reasonably affable manner, though he had risen from supper with a half-gnawed mutton-chop in one hand and a half-finished glass of claret in the other.

Jeffrey Wynne, without turning from the window, reached out and seized the girl's shoulder.

"Peg," he whispered, "I am acquainted with that officer. He must not see you. Crouch down! Draw your cloak above your head and crouch down. Don't ask why or debate the matter! Do as I bid you!"

Peg, breathing quickly, did not ask why; she never debated when there was something (often to her mysterious) which to him seemed so urgent. She overdid her part, actress-fashion, by yanking up the hood of the cloak, crushing her straw hat, and falling straight back against the cushions like a woman drunk or dead. But at least she obeyed instantly. The young captain, emerging a moment later into a glow of lanthorns and carriage-lamps, stopped and stared.

"Jeff Wynne, by all that's holy," he said in high pleasure. "Come, this is well met! What's the bother here?"

"Your servant, Tubby. There is no bother. I but wondered at the reason for a guard on London Bridge. Has the old song come true? Is it falling down at last?"

"Near to falling down, split my bottom," said Captain Tobias Beresford, with a comfortable belch. "To take away the houses will widen it for a press of carts and wagons that's got quite out of hand. They have no choice." He gestured up-river. "Westminster Bridge is too far away. Blackfriars Bridge, only a builder's dream and not yet begun, will be still further away. This old 'un, widened and with the weight of houses gone, may take years to fall." Abruptly he paused. "Come, Jeff, don't you know all this? Where have you been these months and months past?"

"I have been in France."

"Damme, my boy, you can't have been in France. We're at war with 'em."

"I am aware of that, Tubby. When have we not been at war with 'em? Yet I have been in France all the same."

"Oh, ay? In secret, like?"

"In secret, Tubby, and in search of someone who proved devilish difficult to find."

"Oh, ay." Captain Beresford looked vastly relieved. "You're about your old games, no doubt, as you used to be for the magistrate at Bow Street Office. Well, good luck. It's more than I have."

"But the people, Tubby—the people who live on the bridge. What of the people?"

"Well, what of 'em?" Captain Beresford demanded. "That's one cause we're here. They've had a full month's warning to take their goods and quit the houses. Most have gone already; you never heard such a wailing and taking-on, in especial from the old 'uns who say they're poor and have nowhere to go. If any are left by Monday morning, we're to turn 'em out with the bayonet."

"Is it so?"

"It is so, take my oath for it. But many of 'em come skulking back a time or two, to try if they can creep into their old houses and swear they must remain by right of possession. That's another cause we're here, to drive 'em away again, and a cursed nuisance it is. This fellow should never have stopped *you*, though; he's stupid. (You're stupid, fellow!) Good God, Jeff, what's the matter?"

Once more the damp wind veered, carrying soots and smudges. Jeffrey Wynne, casting aside his cloak, half opened the door as if he meant to jump down. The lantern-light fell on a long-skirted coat of plum-coloured velvet. Though of fine quality, it was far from new. At his left hip, beneath the skirt of the coat, swung a smallsword in a silver-mounted Morocco-leather scabbard.

"Tubby," he said, "near one of the openings in the blocks of buildings towards the far side—hard by Nonsuch House, I think —there is a print-seller's called the Magic Pen. An old woman, so very old you must have remarked her if you saw her, either lodges or did lodge above that shop. Tubby, is the woman still there?"

"Now how a pox should *I* know? I've not seen her. What concern have you with an old woman on London Bridge?"

"None." Mr. Wynne hesitated. "No true concern, when all's said. But once, in some sense, she served my grandfather when our fortunes were good. Besides, it seems a most barbarous thing to turn these people from their homes."

"She's an old servant, hey?"

"In some sense, yes."

"Well, the feeling does you credit. I'm a man of tenderness too, split my bottom. The pin-and-needle makers are of some use, I grant; there are ladies who come from as far away as St. James's to buy good wares cheap of the pin-and-needle makers.

But the others—pah! If any suffer loss or hardship here, 'tis the Bridge House Estate; they'll be out of pocket nine hundred pound a year in rents."

"That is all you have to tell me?"

"It's all I know to tell you," Captain Beresford answered in a huff. "Now drive on if you must, or stay and crack a bottle if you will."

"I much regret, Tubby, that I may not linger. Coachman, drive on."

"Stay but a moment more, Jeff!"

Captain Beresford moved his shoulders. Still holding mutton-chop and glass of wine, he glanced suddenly behind him, and then began slowly to turn round and round. The expression on his face was matched in the eyes of the guardsman with the lanthorn.

"If you'll not linger here, Jeff," he said, "then you'll not linger on the bridge either?"

"Why not? Is it forbidden?"

"Not by order, no. Still, I want no more of these odd noises by night; nor does the officer at the bridge-foot end. The men don't like it. If I was a cursed imagining fellow like you, which thank fortune I ain't, I could call this a cursed ghosty place and think things were walking. Hey?"

"It is full of dead men's bones, Tubby. You need feel no surprise if it be also full of ghosts. A sweet good-night to you. Coachman, drive on!"

The long whip cracked. Hoofs and wheels thundered on thick-bolted planks beneath the arch of the gatehouse; and then, as they settled to a gallop, beneath so many arches of timber between houses that echoes reverberated as though in a tunnel.

The young man sat down and brooded. Peg, immediately alert, assumed that fierce stateliness which so ill became her, and flounced to her own side of the post-chaise.

"If ever I despised you ere this, Mr. Jeffrey Wynne, it is as nothing to what I feel now. Why, pray, must I hide my face from that officer?"

"Tubby Beresford? Can you swear, Peg, you never met him? Or even saw him before?"

"I—I—to speak a truth, I can't recall. But I wondered."

"So did I. Tubby goes much into good society, and his tongue wags overfreely. Forget him now. More serious consideration must weigh with you when I deliver you to your uncle at the Golden Cross."

"At the Golden Cross?"

"For sure you know the Golden Cross Inn? Hard by Northumberland House at Charing Cross?"

"You said you were escorting me home!"

"Yes; you shall go home presently. Before that, however, your uncle desires to question you at some place remote from servants and neighbours in St. James's Square."

"Why does he desire to question me?—No, I insist upon knowing! I'll not leave off until you answer."

"To speak plain, then, because you have become damaged goods. Despite the fortune you inherit, it will not be easy to arrange a good marriage after this last adventure."

"Was ever, *ever* a woman made so miserable as I have been?"

"By whom, madam? You grow more fearful, to be sure, as we draw nearer the ogre; and I don't blame you. Sir Mortimer Ralston is not a good-tempered man."

"He'll forgive me; he always does."

"True. Take comfort. In his own fashion he loves you, and he will only question you. He will not, as others might, summon a physician or a panel of matrons for a more intimate examination."

"Oh, filthy!" There were tears of unhappiness stinging Peg's eyes again. "You are offensive. You are disgusting. I'll hear no coarse language, rot your soul; I would remind you I am a gentlewoman."

The wild gallop across the bridge had gone only a few yards before the driver reined in hard. These crazy old houses were built so close together that from a distance they resembled blocks of buildings with only a few open spaces between them so that a man on foot could walk to the rail of the bridge. In some places the road was twenty feet wide; at others it narrowed to twelve. Jutting first floors above the street, with metal shop-signs all acreak in the wind, closed in so tightly that a high-loaded dray could get stuck between.

And now not even the usual dim gleams showed from upper windows; the place, ill-smelling but not so bad as most London streets because of the river-breeze, was pitch black except where the light of a rising moon touched open spaces. It would have seemed dead without the clatter of their own passage, the unceasing current-roar; and, on the approach to Fish Street Hill, a thumping and jingling as great paddle-wheels supplied power for the water-works.

But they did not hear these things. Peg Ralston, for once in her life desperately honest, wrung her hands and wept under the ruin of a straw hat.

"And that you, you of all persons in this world, should tell me I am no maid! When it was you, and only you, who—"

"Peg, be silent!"

"Ah, does that stab your conscience?"

"Yes; I confess I am not happy."

"Jeffrey, if only you had been less cruel to me!"

"By this time, no doubt," said Mr. Wynne, "it has all become my fault."

"I do not say as much, or even think so. It was stupid and s-silly of me to flee from home; *I* own *that*. But I was so extravagant vexed with you that I scarce knew what I did. You vowed I had been abed with a dozen men in London. And now, I dare swear, you think it was a dozen men in Paris. And you'll tell my uncle so."

"Must it be repeated, madam, that your broad-minded views are no concern of mine? I could tell your uncle only where I found you. And he knows that already."

"He knows it? How?"

"By the smuggled letter I sent him, as we were both smuggled across the Channel. Incredible as it may seem, your conduct has troubled him."

"I am sorry! I repent of it!"

"Even if I wished, then, it could not be concealed that you spent some months in the school for King Louis's *Parc aux Cerfs*."

"Some months?" echoed the astounded Peg, leaving off weeping to cry out at the injustice. "It was a matter of scarce two or three hours."

"Two or three hours? Come, madam!"

"I swear—!"

"When it required months to find you? Such enquiries, admittedly, are not rapid in a country where at any moment the enquirer may find himself jailed or hanged as a spy. Yet you had gone nowhere near any friend or acquaintance in France. How did you live during all that time? Was it by someone's disinterested charity?"

"I took no charity; none was needed. I'll not deny that before leaving home I—I took a deal of money from my uncle's strong-box."

"Gad's life, this is still better! Sir Mortimer Ralston's temper must be sweet past all understanding."

"It was not truly stealing; is he not my uncle? And I was in that place at Versailles, I swear, but a matter of hours! I grew affrighted, as you guessed. I had swore to punish you; I was resolved to punish you; but I grew affrighted. Jeffrey, Jeffrey, have you no tenderness for me at all?"

"Well! I . . ."

"Don't you love me?"

"No."

Peg swept up both arms and clenched her fist in a last ex-
tremity of woe.

"So that now," she said, "I am to be haled before Uncle
Mortimer like any strumpet haled before a magistrate? Mrs.
Cresswell will be there too; that odious woman will be there,
who is nothing but my uncle's doxy and yet will take on the
most righteous airs and preach at me. I don't complain; no
doubt I deserve it. But you! That you should desert me too."

"How, madam? Desert you?"

"Yes, you will. Don't gainsay it. When you have left me at the
Golden Cross, it is in your mind straightway to take coach or
chair and return here to London Bridge. For you are minded
to visit an old woman who lodges above a print-seller's shop
called the Magic Pen. Is it not so?"

Jeffrey Wynne whirled round. "Peg, how the devil did you
know that?"

Momentarily all speech was blotted out by the thudding and
jingling of the great paddle-wheels, under the bridge against
the City bank, which pumped water to all London east of
Temple Bar. Then the post-chaise had crossed over it; it passed
St. Magnus's Church on the right, and went toiling up Fish
Street Hill for a left-hand turn at Greater Eastcheap. No guard
appeared. Nobody stirred in the street except an elderly watchman, one of the despised Charlies, skulking with pole and
lanthorn, under the red lattice of a tavern near the Monument.

"Peg, how the devil did you know that?"

"Is it not true?"

"True or false, how did you guess?"

"But I knew it; simply I knew it. How should I not know it,
since it concerns you?"

"Hark'ee, Peg, I'll not desert you tonight so long as there is
need."

"Then you do love me, don't you?"

"No, woman, I do not. But you are in the right of it; I have
every intent to return here as soon as possible. For I have come
to a decision."

"About us?"

"In the main, madam, it concerns the ghost of a woman long
dead, and a portrait in the green-room at Covent Garden. What
I plan is sheer folly, let's allow. It will lead to law-breaking and
may lead to murder."

*"Murder?"*

"And yet I am determined on it. Be silent, now, and try to entrust me! More lives than our own, I can assure you, will depend upon the occurrences of the next two hours."

## II

### Mary, Mary, Quite Contrary

"Good sir and young mistress," the landlord said heartily, "give yourselves the trouble of stepping down. You are awaited and welcome."

He dodged past the horses' heads as the post-chaise halted on the cobbles of the inn-yard, and opened the carriage-door. Jeffrey Wynne, adjusting his tricorne hat, swung out and jumped down to mud and straw on the cobbles.

A thick smoke-reek eddied in the yard, which had a railed balcony round all four of its inner sides. There were lights in little latticed windows off the balcony; they shone on the young man's sword-scabbard and the silver buckles of his shoes.

"'Awaited and welcome,'" he said in no easy tone. "Sir Mortimer Ralston—?"

"Nay, sir, I can't tell you his name. But a gentleman, doubtless the same, awaits you in my set of chambers called the Antelope, with the private parlour. He desires that you and the young mistress shall attend him immediately."

"In good time, landlord, in good time!"

"Under favour, sir," and the landlord made an agonized genuflexion, "he hath awaited you some hours. He said 'immediately.' There is a lady with him."

From inside the carriage came a noise of someone stamping her foot.

"Did he so?" enquired Peg Ralston's sweet voice. "And a lady, God's death."

Flushed and lovely, as tall as her companion but soft of body and with no great physical strength, she appeared at the doorway. She had thrown aside her cloak, to reveal a lilac-and-rose satin gown with skirt slightly widened by whalebone supports in an under-petticoat called a hoop; she was gulping back tears of fright which made her speak like this.

"I am filthy," she said dramatically. "That's to say, I mean, I am much travel-stained. I have not shifted my clothes these four days. Mr. Wynne, I'll not meet that odious woman until I am made ready."

"Landlord," said Jeffrey, "be good enough to escort this lady

13

to another room with a private parlour. Fetch her soap and water, if such be available."

"Sir, sir," moaned the landlord, "I am not certain that—"

"You have a pump, surely? Should all else fail, she can put her head under that. No, madam, I must not permit you to use more white-lead and rouge. You have too pretty a face to daub it like a juggler at Bart's Fair."

"Sir, has the lady luggage?"

"Now how should I have luggage," asked Peg, "when I was catched away in my petticoat? Did you hear this gentleman?"

"Sir, sir, but I must escort you and show you the way to the Antelope."

"I know the way. I can escort myself. Look to the lady."

A gold coin spun into the air, followed by another for the coachman and a third for the postilion astride the off-horse, causing Peg to protest against extravagance in terms that would have been strong if he had just dissipated a family fortune as a famous forebear had done. Then, as ostlers gathered round the carriage, he strode away across the inn-yard.

The Golden Cross, presumably so called because the tavern-standard outside its arch bore the sign of a white cross on a green background, faced towards the statue of King Charles the First. You could not see that statue from the yard, or see anything except the loom of Northumberland House with weather-vane and two stone lions. It was also the coaching-station for the west of England; a powerful smell of horses steamed in night air.

Jeffrey, cloak across his arm, went up an outside staircase to the balcony. He did not touch the leather draw-string at the outside door he was seeking. Instead he peered in through the window beside it.

The room appeared charged with emotion, yes. But it was not quite the emotion he had expected to find.

Two candles burned on the chimney-piece of a wainscotted parlour with a bare board floor. Behind a table in the middle, facing the window, sat a man who had been doing himself well at supper.

He was a big man of past fifty, muscular as well as bulky from a big paunch and a heavy jowl. His rich clothes, flowered satin, were spattered with stains of food and snuff; and he had on a great draggled bag-wig. Sir Mortimer Ralston wore a sword only through custom; he would often say, smiting his fist on something, that he didn't know how to use a sword and sus-pected few men could use one either. At the moment his red face did not seem so much ill-tempered as watchful and thought-

ful, his eyes moving sideways while he drank from a dropsical
glass goblet.

The emotion in that parlour, such as it was, flowed from a
graceful woman pacing back and forth at the fire-place with a
closed fan in her hand. Mrs. Lavinia Cresswell, widow, could
have passed for thirty anywhere except in the broad daylight
most fashionable ladies avoided.

Mrs. Cresswell was very handsome despite rather-too-pale fair
hair and a rather-too-pale blue eye. She was not tall. Yet she
had the true bearing, the true languid haughtiness, which Peg
so passionately desired and could never imitate. Mrs. Cresswell
spoke briefly to her companion; the onlooker could not hear the
words; but it was almost as though Sir Mortimer cringed.

'Now I wonder,' Jeffrey Wynne was reflecting.

It seemed to him that all his joints ached from the long jolting
of the carriage, and his head ached from the anxiety of months.
He watched them a moment more, thinking whatever thoughts
you may attribute to him, before he went softly to the door. Also
softly, so that the latch should not click, he lifted the leather
draw-string. Then he threw the door open.

The effect, on one person at least, was as though he had
thrown a grenado.

"How now?" said Sir Mortimer.

The big man surged up, his paunch all but upsetting the table
amid a clatter of pewter dishes. His mouth fell open. Much of
the ruddy colour drained from his face as he looked first at
Jeffrey and then past Jeffrey's shoulder. He had a deep voice, a
cellar-rumble and hoarse; but it cracked none the less.

"How now?" he said. And then: "Hell's death. You failed
after all?"

"Don't fear, sir. I did not fail."

'But the wench? Is she safe?"

"Quite safe."

"Why, then!" said Sir Mortimer, controlling himself as though
shamefaced. "Why, then!"

Mrs. Cresswell had turned away and was tapping with her
closed fan at the ledge of the chimney-piece. Sir Mortimer sank
into the chair, gulping so hastily at the goblet that red wine ran
down over his chins into the lace at his throat. It was some
seconds before he finished or spoke. The veins of his forehead
began to swell blue and choleric. He whacked the foot of the
glass on the table, and rose up again.

"Afeared?" he said. "Now who's afeared, God damme? Very
well: where's my niece? Where *is* the strumpet? Where's she
hiding? Fetch her out, young man, and I'll kill her. I'll kill
her, egad, and then I'll disown her. Fetch her out!"

"Sir," said Jeffrey, "I ask you to hear me."

"You do, hey? Where is she?"

"Sir, Peg is making ready in another room. For God's sake, sir, deal gently with her. For all her mighty pretences, she has suffered much in her mind."

It was Mrs. Cresswell who answered, turning round coolly from the chimney-piece.

"Indeed?" she smiled. "Before we have finished with her, I greatly fear, the dear girl will have suffered more in her body."

"If I may venture a suggestion, madam—"

"You may not. Mr. Wynne, might I ask your age?"

"I am twenty-five."

"Indeed. You are twenty-five." Mrs. Cresswell raised pale eyebrows. "From your mien and your fashion of speech, I had thought you perhaps a trifle more. But you are twenty-five. Therefore be pleased to speak when you are spoken to; not before."

"Madam—"

"There is another matter, Mr. Wynne. You have been of some service to us, or so I understand. Why did you perform that service?"

"I did it for hire."

"Good. I am rejoiced you should apprehend as much. But your usefulness is over; and so, I must regretfully mention, is our interest in you."

Suddenly Sir Mortimer clenched his first and smote the table.

"Nay, now, Lavvy . . ."

"My dear man, do you fancy *me* not devoted to your honour and your interest, if none else is?"

"Nay, Lavvy, I—I know it. But why be harsh with the boy?"

"Why be harsh with the girl?" asked Mrs. Cresswell.

Gently opening her fan, she advanced towards him with a pinkness on her waxy forehead and her upper lip lifted above a pale, prim, handsome mouth. Candlelight caught gleams from the gold-and-ruby pendant round her neck.

"Or do you fancy me deluded by your bluster, by this play-acting at being Squire Western in the tale by the late Mr. Fielding? I am not deluded. You will 'kill' her, you say? What will you do? How will you chastise her as she deserves, for having run away like this? Will you in truth chastise her at all?"

"Nay, Lavvy, be easy! She's my dead brother's child. I brought her up."

"Truly you did. That's evident in your speech and hers. There is good blood in your veins, no doubt. But you are a country bumpkin and so is she."

"Lavvy—"

"Saw you ever such cozening eyes? Such tricks and wheedles of a milkmaid to gull stupid men? You can't help bringing her up a bumpkin; you need not have brought her up a slut. Is she fit for the company of His Gracious Majesty at St. James's Palace?"

" 'Gracious Majesty,' is it?" shouted Sir Mortimer. "That tub-o'-lard booby who's not even learned to talk plain in English, and with no more wits than anybody else out o' Hanover?"

"Still a Jacobite, dear man? Still with schoolboy's love of the Stuarts? Don't tremble for your neck; these Jacobites are dead and done with. But do you indeed desire to see your loutish girl mingle in good society, as you say you do? Or must there be stronger means used to curb you for your own good?"

"Lavvy, Lavvy, I can't deny you anything. God's death, have it as you please. What's to be done with Peg, then?"

"She must be stripped naked and thrashed with a strap. Afterwards you will have her committed to Bridewell for a month on a charge of common harlotry. What's she to you, or you to her, when there are others who truly love you? And you need not flog her; I would not have it so; you are too soft of heart. My good brother, Mr. Tawnish, is below-stairs to render the service." Mrs. Cresswell swung round to Jeffrey. "*You* spoke, young man?"

"I did, madam."

"May one ask what you said?"

"I said, madam, that your good brother will touch Miss Ralston at his own risk."

"Indeed?" enquired Lavinia Cresswell, who was not impressed. "Have you met my brother, Mr. Wynne? Or his near friend Major Skelly?"

"I have not that doubtful honour."

"Nor are you *quite* an accomplished swordsman, I believe?"

"No, I am not. And I have no taste for heroics in any case."

"Again I commend you. Few fortune-hunters are so wise. Now where is this poor persecuted one? In what room is she skulking?"

"I can't say."

"You mean you won't say. Then I fear I must fetch her for myself. Or do you design to prevent me?"

"Not even that, madam. Yet a moment ago you made reference to a tale of the late Mr. Henry Fielding. Were you acquainted with Mr. Fielding?"

Mrs. Cresswell looked at him. Her gown was of cream-coloured velvet, with a pink sacque and wide lace double-sleeves from elbow almost to wrist; the ruby pendant rose and fell at the very low, square-cut opening of the bodice.

"I am a person of taste; it may be, not ashamed to shed tears at an affecting page. But his work is coarse and abhorrent, unlike Mr. Richardson's. That most moving and impassioned book *Clarissa*—"

"My question, madam, was not as to your literary pretensions. Are you familiar with him in another capacity? Or with his half-brother and successor, the blind magistrate at Bow Street? With those who most stealthily are called 'Mr. Fielding's People'?"

"I am familiar with blind insolence, at all events. May I go below-stairs, or may I not?"

"Be pleased, madam, to go below-stairs or to the devil."

"You will regret this," said Mrs. Cresswell.

The door opened and clapped shut. Two candle-flames jumped and undulated. A wind rushed over Charing Cross into the mouth of the Strand, through streets which one who knew them had described as being 'in a downright state of savage barbarism.' Perhaps it was not so different indoors.

"Sir—" Jeffrey began.

"You never thought, boy," said Sir Mortimer Ralston, "to see me like this. Confess it! You never thought to see me fall so low."

Throughout Mrs. Cresswell's remarks he had not moved from behind the table or raised his eyes from the floor. Now he lumbered out, half turning. His wig was askew. One white stocking, the left one, had slipped the buckles of his knee-breeches and tumbled down over a big shoe. And so he halted, peering red-faced over his shoulder in the firelight, like a gross and swollen schoolboy.

"I'm besotted with the woman, d'ye say? Well, damme, and what if I am? I can't resist her, d'ye say? Well, damme, and what if I can't? Am I the first man to be taken so?"

"Not the first or the last, if it were only that."

"As you are besotted with Peg. D'ye think I don't know you are? Only you hide it the better. I can't hide it. I'm a plain blunt man."

"Sir, you are anything but a plain blunt man."

"Ay?" demanded Sir Mortimer, with his natural colour and truculence flowing back. "You'd fathomed that, had you?"

"Something of it."

"How much of it? D'ye guess why I sent you on that cloud-cuckoo quest of Peg when I could have had her found and haled back a dozen times by a dozen men of mine in Paris?"

The cloak still hung across Jeffrey's arm. He thought of cursing to high heaven, of taking that cloak and hurling it on the floor in a gesture like one of Sir Mortimer's. But he only looked back.

"A dozen men of yours in Paris? Do you emulate Sir Francis Walsingham?"

"Who's Sir Francis Walsingham?"

"He is dead. Once, or so we read, he employed a legion of spies for Good Queen Bess."

"Ay; book-learning," snarled Sir Mortimer. "I respect it, mind; but there's a mort too much of it and too little hard sense. It was not for spying I put capital behind Hookson's the goldsmith's of Leadenhall Street. We've been at war with the Mounseers this twelvemonth and more. But bankers don't go to war; bankers get rich. Keep this to yourself, hark'ee; they'd drive me from home in my shirt, these people of fashion would, if they learned I had interest in trade. Still, there's my answer."

"Your answer to what? What did you send me into France?"

"Why, damme, because *somebody* must wed Peg. I design you shall wed her; who else? I've had a mind to it from the first, when I could make you prove your mettle and show yourself nothing of the cursed timid fellow you affect to be." He caught Jeffrey's eye. "Nay, now, don't resent it. I like you. If you're besotted with Peg, and she's still more besotted with you, now where's the harm in that or in my design either?"

"There is no harm in it. But there is a grave error. The error, sir, is that I won't have her."

"How?" cried the other, outraged. "You won't have her?"

"No, I will not."

Sir Mortimer lumbered forward, his shoulders rising and thickening against candlelight.

"Because she's no virgin, hey? I can't prove 'twas you first lay with her; the wench would spit on me before she said one word against you; but I've no need to prove it like a demnition lawyer. In any case, what's the small matter of a maidenhead in a gel with so large a wedding-portion as Peg? Is it her virtue?"

"No, it is not. This female virtue seems to me a much overprized commodity, and mysterious for the veneration in which they told it. To praise a woman because she has never exercised her sex is as though you should praise a man because he has never exercised his brains."

"Well, that's good sense. Don't say it so loud, mind; you'll have the whole pack o' parsons in full cry after us. But it's good sense, and what ails you?" Then Sir Mortimer stared. "It's not the rhino, is it? You're not too proud-stomached to take Peg's money, when any young man of family expects to mend a ruined fortune with a rich marriage and quite right of him too? For sure it's not the rhino?"

"No, it is not the money. At least—"

"Then what a fiend's name is amiss? Do you deny you love this wench?"

"In my heart I don't deny it. But I'll cut my throat before I wed with her or so much as acknowledge I desire to."

"Now, who are you, sirrah, to say what you'll do or what you won't do? *What* are you? Lavvy may be perplexed when you talk of 'Mr. Fielding's People.' I'm not perplexed. Mr. Fielding's People are the thief-takers from Bow Street, the scum who work in secret and betray robbers or murderers for blood-money. And you're one of 'em. Is there any scavenger worse than that?"

"Have a care, sir."

"Lord, lord," Sir Mortimer said tragically, "but what a generation of vipers we live among. Here's Peg would be a play-actress at Drury Lane, near the lowest of the low, save that I won't have it. Here's you a thief-taker, the very lowest. Here's both of you in love and won't wed, and would break my heart for a pair of moonstruck zanies."

"Your facts, sir—"

"Don't *you* speak o' facts, ecod."

"Your facts, sir, are incorrect. Mr. John Fielding at Bow Street has brought dignity to a magistrate's court at last, and dignity to his officers too. As for the playhouse: those two most chilly-faced and precious men of breeding, His Grace of Grafton and Mr. Horace Walpole, are both proud to boast they dine with Garrick at Hampton."

"Peg ain't Garrick, you young whelp. She's more like that other Peg, the Woffington woman, who fled the stage ere they hissed her off it." His tone changed. "Lad, lad, attend to me! There's not much time. At any minute Lavvy will—"

Sir Mortimer stopped suddenly, his mouth open and one hand at the gold buttons down his coat. Jeffrey nodded.

"Yes," he agreed. "At any minute, you were about to say, Madam Cresswell will return. You will cringe before her like a man in the pillory when they fling stones and dead cats. I mean no offence, sir, but what's amiss with *you?*"

"I can't resist the woman. I owned it. That's all."

"Under favour, sir, it is not all: though some months ago I thought it was."

"Well, damme, shall I neglect Peg's welfare at all times? She must move in good company, else where's the use of our taking a house in London at all? Lavvy Cresswell has the ear of Most Gracious and Fat-Behinded King George the Second, who's as much an impressionable widower as I am. That's true, and you know it!"

"It is also a part of the truth, granted. Yet you were never

over-impressed by good company. I have seen you pitch a baronet downstairs for saying half of what Madam Cresswell said.
What hold has this woman upon you? What threats does she
use to tame you? Or is it her good brother, Mr. Hamnet
Tawnish?"

" 'Hold'? 'Threats'?"

"Yes."

Sir Mortimer spoke after a pause.

"One day, boy," he said in a strangled voice, "you'll awake to
find yourself grown old. No longer so safe or assured of yourself at all times."

"I have never been assured of myself one tenth of a second.
I would to God I could be."

"No longer so assured of yourself, I say. Or so quick to think
and speak, or even to pen a liar in a corner. But will you see
Peg thrashed here, and then jailed on a charge that can be
sworn to at a magistrate's? Thereafter, when she's had her lesson, to be thrown to Hamnet Tawnish if he's still of a mind to
have her?"

"Thrown to Hamnet Tawnish?"

"You said you'd not met him."

"Nor have I. He is known to me by repute as a swordsman
second only to his crony, Major Skelly, and for other things besides. Peg? Thrown to Hamnet Tawnish!"

"Ay; there's the core of it. Who'll help her if you don't?"

"Upon your honour, is this true? With all the resources at her
uncle's command?"

"Lad, I swear . . ."

It was as though Jeffrey caught the echo of another voice.

"Yes," he said. "Peg herself swore to a great deal not long
ago. Sir, I will be gulled no longer either by you or by Peg
either. Thank you, no: I would not stir an inch to help her; no,
not if—"

Quick footsteps rapped along the wooden gallery outside.
These chambers at the Golden Cross consisted of the wainscotted
parlour adjoining an airless bedroom not devoid of fleas. Footsteps passed the bedroom and reached the parlour. Lavinia
Cresswell, followed by a man some half a dozen years older,
opened the door and looked at Sir Mortimer while you might
have counted ten.

Mrs. Cresswell did not appear too angry, except that one or
two spots of bad complexion stood out against a waxy forehead.

"This good Mary Margaret of ours," she said, "has still more
to answer for. She is gone."

"Gone? Gone where?"

"That," replied Mrs. Cresswell, "is what we would wish to know."

"Oh, yes," said the man who accompanied her. "We more than wish to know."

If Mrs. Cresswell was short in stature, her companion stood lean and above middle height. He had long hands with long, supple-jointed fingers. Yet these two seemed unmistakably brother and sister, having much the same expression as well as features and bloodless cast of countenance.

"Your niece, dear man," said Mrs. Cresswell, "bespoke a room on the plea that she desired to wash herself. Hardly a minute later she ran into the yard, calling for a hackney-coach. The landlord, or so he says, followed and would have dissuaded her. Mistress Peg paid no heed. She was driven away eastwards."

"Lavvy, Lavvy," wailed Sir Mortimer, "this is none of my doing."

"I don't say it was."

"And I can't tell where the lass is gone."

"I don't say that either." Mrs. Cresswell nodded toward Jeffrey. "But does *he* know?"

"No," said Jeffrey, "I do not."

"You don't know much, do you?" asked Hamnet Tawnish.

Mr. Tawnish shouldered past the woman. His sleek white wig fitted him neatly, a horizontal curl pressing against each ear. His gold-laced coat was of mustard-colour against a blue waistcoat, the coat-cuffs as wide and deep as pockets. His left hand fell on the pommel of a smallsword with a steel-cut hilt and gilded knuckle-guard.

"You don't know much, do you?" he repeated.

"Stay your hand, sweet brother," said Mrs. Cresswell. Her wide-open eyes were fixed on Jeffrey. "It is known to me, Mr. Wynne, that you have lodgings in Covent Garden Piazza. Almost any coarseness could go unremarked there: Mistress Peg drove eastwards; to the hackney-coachman she gave instructions which, while imperfectly overheard, may be of use. Mr. Wynne, do you lodge at or near any premises with a sign of the Magic Pen?"

Oddly enough, it was Sir Mortimer who uttered an exclamation.

Jeffrey's expression gave no indication, or so he hoped, that the words had meaning for him. But they struck fear for Peg into his mind and heart; instinctively he started towards the door; Hamnet Tawnish, hands dropped, was in front of him.

"Mr. Tawnish . . ."

"Ah, you know me?" enquired the other, lifting his upper lip much as his sister did. "You'll know me better presently. Have you ears, fellow?"

"Mr. Wynne," said Mrs. Cresswell, "I await an answer to my question."

"The answer, madam, is that I lodge nowhere near any premises called the Magic Pen."

"Then where are you going?"

"Where I am going, madam, concerns no person except myself."

A smile crawled under Hamnet Tawnish's nose. With his open left hand, brought up almost negligently, he caught Jeffrey so ringing a crack across the cheek-bone that the tricorne hat jumped on his head. With his right hand Hamnet Tawnish whipped his sword from the scabbard.

"Draw!" he said.

"Mr. Tawnish, I desire no quarrel with you if it can be avoided."

"Belike," agreed the taller man. "But you have one and you'll not creep from it. Now draw."

"Hamnet," cried Mrs. Cresswell, "let him go!"

"Sweet sister—"

"It is plain," said Mrs. Cresswell, with her eyes turned suddenly towards a corner of the ceiling, "that he can give us no aid. And at best, you observe, he is so poor in spirit that to quarrel were a waste of time. Let him go!"

The sword-blade thin and needle-sharp in point, yet had no cutting edge. Hamnet Tawnish drew back his arm as if to throw a round-arm cut, as contemptuous as it was harmless, in the direction of Jeffrey's eyes.

Jeffrey bowed, fully facing him. Then, with a look too detached even to be called derisive, Mr. Tawnish dropped the point and stood aside. Sir Mortimer cursed into his jowls. Mrs. Cresswell contemplated that corner of the ceiling. And Jeffrey ran for the door.

# III

## The Young Woman, and the Old

"Peg!" he called. And again, more sharply: "*Peg!*"

His voice, loud enough to have roused a guard if any had been watching, went up and was lost amid the tumbling echoes of London Bridge. There was still no reply.

Jeffrey, in agony, glanced back over his shoulder.

The clocks on the City bank had rung ten. At such a very late hour there would be nobody in the street except cutthroats or drunken people, the latter even more numerous than the former because the law against cheap gin could not be enforced. Some victim of an attacker or of the horrors, in fact, was screaming on an unearthly note from an alley off the waterside. It sounded like a woman, as often it was.

Jeffrey hesitated. Some ten minutes ago two sedan-chair bearers, at a jog from Charing Cross and trotting fit to burst their hearts, had deposited him in Great Eastcheap at the top of Fish Street Hill. Southwards, near the Monument, was the lattice of a tavern he had seen once before that night. It was more than a tavern, he remembered from a profession he hated despite his brave words: it was the Grapes, a coaching inn which, like the Bull and Mouth in St. Martin's-le-Grand, served travellers to and from the north country.

And so he had pushed into a sanded passage beside the taproom, coming face to face with the landlord.

If the landlord at the Golden Cross had been lean and unctuous, this one was fat and suspicious.

"A lady?" he had asked in reply to Jeffrey's question. "A *young* lady? Come, can you describe her?"

"You will know if you have seen her. Very dark eyes, much alive, with glistening whites. Hair of a soft light-brown, a little piled up and falling in one or two curls at the back of the neck. Very pretty though overpainted. A lavender-coloured gown with red decoration; and, I think, having money in a purse at her girdle."

"A young *lady?* And pretty? And having money? And abroad at this hour?"

"Yes. That is what I fear."

24

"Come, what cause have you to think this young lady called at my house?"

"None whatever, save that yours is the only light in the street. She may have asked the way to a print-seller's shop on London Bridge. She may have asked for a linkman with a torch to light her there."

"I have not seen her. Is she mad?"

"At times. No matter! Since she was not here . . ."

"I did not say she was not here; I said I had not seen her."

Jeffrey, shivering in his cloak and about to retire, swung back again.

"If such an one walked forthwith into my tap-room, no doubt frightened but venturing there all the same and addressing a tapster to the great scandal and vexation of my wife, can I be everywhere at once? Am I to blame for runaways girls who may draw brothers or fathers after 'em? This is an honest house, young sir!"

Here the landlord's round face swam out at him.

"The girl, sir," said this host, "was not in my house above two minutes' time. She then flew away without linkboy or light either. You can't speak to the tapster she addressed; he is drunk and abed. But there's no harm if you have a word with the doctor."

"What doctor?"

"A doctor of physic," retorted the landlord, "but no quack, as most of 'em are. He is called Dr. Abel. *He* dwells on London Bridge, or will until they drive him from it. Each night he comes here to drink his two or three bottles like an honest man. The girl addressed him too. He is in the taproom still. And this is an honest house; there is a clergyman with him."

Jeffrey hurried past.

The taproom, black-beamed and with sweating walls, lay deserted except for a man sitting at each side of a table by the fire. The elder of the two, thick-bodied and of early middle age, smoked a long pipe as he listened.

He wore no sword. The badge of his physician's office, a tall cane with a brass head polished to resemble gold, was propped against the table. For all his weary and embittered air, for all the seediness of poverty that clung to snuff-coloured coat and white stockings, Dr. Abel had in his face a real kindliness—as unexpected, by that bleak fireside, as though you found it in an engraving by Mr. Hogarth of Leicester Fields.

His companion, a thin cadaverous-faced man in clerical black gown with white-linen bands, might have seemed sprightly or even sly by reason of a humorous nose and large soulful-looking eyes. But the parson was too much in earnest. He leaned across the table, speaking in a hushed and grave voice. Jeffrey might have hesitated to intrude if the scene had not exploded in a different emotion.

"Now, God damn my soul," said the clergyman, springing to his feet in tears, "but this is a mighty disobliging thing. 'Twas a civil question, Doctor, most civilly put! If a morsel of female flesh should prove less sweet than it seemed, and a poor unhappy divine should catch the French sickness through no fault of his own, is there no swift and sovereign cure for it?"

"Reverend sir, you must consult a surgeon and not a physician. Besides, as I say—"

"Doctor, Doctor! I am but newly arrived upon a visit to town. Is this London courtesy?"

"Reverend sir," said the doctor, relenting in spite of himself, "I have told you I do not deal in such cures. There are too many people a-dying of causes that can't be prevented."

"And dying with your help, past doubt?"

"With my help, I suppose," Dr. Abel said wearily. "I can't claim to be Hunter of Jermyn Street. But there is no true remedy for the French sickness, I apprehend; certainly no swift one. If we would avoid it altogether, sir, we must try to stop at home and behave ourselves."

"Yes, yes, that's all very well," sighed the parson. "I am wed to a crazy wife, or as near crazed as makes no difference. I could weep for my poor Eliza"—in fact, he was already doing so—"but that she falls into the shrieking vapours if she finds a man so much as fondle a servant-wench behind the door. And it *was* behind the door, Doctor, which showed true delicacy on my part."

"Are you sure you took the French sickness of this servant-wench?"

"Nay; how can I be? And it was not the servant-wench; it was the widow in Cheapside I am here to visit, and occurred scarce an hour ago. But at each small lapse I think I have catched it; I fear I have catched it; and that's near as bad as catching it in sober earnest."

"Reverend sir," said the doctor, sitting up straight, "you have a most singular perseverance in lewd tastes."

"Learned doctor," said the clergyman, "go stick your head in a rat-hole as a fellow of small delicacy and no true feelings. I am the Rev. Laurence Sterne, vicar of Sutton and of Stillington in Yorkshire, and a prebend of York Cathedral too. Were it not for my calling, God damme, I would lay a cudgel across your skull at this minute."

('Now, why is it,' Jeffrey Wynne was thinking, with the same despair he had felt so often before, 'that everyone in this accursed world seems desirous of forcing a quarrel or picking a fight?')

"Gentlemen both," he said aloud, and hurried forward, "I ask your pardon if I interrupt. I also am seeking a woman: though not, that's to say, in the same sense as this good divine. Will you hear me?"

He rattled out as much of the story as seemed advisable, while Dr. Abel stood up in grave courtesy and the Rev. Laurence Sterne listened all agog.

"She is handsome, you say?" demanded the latter. "And I was not here! A pox on it, why was I not here?"

"Sir, be silent," said Dr. Abel. He was much troubled, and put aside the long pipe. "*I* was here."

"And did the young lady question you, Doctor?" asked Jeffrey.

"She did. She asked if I had acquaintance with an old woman, name to her unknown, living above the shop you mentioned. I said I indeed knew the woman, who is called Grace Delight. And I strongly counselled the young lady not to go there, though I did not tell her why. There is no harm in the old woman, or so I think. But those premises have a foolish repute for being haunted; and 'tis said men have died there of fright."

"Sweet Jesus!" said the clergyman, turning pale under his tears. "Is it truly haunted?"

"Sir, be silent," snapped Dr. Abel. "I said a foolish repute."

"Ay, but—!"

"These things are of the mind. Men have scared themselves to death, as I can testify from my own knowledge. I counselled the young lady to go to her home. She replied that she had no home, or at least that there was none anywhere who loved her."

Jeffrey, head down, stalked away from the table and then back again.

"If she would await me while I fetched my case of phials," and Dr. Abel nodded towards a door across the taproom, "from where I had put it against being kicked or trampled by the tipsy people here, I said I would escort her. When I returned she had run away."

"Come, but this is a mighty mysterious and romantical business," said the Rev. Laurence Sterne. "Now, why should a young lady of breeding, if such she be, desire to visit these premises on London Bridge?"

"I can't say. It was none of my business to pry."

Here Dr. Abel, broad-faced and rather blear-eyed under a fraying old wig, rubbed his hand across his forehead.

"No, let's not lie," he said. "Being myself too tipsy and far too comfortable, I did not even follow as I should have done.

There is no harm done, I hazard. And yet, unless I am greatly mistaken, that girl was sore upset and in need to be comforted. I will go now, if you like. But you, young sir: do not wait at all. I counsel you to make haste before me."

And Jeffrey had not waited.

He knew why no sentry challenged him from the gatehouse on this side of the bridge. Half a dozen soldiers of the 1st Foot Guards, grenadier caps laid aside, lounged at a fire-place within the gatehouse. He could see them through the window, with their shadows on a whitewashed wall; presumably they had been there all evening.

He stood some twenty yards out under the dim arches, calling Peg's name, when he heard or believed he heard a woman scream from the waterside. But that was behind him. He ran on towards the first clear, broad opening between the blocks of houses.

Just ahead, occupying the whole width of the bridge, loomed up the Tudor bulk of Nonsuch House.

It lifted five or six floors of plaster and wood once richly carved or gilded; many windows; and four corner towers each with its wind-streaming weathercock. A high-sailing moon lit such of the windows as remained unbroken. The rest were eyeless, boarded up or stopped with rubbish, a last touch of the desolate.

"Peg!"

In that open space, clear and broad to the railing of the bridge on either side, he thought he saw a movement on the right: up-river, towards Westminster. Jeffrey ran to the balustraded walk they had built thirty years ago, outwards and parallel to the houses, so that foot-passengers might cross without being crushed amid vehicles. But he found nobody; the shadows tricked him. He leaned against the balustrade, looking sideways along a humped line of houses towards Southwark.

There was good reason for that roaring water. Too much massive stone-work went into piers and starlings, leaving little room for breadth in the supporting arches. Its widest span—the middle one, with drawbridge against siege or attack, unraised since the Middle Ages—was less than forty feet across.

In the days of the bridge's glory, when rich men were not ashamed to be merchants, they had laid out gardens on the rooftops. From the backs of many houses a box-like little room projected on supports above-water: the jakes or privy, an enormous luxury in past centuries and not common even today.

' "Grace Delight," ' Jeffrey Wynne was thinking. ' "Grace Delight." A bloated old woman with addled wits and a snuff-cankered lip? Can anyone believe that is her true name? What if Peg should have discovered who the woman really is?'

'Well, and what if Peg has discovered it?' whispered another voice in his brain. 'What's the difference? Does it matter?'

'Ah, but it does matter,' whispered the first voice. 'If you are resolved this night to commit a crime, because you must have Peg Ralston despite the devil and the altar, you have chosen a mighty ill time to commit it.

'Or are you truly resolved, after all? Is that why you linger and sweat here, so close to the shop? A man of determination would have throttled the hag long ago, and would do it now in risk of Peg's presence or not. He would . . .'

Phosphorescent rapids boiled far below. A great wind played on London Bridge as though on a fiddle. Again Jeffrey turned and ran, being sure this time he heard a woman's voice cry out.

He ran through the tunnel under Nonsuch House. He emerged into the carriageway beyond, with beams supporting housefronts on either side. And there, without warning, he ran smack against someone in the near-dark.

It is all very well, as Mr. Laurence Sterne might have said, to scoff at superstitious fears. But the thump of his own footsteps dinned in Jeffrey's ears. His hands had darted out to seize and strangle, witlessly, when he touched a woman's soft shoulders and knew the woman was Peg herself.

Afterwards he could only curse under his breath, trying to conquer a husky voice. He took Peg in his arms and pressed her hard against him. She was rigid and near babbling with terror, but at his first word she went limp and then clung back.

"Well," he said at length, "you are safe. Now what's this? What do you think you are at?"

"Jeffrey—"

"Speak up and answer! Why did you come here?"

"Because I thought you might follow."

"Indeed? Was that the only reason?"

"I thought you would follow. And you did follow. And I know why."

"Do you so?"

"I do so. Because you love me."

"Because I thought you might be robbed or murdered. For the last time, Peg, a truce to this romantical foolery! I'll bear no more of it."

"Oh, pray stop! You are more romantical than I am. Only you think 'tis weak, and you won't allow it. Don't you want to kiss me?"

"In candour, madam, I should much prefer to turn you across my knee and wallop you."

"Like that odious Hamnet Tawnish, that man with the long

cold hands and the swordsman's eye? Doing the bidding of his
far more odious sister? I saw him through a window at the inn.
I think that precious pair would kill me if they could. Where
should I take refuge, pray, but in the home of an old and
trusted servant?"

"The home of— *How*? What's that?"

"This woman Grace Delight, though sure it can't be her name.
You told me she had been an old servant of your family."

Faint moonlight filtered down through the timbers and the
crooked jutting gables. He could just discern Peg's face, and
the premises on the right by which she stood. Her terror was
fading, though there was a wild white gleam about the eyes. He
had put her away from him, but still held her arms under her
cloak. Its hood was back, her hat gone and her hair a little
tumbled.

"No, Peg."

"But you said . . ."

"No, sweet wench. I said, Peg, that 'in some sense' she once
served my grandfather. I did not say in what sense she served.
It might much astonish you to learn."

"No, I doubt it would." He felt rather than saw Peg's eyebrows go up. "You would have said, would you not, that she was
your grandsire's kept woman? And once upon a time may have
been very pretty?"

*"How the devil's name do you know that?"*

"Why, because 'twas you who said it," said Peg. "And by your
fashion of saying it. And who but a courtesan, or the like or the
worse, would have dreamed of taking such a name as that?"

"Peg, have you gone into that house there? Have you seen her?
No, no, you could scarce have guessed it by seeing her now."

"Well, well, no doubt it was all very wicked. But 'twas in our
grandsires' wicked times. And 'tis all one. Even if she was a kept
woman years upon years ago, I daresay she is still trustworthy
and dependable."

"No, she is anything but such. There's your romantical nonsense again. Yet it's fitting that today she should cast horoscopes,
and wave spells, and be somewhat horribly mad."

"Dear God!"

When the Great Fire of 1666 had burnt a path from the north
on London Bridge and was checked short of the first gap, it
had jumped not quite so far as Nonsuch House, which was a
far older relic of King Harry's time—or as these houses about
them now, which were older still.

The shop-premises of the Magic Pen had a single broad window fastlocked by wooden shutters. Of two doors set side by
side to the left of it, Jeffrey knew, one door led to the shop it-

self and one to a staircase going up inside. Two more floors in a narrow front lifted above the street; a patchwork of black beams and discoloured plaster with little windows somehow blocked or obscured from inside. The literal sign of the Magic Pen, hanging from a creaky rod above their heads, gave a great jerk and swing as the wind caught it.

"Peg, once more: you did not enter this house?"

"No, I did not! I had thought to do so. A tapster at the Grapes said where I should find it; I told them I meant to take refuge. Yet I touched the door, and could not enter. I can't say why; I did not then fear for ghoulies and ghosties, as I fear now."

"Was it you who cried out?"

"Cried out?"

"A few minutes ago. I had fancied I heard it. Did you cry out?"

"No, I did not. I stood here an unconscionable great length of time, and could not move. I near died when I heard you running at me. But there was none cried out; assuredly not I."

"Well, that's like enough. I have been fancying so much, what with thinking of you and with my own bad conscience, it's like enough I dreamed this too. And you have courage; you are Sir Mortimer Ralston's niece, with so much of his nature you might be his daughter instead. If you did not enter, there is now no need for either of us to enter."

"Jeffrey, I but touched the door there on the left. It was unbarred or unfastened . . ."

"A street-door, here or anywhere else, unbarred or unfastened after nightfall?"

"I can't help that; it was so! I touched the door, and it swung open an inch or two or three. I had thought to see the inside all little and foul and horrid. It's little enough, with stairs as steep as a ladder, though less foul than I feared. Yet I pulled the latch shut and durst not enter. And yet there was a wax-light burning above-stairs even so."

"A wax-light?"

"Mercy upon us, is that so odd?"

"Peg, you have never been poor. None hereabouts would have waxlights, even though—" he stopped. "The woman Grace Delight would burn a wick in a dish of oil, if indeed she had any light at all."

"God, God, do you think I always tell you lies? See for yourself!"

Peg pulled at the door, flinging it open on leather hinges so that it struck hard against the inside wall.

And, just after that door struck the wall, someone did scream.

It came from above-stairs. It might have been mortal terror or agony, or even both. It went up in a kind of bubbling shriek: from a human throat, but hardly human in sound. It pierced into flesh and nerves; it was followed by heavy and gasping breaths, and a noise like a thump on a thick floor. If there were other sounds, they went unheard by these two people below.

He could see Peg clearly, since a small light did in fact shine from up there. Her knees faltered; it was as though some of the colour went from her eyes. Ten seconds passed before anyone spoke.

"Now attend to me," Jeffrey said. "I am going in."

"Are you mad?"

"Go back to the Grapes. You will be safe there. Run!"

"You'd leave me? Or have me leave you? I'll not do it! *Please.*"

"Then follow behind me, but not too close. Don't encumber my sword-arm."

"You would run from a parcel of Frenchmen, yet go to look in the eye at this? Are you not afeared?"

"Yes. But little enough of ghosts or evil spirits. If some living person has come at the old woman and hurt her—"

"Who would come at her and hurt her?"

"*I* would have, for one. That is what shames me. And I am a thief-taker by trade. I must go in."

Taking Peg's arm, he drew her across the threshold and shut the door. A wooden bar lay on the floor. He picked it up and fitted it into its wooden slots, barring them into the dank little space. A set of stone stops so primitive as to be like a pillar with high, shallow treads like ledges, where the least ill balance could be breakneck, went up through a trap-opening in the ceiling. Above were two little rooms, set side by side, making the depth of the house between its front on the street and its back up-river towards Westminster.

"Remain here," he said. "If any should come at *you* to hurt you, he must come past me by those steps."

Jeffrey took off his cloak, dropping it on the floor. Peg saw him start up those ledge-like stairs, left hand supporting his sword-scabbard and head outlined against the gleam of a candle in the room just above. She saw his head jerk and his right hand grip for balance at the trap-opening. Then he crawled over the edge and disappeared.

"Jeffrey!"

He made no answer from above. There was not even a noise of footsteps. There was only a pressure on her breathing from the smoke and grease of more than two centuries.

"*Jeffrey!*"

"Be silent!"

She had crowded back against the barred door, her shoulders pressing it. He slipped and almost fell as he began to descend. Though she could see him only in silhouette—first the buckled shoes, then the legs in grey worsted stockings, then the knee-breeches and plum-coloured coat with silver thread round its buttonholes—yet Peg could sense his complexion must be much the same colour as his wig.

"Be silent!" he said again. "There is none here but ourselves. The old woman is dead."

"Was she hurt? Was she harmed? Was she . . . ?"

"Yes. Yes, in some sense harmed. Though she has no wound of the body, I think, for all the look upon her face. She died of fright."

# IV

## Swords by Moonlight

"Peg, you need not fear. I have thrown a cloth across her face. Give me your hand and come up."

"Must I? Must I? Is there need for that?"

"It is unlikely. The law does not call it violence when a life is snuffed out in that fashion. There will be no opening of the carcase, no coroner's quest. There should be only a pauper's burial by the parish, and no cause for you to testify. Unless . . ."

"Unless what?"

Jeffrey closed off the images in his brain. Taking up the cloak from the floor, he slung it round his shoulders. He lifted the door-bar out of wooden sockets, and propped it against the wall. Then he turned back.

"Are you better now?" he asked, and touched her cheek gently. "I hope so. God knows I had not meant to frighten you."

"Oh, that is different! Oh, if you are kind to me I can do all you ask!"

"Would you also give me aid if I were the one in need of it?"

"Oh, don't you know I would?"

"What's the Cornish litany, and the things they pray to be delivered from? 'From ghoulies, and ghosties, and long-leggity beasties, and things that go bump in the night.' Smile at that, Peg! There are none such in the house, upon my word. Up there," he pointed, "we have two small rooms. On the right, a bedchamber with a straw pallet. On the left, directly over our heads, a larger room and the old woman dead on the floor. Can you accompany me?"

"Yes." Peg stopped, a hand at her breast. "You—you said you were a thief-taker. '*I am a thief-taker by trade*': that is what you said. What did you mean by it?"

"Your uncle knows."

"*I* don't know."

"True; and you must hear. There are no ghosts, but this death of Grace Delight is more unaccountable even than it looks. Peg—"

She ran at the staircase and scrambled up with tomboyish

movements for one so maidenly in appearance. Nor did she
flinch much at what they found in the room above. Mere dirt
was not troublesome, unless so noxious as to become offensive.
Death at its ugliest aspect, common in street and in fine houses
of gilt and mirrors as well, was a fact to be accepted once it
had occurred. Yet he found Peg standing rigid, skirts drawn
round her, when he followed through the trap-opening.

Again Jeffrey looked round the room.

Its floor was of oak, solid despite the humps of age. They
could not see the window in the front wall; a piece of thick
sacking hung across it. But in the rear wall, just above a high
and broad wooden chest crudely carved, a second window overlooked the moonlit river. This window had two leaves like little
doors, formed of round panes in wavy bottle-glass; one leaf had
been propped hard open, admitting what all conceded to be the
unhealthfulness of night air.

The old woman, dropsy-bloated, lay on her back beside the
wooden chest. She wore a draggled mob-cap and a smock of
brown linsey-woolsey. Across her face had draped a filthy
silk kerchief once coloured bright green. At the north-west
corner of the room, shielded from draughts, the candle burned
upright in its own grease from a blackened metal dish on a
joint-stool, and shed steady light on the covered face.

Peg and Jeffrey both spoke at once.

"You said—" the girl blurted out.

"These thief-takers—" he began.

The blood beat in their ears and in their hearts; both stopped
speaking. A gust of wind swooped at the open casement, rattling
it, above a noise of tumbling rapids.

"These thief-takers," Jeffrey went on, "have an evil name and
are much hated. Folk think us all like Jonathan Wild, who was
hanged long before you were born. It's no trade to boast of, I
grant. Mr. Fielding's People work in secret; they wear no dis-
tinctive dress; their names may not be known, else their usefulness is ended. Yet at times, when a man's wits are needed to
sound the depths of a mystery that informers alone can't pierce,
this thief-taker may be none so base a fellow as your uncle
thinks."

"Jeffrey, Jeffrey, why must you so torment yourself?"

"I don't. There are worse ways of earning one's keep than by
taking blood-money."

"You do," cried Peg, ignoring the last sentence. "You have
asked me why I came here to seek this woman. Why did you
come here? You said you had made a resolve. You said it would
lead to law-breaking and might lead to murder."

"Yes. There has been a murder."

Peg put her hands to her cheeks, from which the colour had again receded.

"Oh, not by me," he told her. "Nor by bludgeon nor by pistol nor by poison. Yet there was something took her life by fear. What was it?"

"Could *I* have done it, do you think? I cast open the door, you'll recall. I cast it open, quite suddenly, so that it struck with great noise against the wall. Could the noise . . . ?"

Jeffrey began to laugh. Then he checked himself and spoke soberly.

"Not with that one," he said, indicating the motionless figure. "Not with Mrs. . . . not with Grace Delight. She was addle-witted, to be sure, but most hard of grain. She would have turned no hair to meet the devil himself. Peg, what frightened her?"

"Do you ask *me?* I can't tell."

"Let us try if we can to determine."

Turning round, he strode towards the joint-stool with such intentness that he all but walked straight into the trap-opening. Peg cried a warning in time. He took up the blackened dish with the candle. Holding the light high, its shadows hollowing his cheek-bones and throwing into prominence the intent green-ish eyes, he ducked first through the doorway of the cubby-hole bedchamber. After a hundred heart-beats he returned and moved slowly round this room, studying each object.

"Jeffrey, what are you doing?"

"Peg, look round. Mark what you see; you must bear witness if necessary."

Again he held the light high.

"There is no fire-place, not even a hearthstone with a vent to carry away smoke; it must be freezing cold in winter. The floor is solid. The lid of this chest"—he lifted it up—"carries dust along the under-edge, having no mark of fingers used to raise it within weeks or even months. There's nothing inside, take note, save some old parchments drawn with her astrolog-ical designs, a dried inkhorn, some clotted pens. Stop! Here is a fresher ink and newer parchment; but undisturbed, I think. This old woman has not been robbed."

"Robbed? Who would rob a near-pauper on London Bridge?"

He did not answer, but closed the lid and dropped his cloak on it.

Moving to the front of the room, he pulled aside the piece of sacking that concealed the window above the street.

"This window," he said, "is in design like the other. It has two leaves and a catch between to fasten them. It is shut but not fastened."

"Foh! Now, what window above a street is often kept fastened? There must be too much servant-maids' throwing out of refuse, of slops or offal or the like, to be got rid of and washed away in the kennel."

"Not on London Bridge. Theirs is a wooden street; it has no kennel. All rubbish to be got rid of"—and Jeffrey strode back again—"must be thrown from *here,* from the rear window, into the natural kennel of the Thames. It may cause some inconvenience to passers-by on the footway, though not if it be thrown wide. Observe also— Peg, come here."

"I'll not! You said you had no intent to frighten me, and now you bend your brows like a hangman!"

"Observe also, outside and below the window, how the timbers are set into the wall. A determined man might climb up from the footway. Now, Grace Delight did not fear housebreakers. Both windows are unfastened; this one is open, and one side propped so with stuffed rags which could not have been put there by a retreating thief. Yet this window has no screen or curtain, whereas the front one is thick-covered by sacking on a rope."

"So that none might observe her from the windows opposite? Well, to be sure! Any person of modesty . . ."

"Was it modesty, Peg?"

The candle-flame thrummed and fluttered. Jeffrey set its dish on the lid of the wooden chest, pushing it aside out of the wind, and went down on one knee beside Grace Delight's body. He looked at the coarse loose-woven fabric of the smock, and then up at the green kerchief across her face.

"This kerchief, though old and foul, is of French silk. The taper is no tallow dip, but a wax-light. This platter here," he tapped the edge of the dish, "is much encrusted and seems of base stuff. It is pure silver."

"Do you tell me she was no pauper-woman at all? And had great store of gold hid away? And that this tempted someone to set on her?"

"I tell you only what in honesty I must tell Justice Fielding tomorrow. Your conclusions, like his, must be your own. You are accustomed to reading my mind; read it now."

"Oh, damn you and damn you!"

"Peg . . ."

"At times I know you, and am happy. At times you are the person I know; I am utterly happy. And then you would jeer or go away into cloud. What's your concern with this woman, truly? Is it—is it to keep scandal from the memory of your late grandsire?"

"Come! That's still worse a romantical notion. My respected

grandsire may toast bread in hell for all of me. And I could
wish the old woman at perdition too, save that I almost pity
her." Here he looked up. "We live in a brutal and cursed and
misbegotten world, for all the fine talk of so many! Doctor Swift
knew this, and died mad in Dublin because he knew it. There
are others who know it, and would keep a leaven of decency.
I think, I think, I met a physician who is one. But there are
not many. For the most part—"

Peg's tone changed.

"Jeffrey, don't! Pray don't! You look for too much of the
world. Can't you be content with those who are fond of you
and would love you?—Heaven have mercy, but what's amiss
*now?*"

Abruptly, after bending close to the covered face, he had
thrust his left arm under the inert woman's shoulders, his right
under the crook of her knees, and lifted the body from the floor.
The green kerchief fell away. Over his arm rolled a face with
eyes all but protruded from their sockets and mouth fixed wide in
a grimace that showed the ulcers of snuff-taking between nostril
and lip.

The face in its mob-cap twisted from Peg's sight. With a great
heave Jeffrey lifted the body head down across his left shoulder.

"There was a breath!" he said, swaying to keep his balance.
"The lightest breath, but I swear the silk moved. There's life
in her still, or some measure of it. With luck, and with the aid
of that doctor, we may even bring her back."

"Jeffrey, you are deluded. She is gone. I—have seen death
before."

"So have I. There was a man in my regiment condemned
to die before a firing-party, and denied a bandage for his eyes.
He screamed and fell like a dead man as the muskets were
levelled, before any command to fire. His limbs and face were
limp, not rigid, but otherwise it is the same case. If they had
not believed that man dead, and made the business sure with a
pistol-ball through the ear, they might have revived him to die
again."

"Well, what's your wish? There is a straw pallet in the other
room, you said. Shall I take the candle and light your way
there?"

About to reply, head turned over his right shoulder, he stopped
with a different expression suddenly widening his eyes.

"No, let be! I had forgot. Let be; I can manage well enough!"

"Come, this is absurdity! Surely you would desire . . . ?"

"I desire you shall not touch the light. And on no account go
near that bedchamber."

"Why?"

"Because that is my wish. Peg, Peg, can you deign to obey me in this?"

Emotion boiled in that room above the boiling river. Peg shivered, breathing hard, but she did not move from where she stood.

Also breathing hard, he carried his burden to the little low doorway beyond the open stair. In the bedroom he looked only at the little low wooden frame, with pallet and blanket, under another curtained window at the front. At no time did he glance round at what else was there. Even with eyes accustomed to reading small print by the light of one taper, as must be anyone who could read at all, he could have made out little except an outline.

He dropped Grace Delight face upwards on the pallet. Indecision struck him and shook him; he hesitated, beating his hands together, and then stalked back to where Peg waited.

"I talk bravely," he said, "but I am a dolt; I don't in the least know what to do for her; I can only hope a physician knows. Which of us shall go to fetch him?"

"Neither of you will go, fellow," said someone else's voice.

A human head was rising slowly through the trap-opening, and looking at them.

Both Peg and Jeffrey spun round. Both backed away beside the wooden chest. A lean figure, in mustard-coloured clothes with unwrinkled stockings, gave a great bound through the opening like a rope-tumbler or a character in one of Mr. Rich's pantomimes at Covent Garden Playhouse. But it advanced slowly, long left hand tapping a sword-hilt.

"Has the cat got your tongue, fellow? Are you so much in amaze? Did you truly fancy I would not follow?"

"No, Mr. Tawnish," Jeffrey said, "I never doubted you would follow. That is not to the point now. I must go at once—"

"You will go nowhere, fellow," said Hamnet Tawnish.

"Sir, a woman lies within one gasp of death in the room behind you. A few minutes, even a matter of seconds, may mean her life if we can fetch a physician who is not far away. For God's sake, sir, allow me to pass!"

"You beg this?"

"If need be, I do."

"When your manners deserve a cane for your incivility to my sister? You won't fight, it's true. But the sword can be a mighty effective cane for a whipping. Stand aside? Come, that's good!"

"I can't urge other considerations upon you? I can't persuade you to forgo this?"

"Do you truly think you can?"

"Why, then," said Jeffrey, with left hand pushing back the

two embroidered slings which held the sword-scabbard to his belt, "let it be as you wish. —Draw!"

*"What's that you say?"*

"You have been very free with your threats, Mr. Tawnish. Now try if you can to make them good. Draw!"

Both blades were out of the scabbards, soundless from leather sheaths lined with wool. Jeffrey had moved still farther back beside the chest; they were too far apart for a lunge. But Hamnet Tawnish made no move to lunge. Instead, unexpectedly, he took a savage backhand cut at the candle.

The light leaped and vanished, metal dish clattering against wood. Peg was crying out, "Stop, you'll be killed; stop, you'll be killed," on a high frantic note that ended in a scream. Jeffrey, body turned sideways, heard the other man bound forward in the dark.

Then moonlight lifted outside a half-open window, flooding through round panes of blurred and wavy glass. Hamnet Tawnish stood with wrist carried high and a little downwards. As the moon entered he flung out at full-length lunge, right knee far bent and point driving for the right side of Jeffrey's chest.

Steel rang on steel, striking a blue spark of friction below the knuckle-guards. Jeffrey, sweating, parried with an outer wrist-turn and cross-lunged in riposte at the inside of the other's sword-arm. He misjudged, but so did Hamnet Tawnish.

Though it might have been an effect of the distorting light, an onlooker would have thought Mr. Tawnish suddenly uncertain, even clumsy, after a stab that had failed to pierce through Jeffrey's lung. He caught the return thrust well enough; his fencing-style had the full flourish of 'grace and deportment' taught by Signor Malevolti Angelo at Carlisle Street in Soho. But his own riposte was slow, and his dart-back even slower for so agile a man.

Jeffrey parried point downwards, whacking the blade aside, and again cross-lunged for the same target. His point ran upwards and stabbed deep through the inside of his adversary's exposed right wrist.

Hamnet Tawnish stood stupid, mouth open. The sword with the gilded knuckle-guard rolled over and fell clattering from a useless right hand. A blackish-looking fluid, blood by moonlight, welled up over wrist and cuff.

Mr. Tawnish stared at it. The spasm that crossed his face was not one of fear; it was of shock, of outrage, of some deeper cause he himself may not have understood. But he turned and ran—towards a trap-opening now invisible. The cry he uttered, as his weight met nothingness above a staircase as steep as a ladder, went up in the same kind of bubbling shriek they had heard before. There was a crash from the passage downstairs, and then silence.

Jeffrey stood motionless, head down. More sweat had started out on his body and under his wig. He did not speak; it was Peg who said the wrong thing.

"You beat him," she cried out, shivering and raising her elbows and with tears brimming over. "I like to have died because I was so afeared for you. But you did not run from him; you beat him."

"Peg, be silent!"

"You took the hazard—"

"Be silent, in all stupidity's name! I took no hazard at all."

And he began to clean blood from his sword by wiping it on the inside of his coat-skirt.

"That lout can't fence, or at least mighty little. Have you never heard your uncle say most men know little of swordplay? That is wise: they want duels no more than I want 'em. Hamnet Tawnish has gained great repute by his sneer and his mighty bearing; none has challenged him. He may have had a lesson or two from Angelo, and come truly to think himself invincible. That is all."

"But *you* challenged him. You could not have known this."

"Not know it? I should have been a great dullard not to know it. Tonight, at the Golden Cross, he lunged out and pulled back his arm as if to throw a harmless cut at my head. No swordsman would have been fool enough to behave so. A man of knowledge could have drawn and thrust through him while his guard was open."

"Then you had no fear for your own skin?"

"Pray believe me, I had great fear. A chance thrust from a novice may puncture Angelo himself."

"And I thought you had done something heroical. 'Fore God I did. Or, if you had not, could you not at least have pretended you had, and made me think of you the more highly?"

"Peg, Peg, will you have done with this play-acting?"

"Play-acting?" said the astounded girl.

"Yes, madam. Make up your mind how you would have me be."

"No. Oh, no! Make up your mind how you would have *me*. I tried to be loving, as I desire to be; and you won't bear it. I try to provoke you; and you won't bear *that*. I try to show I am most honest touched; and you'll bear that least of all. What's a poor loving dolt to do with such a fellow?"

"I—I must own, Peg, I am not always easy."

"Easy? You are the hopelessest person that ever lived on this earth. And now you have killed a man; foh, you have murdered him; he lies dead down there; and here are two people dead or a-dying with us now."

Jeffrey's expression changed.

"Two!" he repeated. "Ay, two. It's well done to remind me."

Moonlight drew wavy shadow-circles across his face as he craned from side to side. He might have been in desperate straits from a wound, and was in fact thinking of flint and steel to kindle a light. He returned the sword to its scabbard. His next actions seemed almost demented.

He ran to the front of the room, tore down the sacking from its rope across the window, and wrapped the rotted fabric round his right fist. The crashing and falling of glass, as he drove his fist at the closed window, must have wakened any dwellers who still slept on London Bridge. The glass, old and bent and brittle inside lead circles, tumbled partly outwards and partly inwards at his feet.

Picking up one such fragment intact, he scrubbed dirt from it with the sacking. Then he hurried back and retrieved the fallen candle from beside Hamnet Tawnish's sword. Though knocked askew when cut from the dish, it still showed an edge of wick."

"Remain here," he said to Peg. "She must have struck a light; and in the bedchamber, to be sure, I recall . . ."

In the bedchamber, groping through darkness, he found at the back a small bricked fire-place at a position corresponding to that of the rear window in the other room. His hands ran round the hearth until he found a small tinder-box. An oiled spark sprang up and caught. Carrying the crooked taper, he went to the old woman's body and held the segment of glass close to her grimacing mouth.

Then he stood unmoving, head down.

Whether it had been illusion that he saw breath flutter through her lips he did not know now, and did not know until afterwards when he began to suspect everything. By that time he had still more reason to curse himself. Indubitably she was dead now.

Peg stirred in the other room. Heavy footsteps, the sound of several men approaching, clumped along the arched thorough-fare of London Bridge towards the front of the house.

Hot wax splashed across Jeffrey's hand, rousing him. He had one act of concealment to perform here, and he did it hastily before he went back to the room where Peg waited.

At the same moment a young and throaty voice, a voice he recognized, rose up from outside.

"Hold, there!" the voice called. "Whoever's within-doors, in the house with the burst window and the part-open door, hold as you are. —You, Johnson," and here Captain Tobias Beresford, of the 1st Foot Guards, seemed to be speaking over his shoulder, "push the door full open. You, Macandrew, remain with me. Whoever's within-doors, stand and give account of yourself. D'ye hear?"

# V

## Dilemma at the Magic Pen

JEFFREY turned the catch of the front window and pushed open its shattered right-hand casement.

"You go too fast, Tubby," he called back. "There are no law-breakers here."

The light of two lanthorns made almost a dazzle round Tubby Beresford and two guardsmen in grenadier caps. These lanthorns were held by one of the guardsmen and by Tubby himself, his black tricorne hat and black jackboots contrasting with the scarlet and buff of the uniform. The second guardsman, a Brown Bess musket held level at waist-height, had jabbed open the door to the passage below.

"Ecod," said Tubby, looking up. "Ecod, I might ha' known it."

Clearly he was ill at ease. His pouchy eyes kept turning round, almost as though he were interested in the dingy shuttered shops across the way.

"Now hark'ee, Jeff, I don't know what you're at. But I gave you warning not to tarry on the bridge. If you've been at what you shouldn't, friend or no friend, you'll pass the night in a watch-house."

"I trust not, Tubby."

"You do, hey? I am about my duty—"

"So am I," retorted Jeffrey, stretching the truth a little. "But you're far from your post at the Southwark side, surely?"

"That's as may be. If Captain Mike Courtland—" and Tubby stabbed a finger northwards, presumably towards the gatehouse at the City end—"if Captain Mike Courtland is too slothful or too tender of poor people's feelings to set proper sentries, I'll not take the blame for it. Now what's afoot, Jeff? Damme, you're all a muck of dirt. What's afoot?"

"In the passage below you will find a man, quite probably stunned and insensible."

"Sir," interrupted the guardsman with the musket. "Sir, or else Macandrew, that's to say. Show a glim, can't you?" And a moment later, as the lanthorn was held up: "There's nobody in the passage, sir. But there's blood-drops from the stairs to the street-door here."

44

"He crawled away, then" said Jeffrey. "I did not hear him. But I counted him more humiliated than harmed."

"Who crawled away?" demanded Captain Beresford. "For the last time, Jeff, what occurred here?"

"A certain man forced a quarrel despite all attempt to prevent him. I ran him through the wrist; I had no choice."

"A sword-brawl, hey? And *that's* not against the law? Damme, Jeff, this means Newgate. *I'm* the man who has no choice."

"Tubby, will you attend to me? Unless martial law be declared, which it is not, all breaches of the peace are under authority of the magistrate-in-chief at Bow Street. The military must aid and obey if called upon by him or by an appointed deputy. You are aware of this, are you not?"

"Ay, it's true enough. Still . . ."

"And upon this occasion," said Jeffrey, again stretching the truth, "I am his appointed deputy. Sure you know this too? Or, from your acquaintance with me, at least you had divined it?"

Across Captain Beresford's darkish brows went a shade of what might have been relief.

"Now, why a pox couldn't you ha' said this before?" he asked. "I suspected, it may be. I couldn't know. You'll take upon yourself the burden of responsibility?"

"I will."

"And make report to old Fielding?"

" 'Old' Fielding? Justice Fielding is thirty-six: no more."

"Is it so, split my bottom?" asked the other, momentarily impressed. "And not so young either, though he carries himself like a man of fifty and a court-chamberlain at the very least."

"He is blind, Tubby. Justice Fielding is not the least vain-glorious of men, or the most lovable. But he is honest; he has wits in his head, and more charity than he will permit to be seen."

"Charity? Oh, ay, charity. Well, have it as you please. What's to our purpose is that I have no mind to meddle if you render yourself responsible."

"I do. Not only for Hamnet Tawnish—"

"For . . . *who?*"

"Hamnet Tawnish. The man with whom I was embroiled. Why, Tubby, are you acquainted with him? Have you played at cards with him? And lost money to him, as so many have?"

It seemed as though some ripple passed across the lanthorn-light; an illusion, since both flames remained steady. But Captain Beresford swung up his own lanthorn, illuminating his face while he tried to illuminate Jeffrey's. The latter would always remember afterwards a cluster of shop-signs opposite: the Two Bibles, a book-seller's long abandoned because so few sought

books on London Bridge; a mirror-maker's called the Dear
Vanity, also deserted; and one of the pin-and-needle makers'
shops, this one called the Knitting-Needle, still open for trade by
day but fast-shuttered now. The signs, rusted and in need of
paint, made a sombre background for Tubby Beresford's bright
uniform.

"What's my affair, Jeff," he snapped, "is my affair."

"Well, that's unanswerable."

"Ay, and more. If 'twas Hamnet Tawnish and no other you
say you ran through the wrist: *if* it was Hamnet Tawnish, I
say . . ."

"He is only a bully-rook, Tubby, a sham swordsman and not to
be feared."

"That may be. Some have suspected it. But a friend of his
named Major Skelly, the one who smiles and smiles, is no sham
swordsman at all. He'll carve your guts as soon as look at you.
Have a care, Jeff."

"I have worse cares, Tubby, and worse luck."

"As how? What else is up there?"

"A dead woman is up here. I have great need of medical
counsel. If the old woman did not die of any wound, then she
died of fright at what visited her, or at what some might call
the Visitation of God."

Tubby Beresford uttered a ringing oath. The guardsman with
the musket drew back from the door. Momentarily Jeffrey
missed Tubby's response in turn of eye; for some time he had
been listening to more footsteps approaching, on this occasion
from the London side. Jeffrey raised his voice to speak the last
words just as Dr. Abel emerged into the lanthorn-light and
stopped short.

Though Dr. Abel carried both the long brass-headed cane and
the wooden box of instruments and phials which marked his calling, Captain Beresford was from one cause or another too off-
balance to remark this.

"Now here's a pretty kettle o' fish, upon my soul," he bawled.
"Is all the world walking on London Bridge at this hour? Who
are you, fellow? What are you doing here, fellow?"

"Sir," replied the newcomer, "I dwell here. My house is some
hundred yards farther on. I am a doctor of physic, as you may
observe."

"Oh, ay?"

"You need not remind me, Captain," said Dr. Abel, correctly
interpreting the other's look and speaking with bitterness, "that
my trade is a somewhat low one. I beg also that you will spare
me any jests concerning it. This night, believe me, I have had
a surfeit of such jests from a clergyman who desired to accom-

pany me. However, low trade or not, I pursue it as best I can."

"Well, well," growled Captain Beresford, recovering something of his usual good manners, "no offence was meant. 'Tis
not as low a trade as a surgeon's, at all events. And, if Jeff
Wynne thinks he has need of a physician—why, in God's name
go to him! There's a clergyman with you, you say?"

"Not now." Here Dr. Abel glanced up and saw Jeffrey at
the window. "That, young sir, is the reason for my lateness."

"Doctor, Doctor, there is no need for apology."

"I fear there is. The Reverend Mr. Sterne first insisted we
must take still another bottle: to give us both courage, so he said,
to venture here. Whereupon he recalled, or said he recalled,
still a second appointment this night to visit his frisky widow in
Cheapside, and went reeling off to find a sedan-chair. Therefore, though I had promised most faithfully to follow you and
the young lady—"

"Young lady?" demanded Captain Beresford. "What young
lady?"

"Under favour, sir," asked the guardsman with the Brown
Bess, "had we not best return to our post?"

"Under favour, sir," said the guardsman with the second
lanthorn, "may *I* say that's good advice?"

"It is indeed good advice, Tubby," said Jeffrey, whose nerves
had begun to crawl again. "There was a young lady here, but she
is gone long ago. It's of no consequence. I have promised to assume responsibility."

Captain Beresford clapped his hand on his sword, looking
round narrowly.

"Ay, but can you assume it? Hark'ee, Jeff, if you think I am
satisfied with the tales of what's happening here, I tell you in
your teeth I am not. I'll go, yes; but not back to my post. I'll
go and have a word with Captain Courtland, to find if *he* knows
one word of what I ought to know. Johnson, Macandrew, accompany me."

"As you please, Tubby. Before you go, though, may I humbly
request that you will leave one of those lanthorns with Dr.
Abel?"

"One of the lanthorns? No, I'll not! Why should I?"

"That also is as you please. But I had not thought you too
frightened of ghosts to cross London Bridge with only one light."

"Afraid, am I? Macandrew! Give the doctor your light."

"Sir . . ."

"D'ye hear me, man?"

From the guardsman Tubby Beresford snatched the lanthorn
with such haste that the hot metal burnt his fingers. He thrust

it at Dr. Abel, who, after an impassive glance at the window, received it in the same hand that held the cane.

While two lights danced wildly outside, Jeffrey backed away. A cold draught between the windows, one half open and one shattered, had already blown out the taper he carried. He backed away through shadow and moonlight to where Peg was waiting, rigid, and shushed her to a whisper when she would have cried aloud.

"Wait!" he said. "They are going now. When you can no longer hear their footsteps, follow me down the stairs to the passage."

"Dear God!" Peg whispered. "Am I a fugitive from justice, that you still hide me away like one?"

"Yes. You may well be. I doubt we have finished with Hamnet Tawnish."

"But you defeated him. You made him run."

"And does that end all things, as in some happy tale for a ladies' drawing-room? Depend on it, it does not. —Now, Peg!"

In the passage below, his back to the open street-door, Dr. George Abel stood holding up the lanthorn. He held it still higher, stiffening, when he saw the bloodstains that spattered the floor.

"Sir," began Dr. Abel, and cleared his throat, "sure I heard you say the old woman of this house is dead?"

"She is dead."

"And that she died of fright?"

"I believe so; I can't tell."

"Then how come this blood in the passage?"

"It is not her blood. Doctor, may I make you known to Miss Ralston here? The two of you spoke together at the Grapes, or so you told me. And you lent her sympathy when she was much in need of it."

"Young sir, sympathy is my trade. Often enough, God knows, I have little else to give. But you may believe me, madam, to be your most obedient servant."

"*I* believe it, Doctor," said Jeffrey. "Well, then—"

He strode past the other man and closed the door. He picked up the wooden bar and dropped it into the sockets. If he had not left that door unbarred, he was reflecting bitterly, tonight's course might not have turned towards ruin.

"At the Grapes, also," he went on, "I told you something of the story. If I told you little then and must tell you little now, that is partly because we have small time at our disposal."

"Sir, is time so important?"

"Yes; pray hear me. Miss Ralston and I entered this house together, when we heard Grace Delight cry out. Or at least—"

Briefly he paused, turning his gaze towards the bloodstain at the foot of the stairs, and then dismissing some notion that had begun to nag him like minor madness.

"We found her dead or dying, as you shall see in a moment, with a face to affright children but no visible mark of violence. We were then interrupted by a certain gentleman called Hamnet Tawnish, who moves in the best society of St. James's and Kensington Palace. None can say how he has entry there, unless it be his sister's doing. He is a rogue and a card-cheat, though too nimble to have it proved against him."

"Jeffrey," cried Peg. "I loathe the odious man. But are you sure of this? *I* had not heard it."

"Perhaps not. You have seen his hands, though; they are a card-cheat's hands, not a swordsman's. You have seen the wide, deep cuffs of his coatsleeves."

"Well, so are all men's cuffs above the wrist-ruffle. So are yours."

"Mine, Peg, are not stiff-wired on the inside to hold hidden cards. And I know this, Dr. Abel, because I am a thief-taker of Bow Street."

"A watchman, you would say? Come. You are not one of the Charlies?"

"No, though I have the same authority as a watchman to arrest and take into custody. I am one of the more despicable officers, Doctor, who do this for blood-money."

"And boast of it?"

"Sometimes; but hear me. Hamnet Tawnish interrupted us. There was a scuffle of swordplay, and I wounded him. He said he had followed me to punish a slight against his sister, which was a lie. He followed because he knew I should lead him to this girl here. If any person stands in danger of arrest, it is Peg Ralston herself."

"Arrest?" breathed Peg. She took a step backwards, her very dark eyes widening and glistening against a flood of pallor. "*Arrest?* Foh, you are mad!"

"No. You were not in that upper room at the Golden Cross; you failed to hear what sweet Madam Cresswell has in store for you. I am not mad, though I may be mistaken and I hope I am."

"Then where is the need," snapped Dr. Abel, "to alarm her so much? Has this young lady committed a crime? Can any say she has?"

"There will be no charge of felony that means Newgate Prison. But there may be a lesser charge, a false one, that could get her committed to Bridewell if they dare lay information before a magistrate."

"Sir, this is fantastical."

"Doctor, do you truly think so?"

"I do, and even in a world like ours. Young ladies of birth and breeding are not put in Bridewell to beat hemp or pick oakum as though they were—as though they were—" Dr. Abel stopped. "What of her parents? What of her friends? Surely there must be someone who cares for her?"

"No, there is none," Peg said clearly. "I have thought there was; I had prayed there was; but I know now there is none."

"Peg, for God's sake!"

"Bridewell!" said the girl, as though a spider had crawled across her flesh. "Bridewell. Do you know what else they do there?"

"Yes. But I have every hope of your uncle. *He* loves you; and he is the only man with authority. I take precautions, that is all."

"Then let us take precautions," said Dr. Abel, "but try to understand what we do. Why do you tell me this, young sir? How may I serve you?"

"You may tell me, if you can, how Grace Delight died. Or, at least, whether there is a physical wound. Afterwards, if you will, you may take Miss Ralston into your home and guard her there while I explore the rooms above-stairs for ten, fifteen, perhaps twenty minutes. Will you oblige me in this?"

Broad-faced under the shabby wig, his eye now grown so bleary as to seem almost blind, Dr. Abel stood clutching cane and lanthorn-handle and instrument-box.

"Doctor," Jeffrey said in desperation, "Much is being asked of you. Yet I take my oath it may be the only means of delivering Peg from two most unsavoury rogues; or, if the worst should befall, of delivering her from a month in Bridewell as a common strumpet."

"As a—"

"Yes. Forgive my bluntness. Will you do this?"

"I will do it."

Taking up one corner of his coat-skirt to avoid burning his fingers, Jeffrey opened the panel of the lanthorn and kindled the wax taper he carried at the broader, larger flame inside. He thrust the taper at Peg, who took it so uncertainly that she almost let it fall.

"Now, Doctor, be pleased to light the way upstairs. Peg, remain here."

"Here? Alone? And at a time like this? You'd use me so, would you?"

"Yes; I fear I would."

"Then go," the girl said angrily. "Go, God damn you! I'll

have no more of your mock sympathy, either now or in future."

"Young sir—"

"Doctor, there are the stairs."

Rather blindly, though with some agility despite his encumbrances, Dr. Abel mounted the steps. Still blindly, with the lanthorn-light in his eyes, he had turned towards the rear of the living-quarters before Jeffrey guided him into the bedchamber.

For Jeffrey it was not easy. He could hear Peg, half sick with uncertainty and fright, sobbing her heart out in the passage below. He could hear the noise as she struck her clenched fist against the wall. But he shut his mind to this. And Dr. Abel, once bent above that grotesque figure on the bed, had eyes or ears only for the task of examination.

Handing the lanthorn to Jeffrey, he put down his other burdens and fitted on a pair of oval spectacles. All bleariness dropped away from the broad, shrewd, ugly face, though it grew even broader and redder. At length he rolled the old woman's body on its back again. He closed the staring eyes, put two pennies in them, and straightened up.

"There is no wound here. Or, that is to say, . . ."

"Is it to say, Doctor, only that you can find none?"

"Sir," retorted the other, straightening up still more, "I could not swear my findings at the Almighty's judgment-seat. Yet I can so testify to the parish clerk, and abide in honour by a verdict I now to be true. A stab-wound to the heart, for example, hath at times caused that same simulacrum of terror and that same rigidness of the muscles. But there is no wound. This shock was of her mind; it stopped the heart from fright."

"You said you were acquainted with her. Did she consult you in the way of physic?"

"Yes; I have been here more than once."

"Was it a heart-ailing, then? So that a sudden fright might carry her off?"

"No, it was in the matter of her dropsy. I urged her to consult a surgeon and be tapped for it. She would not do this, though to be tapped for dropsy is a small thing. And so I could only dose her with Bishop Berkeley's tar-water, which is useless." Dr. Abel looked down. "But certes the dropsy would enfeeble her heart. And now it is not seemly she should be without face-cloth or decent covering. Are there no bedclothes here?"

"She had a blanket. It is otherwise employed now. When Tubby Beresford came shouting under the windows, I used it to hide that painting in the corner there."

There was a pause like the impact of a blow.

"Painting? What painting?"

"You shall look at it," Jeffrey said, "but speak low when you answer. We must not be overheard."

He held the lanthorn high.

Rats scuttled inside the wall. Another breakneck stair mounted towards a trap-opening to the stationer's abandoned lumber-rooms above. The painting, half-length canvas unframed save for its own wooden binding, had been propped in the angle of the wall beyond the fire-place and hidden by a fouled and greasy blanket draped from the top. Jeffrey strode towards it, stamping hard on the floor, and then swung round.

"Doctor," he went on, "you have divined already there is some secret as touches that old woman on the bed?"

"Granted; yet what's the manner of it? She had some educa-ion, I thought. She was miserly, they said. But who shall call his neighbour miserly when all on the bridge are poor? There was no painting when I called here a fortnight past."

"It was here, I think; she kept it hid in the cupboard. Would you see Grace Delight as she looked in the prime of her beauty, near to sixty years ago? Would you remember her if you saw the image?"

"Remember her?" said Dr. Abel, stung to resentment at last. "Come, sir, I have lived in this world scarce more than five de-cades. I am not so ancient as you seem to think."

"True." Jeffrey bit at his fingernails. "True; pray forgive me; I had been thinking of another man who must be of much the same age. Are you familiar with the green-room at Covent Garden Theatre?"

"I go seldom to the play, Mr. Wynne. Above all I avoid green-rooms."

"A dissenter? A methodist-man? A scorner of all play-acting?"

"Why, to speak truth, the sight of these actresses in the green-room, only half clad and with breasts showing, is not a sight that is good for me. Do you find this ridiculous?"

"No; I find it honest. The same thought has been expressed by so staunch a moral man as 'Dictionary' Johnson. But it is not to our purpose."

He began to pace beside the canvas, still without touching its blanket.

"A painting similar to this—not alike, but similar—hangs in the green-room at Covent Garden. The one at Covent Garden is a portrait of Mrs. Bracegirdle as she appeared in *Love for Love* at the end of the last century."

"Mrs. Bracegirdle? Anne Bracegirdle?"

"The name is familiar to you?"

"It is familiar to all. She was kind of heart, they say. Alone among actresses she was virtuous. She left the stage when she was still young; she is buried now in the Abbey. That portrait there," and Dr. Abel pointed, "is also of Anne Bracegirdle?"

"No. It is of her younger sister. There have been doubts of Anne's great holiness; there can be no doubts regarding her sister's. Rebecca Bracegirdle, who took the name of Grace Delight, was more greedy than a Mincing Lane pawnbroker and less virtuous than a Covent Garden drab. Now see for yourself why I am at my wit's end."

He threw aside the blanket.

Dr. Abel's stolidity wavered. "But that is . . ."

"Hush, for God's sake. Lower your voice."

A woman's face and figure had sprung out as though alive. Her gown, of orange-and-blue silk, was in a mode fashionable when King William coughed with asthma at Hampton Court. A great web of diamonds circled her throat and fell to the opening of the bodice. The head was carried a little back, the mouth smiling, the fair conplexion set off by wired ringlets. Her face and figure were the face and figure of Peg Ralston.

"Young sir," said Dr. Abel, "I begin to understand."

"No, Doctor. Attend to me."

"I am waiting."

"My grandsire," Jeffrey said, "was this woman's lover for some years. He flung away a fortune for her whims. He decked her with half the jewels of Golconda. When she took a fancy to a younger man as the first wrinkles grew round her eyes, he cut his throat in a warm bath at the Hummums."

"I understand still better. You are much in love with Miss Ralston, it is plain."

"And if I am?"

"I could wish you were not. She is blood-kin to the old woman who died here. You and this girl may well have the same grandfather, and be bloodkin to each other."

"No, Doctor. No, I say! I have sifted the matter too thoroughly. We are no kin at all."

"Then it need not trouble you, need it? Have you made mention of this to Miss Ralston herself? Have you shown her the portrait?"

"No, damme! I had thought to; I had meant to; but at the pinch I could not bear to have her look on it."

"Would you wed the girl, feeling as you do?"

"Why not? Even if the lie were true, our blood-line is none so close. And she shall never hear this tale from me."

"But what if she should hear it from another? As she is bound to hear soon or late. What then?"

"I don't know."

"Young sir," returned Dr. Abel, rubbing a hand heavily and

wearily across his forehead, "I am myself weak and I would
not preach. Yet I count myself a judge of men. You can't wed
her; you can't even tell her. 'Behold this old woman,' you would
have to say, 'first in her beauty and then in her obscenity. We
share an incestuous passion, you and I; let all custom go hang;
let's marry and gratify ourselves, no matter how the world will
behave towards you afterwards.' Could you say as much to
her?"

*"Doctor, have done with this!"*

"And yet, if you were wed to the girl, there could at least be
no nonsense of haling her before a court to be put in Bridewell.
You would be her master, her legal protector. How can you
protect her now?"

The whispered voices struck at each other and clashed. Jeffrey
lowered the lanthorn; his arm was shaking. Then both of them
started. Though they had heard no footstep in the street, they
heard the fusillade of knocks as a fist hammered at the door
from outside. They heard Peg cry out. Once more Captain
Beresford's voice rose up.

"Open this door, Jeff. There's a woman in the house, for all
you told lies and denied it. She was seen at the Grapes; she enquired her way. Now open this door!"

Jeffrey moved forward, thrusting the lanthorn at Dr. Abel.
His right hand flew to his sword-hilt, and he drew the blade.

"Doctor," he said, "go below-stairs with the light and stand
at Peg's side. But don't open the door."

"I have a kindness for you, young sir, though God He knows
why I should have it. You'll add no more to folly on folly.
Put up that blade! What can a toy smallsword do against the
military?"

"Do you hear me, Doctor? Pray do as I ask. You don't know
at all what I have in mind."

Nor did Jeffrey himself, though by instinct he ran into the
other room and towards the shattered window. Then his heart
sank still further. He saw not only Captain Beresford with the
two soldiers; there were also two watchmen who might not have
dared approach without the backing of the Guards.

"You exceed your authority, Tubby."

"Do I so? The woman's name is Mary Margaret Ralston.
This Charlie here," and Tubby tapped one watchman's shoulder, "has a magistrate's writ to take her in custody."

"The value of a writ, Tubby, may depend on the person who
laid information against her. Since it must be Hamnet Tawnish
or Lavina Cresswell . . ."

"Hamnet Tawnish? Lavinia Cresswell? The information was
laid by her uncle, one Sir Mortimer Ralston."

Jeffrey lowered his head. Dr. Abel stumbled on the stairs.

"Tubby, that can't be! You are somehow mistaken!"

"If you doubt me, come below and see the writ. She is to be conveyed to the nearest round-house and appear before Justice Fielding tomorrow. Now, do you open this door or is it to be smashed with a musket-butt?"

Jeffrey waited while a man might have counted to ten. Then he walked to the trap-opening. Peg and the doctor were both staring up at him.

"Dr. Abel," he said, "you had best open the door."

"But you won't let them take me, will you?" Peg cried. "This is mad and I am dreaming and you won't let them take me?"

"They may take you, Peg—"

"*No!*"

"They may take you, I say, but they will not hold you long. The damned world must be fought with its own weapons; let that be so henceforward. Dr. Abel, open the door."

## VI

## *Of Lavinia Cresswell in the Alcove—*

IN COVENT GARDEN, towards seven o'clock on the following morning, a murky sky stirred with smoke above the roof-tops.

The day's brawling, shrieking, whistling had hardly begun. These houses, still high and handsome in red brick with white window-facings, looked very little gone to seed from outside. But the fruit-and-vegetable market, though not yet large, set up a din amid stalls and booths round Inigo Jones's column in the centre of the square. And so any inhabitants with pretentions to gentility had moved away years ago. From arcades called the piazzas along the north and east sides to a bagnio called the Hummums at the south side, it was full of dubious places and still more dubious people.

Prostitutes in some finery haunted the piazzas, picking pockets when they could not entice. Apprentices yelled at football round the market, using this as an excuse to run head-down at any stranger and butt him flat. Fishwives with covered baskets screamed their wares in language thought to be highly humorous. Law or no law against the sale of cheap gin, you could buy it anywhere and get dead drunk for twopence.

Jeffrey Wynne, at his lodgings above the snuff-seller's in the northern piazza, awoke with a headache from efforts on Peg's behalf that had lasted until two in the morning.

Hopeless! So far, entirely hopeless. The law had her fast.

It was true that those he tried to find had avoided him or refused to see him. And, though this might be fraying on the temper, it meant no more than a postponement; he had still to play whatever cards he held.

'Or if not . . . ?' it occurred to him.

He was served his morning chocolate by a landlady who expected curses from all her lodgers and was astonished only when she got them from Mr. Wynne. He washed and shaved in the bucket of cold water provided (usually) each morning for that purpose. He put on his only other wearable suit of clothes: cheap fustian coat and breeches, though with clean linen and a sword to be proud of.

But he had no money.

On a post-chaise, on unaccustomed coaches and chairs, on a

certain secret business too, he had spent every farthing received before yesterday from Sir Mortimer Ralston. If much more had been promised by the loud-mouthed old braggart in St. James's Square, he swore to himself he would not accept it now.

'When will you learn?' he was thinking. 'When will you ever learn?'

There was a chilly bite in the air outside. A dozen or so people were still sleeping off fumes under the shelter of the arcade. Towards his left, where Covent Garden Theatre loomed above the houses on the west side of Bow Street, Jeffrey glanced along and thought instead of Justice John Fielding preparing to hear this day's causes in a cramped courtroom adjoining Justice Fielding's house on the east side of the same street.

But he must not seek Mr. Fielding yet; or, at least, so he imagined. There should be another attack first. Jeffrey set out at a walk nearer a trot.

Less than twenty minutes later, less than a mile's distance away, he entered another square which was the exact centre of all gentility: as different from Covent Garden as old Lady Mary Wortley Montagu differed from Big Nell or Flash Kate.

Stately aloof houses faced out across cobblestones towards the octagonal fence of iron railings round an immense circular pond of water. His Grace of Norfolk dwelt here, and my Lord Bristol, and Sir George Lee. So did Admiral Boscawen. So did Mr. William Pitt, not yet created Earl of Chatham but already the genius of victory who would set British colours above half the earth.

Jeffrey, emerging by way of Charles Street into St. James's Square, was conscious of his own shabbiness when he ran up the steps of a house on the north side. It surprised him a little to see that the street-floor shutters had been opened at so early an hour for this district.

He plied the knocker, as he had plied it late last night without response. There was still no answer. Jeffrey hammered again, and waited a full two minutes with his temper on the rise. Whereupon, as though someone inside had been counting, the door was suddenly opened by a major-domo with a supercilious eye.

"Yes?" said the major-domo.

Jeffrey was startled enough to draw back.

"Where is Kitts?" he asked. "Who are you?"

"Well," said the major-domo, eyeing his clothes up and down, "who are *you*, then? What's your business here?"

"You are new-employed, are you not? Within the past few months, at all events? Is Kitts no longer employed?"

"Now what's that signify," asked the major-domo, "to any but my master? Who are you? What's your business?"

"My name is Wynne. I desire to speak with Sir Mortimer Ralston."

"Well, so you may. It don't mean you'll speak with him, though. What's your business?"

"I said," Jeffrey raised his voice a little, "that I desire to speak with Sir Mortimer."

"And *I* said: what's your business?"

Yet the major-domo began suddenly to back away, first with one long stride and then two, leaving the door wide open. Jeffrey had more than a stealthy sense that he was expected, and that the house had been waiting for him.

He crossed the threshold into the foyer.

You may buy the craft of builder or architect, as had been done here. You may have your foyer set out with a marble floor, with Ionic columns rising to scrolled and gilded capitals, with a wide noble staircase of dark wood against a white-panelled wall.

But a dank, unpleasant wind stirred through the foyer. It was nearly dark because of curtains that shrouded the tall windows. In a matter of months this house's whole atmosphere had altered as had its servant-in-chief.

The major-domo, carrying a staff which was the badge of his office, retreated to the middle of the foyer. Jeffrey, glancing left and right into the room on either side of it, saw that much of the furniture was different too.

Not long ago the world of fashion had been swept by a craze for the 'Chinese,' or so-called Chinese. The new furniture here—clocks in wooden cases wrought to spirals and curlicues, chairs patterned after dragons or lions' heads, gaudy cabinets built like pagodas with little bells at the corners—stood up floridly against each white-panelled wall.

Jeffrey looked round.

"I should have taken thought," he said. "How long has she governed matters, then?"

"Who?"

"Mrs. Cresswell. How long since she took up residence in this house?"

The major-domo's eyes narrowed.

"*I'll* tell you what," he snapped, pointing with his left hand. "You won't say your business, so you'll not see Sir Mortimer. You'll not see Sir Mortimer anyway. Sir Mortimer's in care o' the Scotch doctor from Jermyn Street; Sir Mortimer's been took ill."

"That is most distressing. Now will you be good enough to

conduct me to him? Otherwise, since I am acquainted with the way to his room, I will—"

"Yes?" interrupted the other.

Lifting the iron-shod staff, he brought it down sharply on the marble floor. He brought it down twice more for good measure. From the room on each side, from the rear of the foyer, from the staircase-landing high up, four liveried flunkeys emerged and stood motionless in the half-light.

"Yes?" repeated the major-domo. "Yes, cully? You'll do what?"

Jeffrey said nothing.

"*I'll* tell you, cully. If you was by any chance to call, madam said, you could have a word with madam herself if you'd a mind to. That's all; that's a favour. Do you want to speak with madam, cully? Or what else?"

"I will speak with Mrs. Cresswell."

"You'd better."

Jeffrey did not comment. This, incredibly, was Peg Ralston's home. This, now breathing slyness and full of servants like jailers at Bridewell, was the only home Peg had ever known. It had been a fool's act for him to come here first, but something might be learned. Still silent, stifling fear as well as rage, he followed one flunkey upstairs towards a closed door at the front of the house.

"You may enter," came Mrs. Cresswell's voice, a full voice for a small if sturdy woman. "Come, don't be about it all day. You may enter."

Jeffrey entered and bowed.

"Your servant, madam."

"My compliments, Mr. Wynne." She spoke almost coquettishly. "And how may I serve *you?*"

There was no Chinese furniture here. The large and lofty room, airless with windows still shuttered, might have been the dressing-room of any other fine lady.

The mirror of the dressing-table was draped in blue silk, as the table itself was draped in folds to the floor. Against more white walls there were chairs with cabriole legs. Within the arch of the alcove, narrower side outwards, stood an immense tester-bed with elaborate cornices from which yellow-brocade curtains had been looped back. Lavinia Cresswell sat propped up in bed to receive him, as the fashion was.

It was no longer fashionable to breakfast heavily off beef-steak with oyster-sauce, in addition to a pint of steaming chocolate and many rounds of toast. But Mrs. Cresswell had just finished every crumb of such a meal from a table beside the head of the bed. She was replete, she was glutted; and something more.

A candle, burning in a silver holder on the table, lighted her intimately. With great decorum the bedclothes were pulled up to her midriff. Otherwise she wore a fur-trimmed robe which had been permitted to fall open. Her hair was concealed by a lace cap: under this, under her waxy-looking forehead, the pale-blue eyes regarded him with a coquetry as unmistakable as it was startling.

"La," said Mrs. Cresswell, with a small laugh. "You are a most objectionable young man, Mr. Wynne. I have declared it often, above a year or more. Yet I am rejoiced to find you in better mood since last night, and resigned."

"Resigned, madam?"

"That this loutish girl shall be dealt with as befits her. I take pains all my enemies shall be dealt with as they deserve. Afterwards, to be sure, there is time for other matters."

"If I may say so, madam, you yourself seem in different mood since last night."

"That is weak woman's privilege, is it not? Besides, I had not then seen the letter you wrote—" Mrs. Cresswell stopped. "You are looking at me, I observe," she added. "Do you find me pleasing?"

"Madam, perhaps I do."

"La," said Lavinia Cresswell.

With more coquetry she extended her hand to be kissed. Jeffrey, wondering how much she knew and how much he might learn before he betrayed his longing to strangle her, was about to move sideways into the alcove between bed and wall. She looked past his shoulder, pale eyes widening, and uttered a small scream.

"Kitty!" she said. "Kitty!"

A tall and dark-haired young servant-maid, all eyes, now stood hesitating by the dressing-table. This, Jeffrey remembered, had been Peg's own maid.

"I had thought you gone, Kitty. Don't you heed my commands? Don't you even hear them?"

"Oh, pray, ma'am . . ."

"Be off, then. Be off at once, I say, or it will be the worse for you."

There was a scurry of skirts, the flutter of a mob-cap, followed by a soft slam of the closing door. And it was as though this exchange had intensified Mrs. Cresswell's emotion rather than lessening it.

"Come, Mr. Wynne, you need not start as guiltily as though Kitty had been your loutish Peg herself."

"I was not aware I had started."

"You are asking yourself, no doubt, whether I try a trick against you?"

"In candour, some such thought had occurred to me."

"There is none, I swear it! I have altered my mind since learning more of *your* mind—"

('Learning what? How?')

"—and of your country bumpkin too. I have gained so little in my life, so very little. You are impoverished, as once I was. We are much the same, you and I."

"As touches last night, madam . . ."

"Mr. Wynne, Mr. Wynne, can't we forget last night?"

"I hope so, if you are sure you know what passed then. Have you spoken with your brother, for example?"

"No, I have not. This I do know: Hamnet suffered a fall on some stairs, it appears, and badly bruised his right wrist. But this was only after he had followed your sweet miss. She had *not* gone to your lodgings in Covent Garden. She had gone to the house of an old astrologer-woman, a fortune-teller on London Bridge. The superstitious, such as this girl is, would give much credence to such kind of cattle. You are well aware of all this, since you followed her first. But at least it was not what I thought."

"It is seldom what we think. Yes, madam?"

"Oh, need I continue?"

"It is necessary; you know it. Yes, madam?"

"Well, bruised wrist or no, Hamnet persuaded a tapster at a nearby tavern to write a note for him, and sent it by street-porter to the Golden Cross. Thus apprised of her whereabouts, poor Mortimer could drive in person to Bow Street and lay information against her before Mr. Fielding. A later note apprised us she had been taken by the watch and will come up for sentence at ten o'clock this morning. There! Are you content?"

"Almost content. Is her uncle truly ill?"

"Unhappily, yes. Oh, most unhappily. I have never seen the poor man so disordered in his mind; he is quite confined to his room by Dr. Hunter. Now, you were saying?"

"We were suggesting, madam, that you and I might combine our forces."

" 'Combine our forces'?" repeated Mrs. Cresswell, looking up from under her eyelids. "La, Mr. Wynne. Now, what *can* you mean?"

"I meant—"

"Yes," interrupted the woman, looking him fully in the eyes, "that is what I meant too."

"We run a grave risk, madam."

"Risk!"

"Yet we run a grave risk notwithstanding; you know this too. For prudence' sake on both our parts, I would ask a question."

"Do you esteem me so little that you would put questions now?"

"I think you will see its necessity."

"Ask, then."

There was a pause.

Lavinia Cresswell's breathing fluttered the flame of the candle as abruptly she turned her head away from him. She turned her body away too: left hand supporting her weight on the bed, the white silk and dark fur of her robe outlined against the looped-back yellow-brocade curtains.

Though no clock ticked in the room, Jeffrey had never been so conscious of time pressing on. A coach-and-four rumbled past outside, the only noise in this all but rural square. Just as abruptly Mrs. Cresswell flung back round to look at him again. She was not at all ill-shaped under the open robe. But to Jeffrey, who ordinarily might have felt as Dr. Abel felt at Covent Garden, this seemed only to heighten and intensify dislike.

He spoke with the same abruptness as her own movement.

"We have no scruples, you and I. We can afford to be frank. You allow this?"

"Why not?"

"Are you wise in your conduct towards Sir Mortimer Ralston?"

"I have been wise for so very long. I begin to grow weary of it."

"Even so, is this a time for folly? You have been poor, as you say. Your own cosseted life and mine too (if you do me the honour of sharing it) depend entirely on your influence over Sir Mortimer. He was not happy, as you also say, when you persuaded or forced him to jail his own niece. Don't you endanger all things for too little? Why must you pursue this girl with such hatred?"

"I have a position to keep up in the world, I thank you. It is fools of her sort who would undermine us all. They must be made to suffer."

"Their loose morals impugn your virtue. Is that it?"

"That's the world: rightly so. And do *you* ask this, considering what we have both just learned concerning her? Would you yourself wed her now?"

Danger seemed suddenly to show the edge of a dagger.

"There is no mystery regarding Peg, or so I think?"

"Hardly a mystery. She makes her own lewd desires quite plain."

"Madam, you seem over-fanatical in this matter of lewdness. I referred to her birth and blood-line."

"Did you, indeed? What then?"

"She is niece to Mortimer Ralston, baronet, of Headingley Hall in Essex, who controls her money until her twenty-first birthday three months from now. Her father was his younger brother, Gerald Ralston; he married a lady of wealth and unimpeachable family. No mystery there, surely?"

"No mystery there," the woman said in a curious tone, "that I am aware of. Why do you ask?"

"Because all your behaviour has been so very odd. You hate Peg, granted. But she *is* an heiress, and you a shrewd woman without scruple. You must desire to provide for your brother, as impoverished as yourself, who would be a likely suitor for the hand of an heiress in marriage. He could wed her without open scandal, without any scandal at all, if you had not screamed she must be flung into Bridewell. You went further; you wished her to be stripped and thrashed by that same brother. Surely this is all a trifle odd?"

"Odd? I have given my reasons. Shall Hamnet wed with a girl like that?"

"Then your own course, as regards marriage, is still more odd. Mortimer Ralston is a rich man and of excellent repute. Already you hold some threat above his head to keep him obedient. You could make the future secure, you could gain all things you desire, if only you were to wed him. Why don't you?"

Jeffrey stood motionless, staring at the candle-flame.

"Mr. Wynne, attend to me."

"I think not. You have had your own way long enough. Last night there seemed no conceivable reason for this reluctance. This morning I find you, so tender of the world opinion, openly installed in his house. Yet you are not Lady Ralston in secret; you could not have forgone the pleasure of showing that authority. Is it possible you are no widow at all, but still with a husband who must not be acknowledged? That you don't wed Sir Mortimer because you dare not? Is it even possible—"

He broke off short, hiding a different kind of thought, and looked at Lavinia Cresswell's face.

The woman of a while before might never have existed. She sat up straight, as poised and aloof as she had been last night. What breathed from the alcove was only a cool, deadly hatred.

Some lighter vehicle, perhaps a hackney-coach, rattled past

over the cobbles outside. The candle-flame drew steadily, shining through dustmotes on a breakfast-service of heavy painted tableware. Then Mrs. Cresswell lifted the tip of her finger and touched one eyebrow.

"Indeed," she observed. "Now, do you truly imagine, young sir, you were leading me where and how you pleased?"

"I make no reference, madam, to the question of who was leading whom."

"Are you proud of yourself, Mr. Wynne?"

"At least I am content. Madam, are you content?"

"Then it is as well," said the woman, with a little shiver, "that your unprovoked advances did *not* succeed. I am surrounded by those who would delight to avenge me. It would go very ill for you, very ill indeed, if I were to cry out for help."

"That must be as you choose. And yet, even as an enemy, can't I persuade you to be generous towards Peg? You will not rise in the world's esteem by harming this girl. A word from you could set her free even now."

"So it could. Let her rot where she is!"

"Madam—"

"And did you also imagine, young sir, I should let you go even so far without holding a card in reserve? Are you so sure Mortimer and I are not wed?"

"No, I am not sure. There is a means to be sure. Pray cry out for help and let's test it."

"This is not the time, young man," and she smiled skeptically, "to display all the cards I hold. You will look upon them soon enough. But I must dispose of at least one vile insinuation against my character. My presence in this house is, and has been, quite proper. My brother has been here to make it proper."

"Yes, your brother," Jeffrey said. "Your *brother*. That may be the key to the whole riddle."

For a moment she sat looking at him as though from well behind the pale-blue eyes instead of with them, her forehead appearing more shiny. Then she flung her body sideways in a movement of catlike swiftness. He did not see the bellrope at the head of the bed until the thrust of her arm swept back brocade curtains. Those curtains upset candle and candle-holder, extinguishing the light. But there was time to see the savage tug she gave at the rope.

In the dark, at first without haste, Jeffrey groped for the door. No sound was uttered from that alcove; it seemed an age before he could find the knob. He opened the door and closed it behind him. That was where he began to hurry, left hand supporting his sword-scabbard, along a hall with an arched roof and a marble floor now softly lighted by a few candles in wall-sconces. He was only a dozen feet from the head of the staircase when a door opened at his left.

In the doorway stood Sir Mortimer Ralston, huge and swaying, a man clearly in illness near to collapse.

He had raised one hand as though for an appeal. His mouth was open, jowls sagging; he seemed trying hard to speak. And yet, either from illness or from the violence of his own emotion, he could force out no words. He stood holding to the doorjamb, in a flowered chamber-robe and with the usual blue-and-red dressing-cap pulled down over the ears on his wigless head.

Jeffrey, as much appalled as seeing a possible way out for Peg, halted and went towards him. But Sir Mortimer did not speak. Evidently he heard, as Jeffrey heard, the stealthy movement from the foyer below. He lurched back into the room, gasping; the door closed, and there was a metallic click as he bolted it in the visitor's face.

Then Jeffrey ran.

He ran as lightly as he could down a polished black-and-white stairs of such solid wood that it might have been marble. A grandfather clock on the landing showed the time as three minutes past nine. Though the foyer remained nearly dark with curtains still drawn and no candle lighted in its carved and gilded chandelier, a little glow shone through the balustrades above. Jeffrey reached the foot of the stairs, and someone touched his elbow from behind.

"Sir, I can help," whispered an all but inaudible voice. "Miss Peg, Sir, I can help."

The tall and dark-haired lady's maid Kitty slipped round in front of him. Against the right-hand wall near the foot of the stairs was a high, solid cabinet built in the gilded ridges of a pagoda, with a grotesque little bell at each corner of the top.

Kitty, wringing her hands in a gesture reminiscent of Peg, stood facing him with her back to the cabinet.

"Mrs. Salmon's Waxwork," she whispered. "Mrs. Salmon's Waxwork. Fleet Street. Four o'clock. Sir—"

Whereupon so communicable is panic, she whispered some blurted words which he could not hear and which nobody could have heard.

"Yes?" Jeffrey whispered back. "What is it?"

"Sir—"

"What is it, Kitty? What are you saying?"

"Yes, girl?" struck in another voice. "What are you saying?"

Kitty jumped and shrank away with the effect of disappearing. Just in her place, as noiselessly as ever, loomed up the major-domo with the supercilious eye and the iron-shod staff.

"It's you, cully," he said with pleasure. "Madam rang. I know what to do. Now, cully—" He lifted the staff to bring it down on the floor and summon help.

It did not touch the floor. Jeffrey's left hand snatched it away; his right hand, closing hard round the man's throat, jerked the major-domo high on his heels as though lifted in a noose. The back of the man's head struck with a crack against the edge of the pagoda-ridge that was just above. You could see the white eyeballs roll up and glisten against light higher up. Grotesquely, too, there was still a faint clashing from toylike bells as the man's body slid down.

Panic caught Jeffrey too; he had not meant to strike so hard. And it was all for nothing. Kitty had gone; he could not see her anywhere. He did see the two footmen, who must have been close behind the major-domo in any case, emerge from the back of the foyer.

He ran for the street-door, got it open, and avoided slamming it or bolting down the steps into the square. There was no hue-and-cry as he walked casually, looking back over his shoulder; he had not expected one.

But never had fool's errand been so botched.

Even if he escaped a charge of assault or worse, even if he believed he had learned some truths about an enigmatic pair of rogues, there was nothing here to assist Peg. Only Justice Fielding could help him now.

# VII

## —And Justice Fielding in the Parlour

"No," said Mr. John Fielding. "Regrettable as it may seem, I think I can't interfere in this."

"Can't or won't?"

"My reasons, though I don't choose to disclose them, are just and compelling. They are in your interest as well as hers. The girl must go to prison."

"Sir, this is a lady of quality."

"I am not unaware of it."

"Nor will you be committing anyone for trial," said Jeffrey. "You sit in judgment on a light offence; yours is the sole decision, even when you sit with one or two brother justices. You can let her go if you will."

"I am not," Justice Fielding remarked dryly, "unaware of that either."

Jeffrey, turning away, put his forehead against the window-pane and looked out into the street.

Justice Fielding sat in rather complacent fashion before the fire-place of his front parlour. There was no fire in the grate; the September sun had turned warm. He sat as he usually did when at home: under the row of blue-china plates along the chimney-piece, his sightless eyes turned towards the speaker, a table at his right elbow and a switch in his hand. He would carry that switch on the bench, waving it gently in front of him to clear his way when he descended.

It was a strong, calm face, if a trifle pompous. The sightless eyes, lids nearly shut, were without patch or bandage. They said of him that he could recognize two thousand lawbreakers from the sound of their voices alone.

"Jeffrey!"

"Justice Fielding?"

"I desire my people to be runners, yet not to use their legs on every occasion. You need not have run from St. James's Square."

"I ceased to run ten minutes ago."

"I am not unaware of it. But it is still discernible in your breathing. You should have taken a sedan-chair."

"Perhaps."

"Ah?" said the justice, catching even the inflection in a voice. "You have been thriftless again? After I gave you special leave of absence for your profit? This won't do. You might belong to the lower orders, for all I can teach you providence. It won't do. We can't have it. Here."

Diving with his hand into a capacious side pocket, he let a handful of coins roll out on the table.

"Sir—"

"Take it," the magistrate said gruffly. "This is no charity, understand. It shall be earned. You have been too long away, and I have need of your wits. There is work today, in particular at Ranelagh."

"Under favour, my only work now concerns Miss Ralston. When they carry her from round-house to court . . ."

"She is here already. By my particular order she was fetched two hours ago."

The images in Jeffrey's mind had been growing progressively worse.

"Here? In that foul place behind the court? Amid a parcel of prigs and mill-kens and bridle-culls? * Not to mention the whores?"

"Patience. She is above-stairs here in my own quarters. Under guard, but apart from the rest. I have questioned her closely with regard to last night."

In this wainscotted parlour, with the blue-china plates above the mantelpiece and the Dutch clock on the wall, there were two doors. One door led to passage and staircase; the other led to more living-quarters at the rear. The Dutch clock, ticking busily, pointed at half-past nine.

Jeffrey took a step forward.

"May I see her?"

"No, I fear not. Patience, I say. Before I am resolved on my decision concerning this girl, there are questions for you to answer on other matters. Can you put your mind to this?"

"Why, if you are not yet quite resolved," Jeffrey told him with a violent uneasy surge of hope, "I can put my mind to it fast enough."

"Very well."

Taking up the switch, which he had set aside when he shook out coins, Mr. Fielding moved it absently in the air as he gathered up his thoughts.

"The woman Cresswell and the man Tawnish." He spoke abruptly. "How is it that these two, of questionable antecedents

* Thieves, burglars, highwaymen.

and still more questionable behaviour, seem to move as they choose in good society?"

"I can't tell. None can tell. My late father, quoting my grandfather, used to say . . ."

"Your grandfather was called Mad Tom Wynne? And your father, regretfully, sometimes of judgment just as loose?"

"That is unimportant. Such people as Mrs. Cresswell and Mr. Tawnish are forever found in the great world. They are *there;* they seem always to have been there; nobody knows why."

"*Imprimis,* then, I think we may forget this adventure in St. James's Square. Your account gave facts, not conclusions. But we can't touch the woman yet. You agree?"

"I fear so. It was botched."

"It was. You should have got authority for going there; a word would have sufficed; still, I doubt there'll be a charge against you. And this major-domo fellow belongs to the lower orders, who must be held in strictest suspicion lest they turn to bad ways and find a good gallows awaiting them."

Again Justice Fielding meditated.

"As for the swordplay last night, which your young lady seems so much to admire in her telling of it: duelling is abhorrent. But you were provoked to it, and you rendered great service. We know the man Tawnish for a common cheat, enjoying every means from packed cards to the rigger's device of trumps in the sleeve-cuff. Thus far he has been safe from the law. Now, thanks to what you did, we'll lay him by the heels in a short time."

"Thanks to what I did? How?"

The blind eyes were turned full on Jeffrey.

"Come, use your wits. He has not been safe because of his dexterousness. He has been safe because of his repute as a swordsman. The victims he plucked were too much in fear of him to protest or lodge complaint with the law. Since that bubble has been burst—and such tales are heard very quickly —they'll run to lodge complaint with me and state their evidence. Then we have him, and so has Newgate or Tyburn."

"True." Jeffrey looked out the window. "It had not occurred to me."

"It should have. You have some few things still to learn. Now, then, with regard to last night's events in general; with regard to the girl Peg Ralston, and the woman who called herself Grace Delight."

"Sir, how much do you know about what occurred last night?"

"All the girl herself knows. More, I fancy, than she desired to tell me."

Jeffrey stared down at the raucous throng in Bow Street,

bracing himself. Though the eyes might not see him or read his face, he felt John Fielding's mind plucking at his mind to draw out secrets. At least, he reflected, Peg had not seen that portrait in the upper room above the Magic Pen. And also . . .

"Yes?" he said.

"Turn your head," Justice Fielding said sharply. "You are speaking away from me."

"So I am. Do you desire to hear of the events leading up to Peg's arrest?"

"No. She has already told me those. I desire to hear what occurred afterwards."

"Well, she was taken in charge by the watch, two of them, backed by an over-zealous friend of mine named Captain Beresford."

"This is also known to me. Did the watch question her? Did Captain Beresford question her?"

"They attempted to do so. I had told Tubby of an old woman dead of fright, but denied Peg's presence. They now seemed seized with the notion Peg must be responsible for the death, though this bore no relation to the charge against her. I prevented questioning, but Peg was in very ill condition. Sir, how is she now?"

"Not well. To continue: did they go above-stairs? Or make a search of the premises? Or see the dead woman's body?"

"No. They accepted Dr. Abel's account of the woman's death, which was a true one. Peg was already below in the passage. And they were not at all easy or happy on those premises; they left in all haste, except . . ."

"Except what? You have a thoughtful sound."

"Tubby Beresford swore the place must be locked up. I said there was no key, and believed so; but Tubby found an old key hanging on a nail beside the stairs. The street-door was locked; Tubby kept the key, and set stricter guard on the bridge. He is as scrupulous as you."

"And then? Continue."

"There is little more to tell. Dr. Abel went to his home; he will make report to coroner and parish clerk this morning. And I, as perhaps you know, presently went banging at your door and Sir Mortimer Ralston's to enlist aid on Peg's behalf. Nobody so much as looked out a window, let alone opening to me."

"It was in the small hours of the morning, I think. What else could you expect at such an hour? Even so, why were you so long about it? Was there nothing else?"

"Nothing else?"

"Nothing, for instance, that took place between the time of

the arrest and the time you went hammering at doors to no purpose?"

"Yes," answered Jeffrey, bracing himself again. "Yes, there was."

"You followed the two watchmen when they carried this girl to the round-house in Great Eastcheap? And you offered them a bribe to release her. Is this true?"

"Yes."

"Since the girl wore handsome clothes and was of evident position in the world, these hearties named a high price. When you agreed, they doubled it. You agree again. But they knew you for one of my secret officers and feared you would betray them. Whereat, having taken your money and got the girl behind bars, they would not release her. In such fashion you spent the last of what you had received from Sir Mortimer Ralston. Is this also true?"

"It is."

Justice Fielding's voice grew more harsh.

"Do you think it unknown to me," he asked, "that all the watchmen, and nearly all my secret officers, are as open to bribes as any menial of the late Sir Robert Walpole? If they thought they could escape detection they would arrest an innocent person for a crown-piece or release a guilty one for half as much. But I had expected better of *you.*"

"Then you were mistaken."

Even forgetting in his rage that he could not be seen, Jeffrey walked up to the magistrate and gestured at the coins on the table.

"There's your own money. If you are finished playing at cat-and-mouse, let me bid your tactics to the devil and you too. Dismiss me from your service and have done with it. Or, if there is a charge to be preferred—"

"Now, who spoke of dismissal? Am I so well provided with good officers that I can afford to lose my only honest one?"

"Honest?" Jeffrey repeated, and eyed the Dutch clock. "That is what I begin to wonder."

"*I* don't wonder, when you are open with me. The bribery I overlook. You are fond of this girl; you would not take a bribe, though you don't hesitate to give one. And what sort of example does this set? Good God, what's to be done by a magistrate-in-chief who would stamp out all wrongdoing—ay, and will contrive it too—if he have no help from those about him? In any event, what could you have hoped to gain by it? The girl would only have been taken in custody again."

"Guilty or not? That is one of the things I desire to mention. May I speak frankly?"

"By all means, if you speak civilly."

In desperation Jeffrey stalked towards the window, and turned back again.

"If I have offended you, sir, I make apology. But not one question you ask, or one matter with which you seem concerned, relates to the only offence charged against Peg. It is not said, I think, she was guilty of any wrong-doing on London Bridge last night? Or might be implicated in a murder?"

"A murder? What murder? The old woman affrighted herself to death, or was affrighted by shadows. Though there *is* a mystery here," Justice Fielding's thoughts seemed to turn inwards, "and this may be useful. Why do you suggest murder?"

"I don't suggest it!—not in sober earnest."

"Well, then?"

"The charge against Peg is of common harlotry. And that is a lie. She is innocent."

"Under the law, Jeffrey, she is whatever her uncle and guardian declares her to be."

"Under favour, sir: not altogether. In addition to the information laid by her uncle, some person must appear in court and give evidence of harlotry. The witness may be challenged and cross-questioned to sound the truth of the business. This is so, surely?"

"It is so," Mr. Fielding assented.

"Well, whoever shall appear against her, I propose to challenge the witness. And, if you lend but half a sympathetic ear for honesty's sake, I am sure I can convince you the charge is false."

"The evidence before me," Justice Fielding said slowly, "may be given by written statement."

"But such testimony may also be challenged in the same way?"

"Oh, it must be still more closely scrutinized."

"Then for the life of me I can't fathom why you should be so dubious, or regard Peg's jailing as an all but foregone conclusion. Since she is innocent, and you will scrutinize all evidence, whose testimony then can convict her?"

"Yours," replied Justice Fielding.

During a long silence, while the Dutch clock ticked remorselessly, he put down the switch. Touching sure fingertips across the coins on the table, he took up a small handbell and made it clatter.

"You *would* have this," he said. "I tried to spare you, but you would have it. Now you needs must have it whether you like it or no."

The door to the passage opened. Joshua Brogden, his ancient

clerk, entered with spectacles on nose and sheaf of papers in hand. Justice Fielding sat back in stately fashion, fingertips together.

"Brogden!"

"Your Worship?"

"You are acquainted with Mr. Wynne. Pray read the letter you have by you."

"Yes, Your Worship. It is dated," continued Brogden, turning over papers without looking at Jeffrey, "it is dated at Paris, as of some days ago, and addressed to Sir Mortimer Ralston in care of Hookson's, the goldsmiths, of Leadenhall Street. It reads—"

"No, stop. We need not distress a man unnecessarily. Give us the matter and substance of the letter."

"It states that Sir Mortimer's niece has been recovered from a house at Versailles used as a school for young women in— in some place with a foreign name—"

"The *Parc aux Cerfs.*"

"Yes, Your Worship. At this place with the foreign name, which is the private brothel of the French King. It further states—"

"That will do. Is it signed by Mr. Wynne?"

"Yes, Your Worship. It is an angry letter."

"An angry letter, and a pretty affair." The shuttered face turned towards Jeffrey. "Will you appear before me to challenge *this* evidence?"

"No."

"No, I had thought not. And don't tell me the offence occurred outside my jurisdiction. Since the complaint was lodged by her guardian, such offence may take place in China and still be within cognizance of our law."

"Yes. The law has mighty moral views."

"You would further say, no doubt, that you no longer believe what you wrote? That you were only a man distracted by rage or jealousy when you wrote it? You would say this too?"

"No, I don't say it. What in God's name would be the good if I did? But it is true none the less."

"Hear me," said Justice Fielding, picking up the switch and pointing with it. "You appear to think such offence a trifling one. It is not so. This girl, being a lady of quality, should have set a better example too. Here's the very irresponsibility which tempts humbler folk, servants or the like; it leads them through gaming-house or brothel (ay, and even theatre) to the robbery that will hang them. All pains must be taken, all care employed and every farthing spent in charity at the limit of a man's purse, to ensure that these people shall not go wrong.

If they go wrong then, we can do no more. Hanging is hanging; a rogue's a rogue, and there's an end on't."

"Is it so?"

"It is so. But I will spare the feelings of this girl's uncle
as far as I can. She shall go to prison for a month—"

"Do you conceive, sir, the effect on a gently nurtured girl
who must pass a month in Bridewell?"

"Who spoke of Bridewell? It's the custom, true, to lodge
prostitutes and vagrants at St. Bride's Hospital. But the place
of confinement is at the discretion of the magistrate. She shall
go to Newgate."

"*Newgate?*"

"Well, which is the worse? At Bridewell she would wear
fetters. She would be put to beat hemp—to mill doll, as they
call it—in company not the most savoury. She could be tied
to the post and flogged if she proved refractory."

Again John Fielding pointed with the switch.

"At Newgate, also granted, the company is none too savoury
either. But it is different for a prisoner with funds in his (or
her) pocket. She may buy private lodging. She may dine at
the governor's own table with others in funds. She may have
liberty within the confines of the prison. Now this girl, as I
understand, is supplied with money she stole from her uncle.
Even if she were not, Sir Mortimer . . ."

He hesitated slightly, with not quite a pause. And, just as
he had caught an inflection in Jeffrey's voice, so Jeffrey caught
some uncertainty in his.

"Sir, what game is being played here? What game are *you*
playing at?"

Brogden, the clerk, jumped as though he had been stung.
There was a fight going on in Bow Street, evidently between
a ballad-singer and a milk-girl; its screeching rose up.

"Game, sirrah? Do you question my honour?"

"No, never that. But there are times when you seem to have
confused yourself with God."

"Well, well, you have already consigned me to the devil.
I must make shift to find my spiritual home as best I can.
The girl goes to Newgate. And how, let's ask ourselves, will
you behave at this decision?"

Once more the switch was extended.

"Can I predict it? You will strike a great attitude, vowing
to quit my service of your own accord, and bid me to the
devil as you did before. Or you will run from here like a
birched schoolboy from the master's study, railing at monstrous
injustice because you can't abide the rules of the school."

"Under favour, you don't truly believe I will do either of

those things. And you are in the right of it; I will do neither."

"Which only means," the magistrate said instantly, "you plot other mischief. I have a kindness for you, it may be, but take care how you yourself trifle with the law."

"I will take good care, believe me. Is there any means of procuring Peg's release in less than a month's time?"

"She may be released, as you should know, at any time her uncle shall withdraw the complaint against her."

"Then I shall take still better care. May I see Peg?"

"Not in the justice-room; it would not be pretty for either of you, and I mean to have the court cleared. At Newgate you must please yourself."

"But in the meanwhile?"

The exchanges went like sword-thrusts. The clerk, on a wire of apprehension, turned from one to the other.

"Brogden, what is the hour?"

"Your Worship, it lacks ten minutes to ten."

"If you insist," Mr. Fielding said to Jeffrey, "you may have the ten minutes before I go below-stairs. But I strongly advise you against seeing her at this time."

"Why?"

"For one thing, she is not alone."

"I don't count guards."

"Nor do I. There is also a drunk clergyman."

"A drunk clergyman?"

"Another prisoner. If he had in fact continued assaulting and beating the watch outside the widow's house, as he began to do, it would have gone ill with him. As it is, since we must re-spect the Church and all order established, I am prepared to be lenient with him too. But no matter. That is not the main reason I advise you against seeing this girl until later."

"Then what is the reason?"

"Come, don't you understand? She holds you responsible for her plight; you will not be well received. That is ever the way of women. In this case, however, I think she has reason on her side."

A whooping, whistling din arose from Bow Street. If the magistrate seemed impervious to all this, Jeffrey was not. He pressed his hands to his forehead, and then dropped them.

"None the less, I will see her if I may."

"As you choose. Brogden, go with him.—One moment!"

The expression of the shuttered face, pompous and yet terrify-ing, followed Jeffrey as he crossed the room after Brogden.

"I would draw your attention," John Fielding said, "to a matter in your behaviour which was remarked as suspicious.

Why, last night, did you desire to remain for some time alone in rooms that contained only a dead body?"

Jeffrey, who had halted and was staring at the floor, swung round.

"Did Peg tell you so?"

"No. And pray don't answer each question by asking another."

"Sir, I think you expected no answer to that. You gave a warning, for which I thank you."

"Whatever I expected, you will be good enough to answer another question put some while ago. There is work for you today: it concerns some thefts in Ranelagh Pleasure Gardens at Chelsea. Will you undertake this errand?"

"If I must."

"You have other errands of your own in mind, perhaps?"

"Only one," Jeffrey lied. Then, still without speaking out, he spoke truth. "I was a great fool this morning. I fled from that bedchamber when I could have wrung a confession from Lavinia Cresswell. Then I lost my head and bolted. But all this may have been good fortune. It made other facts observable, and led to the errand."

"What errand, Mr. Wynne? Where?"

"You will have guessed it. Mrs. Salmon's Waxwork. Fleet Street. Four o'clock this afternoon."

# VIII

## The Crossroads of Perplexity

THE clock at the Church of St. Dunstan-in-the-West, a short way within Temple Bar and not far opposite Mrs. Salmon's Waxwork, began to hammer out three as Jeffrey approached from the east in Fleet Street.

He was still too far away to see the two metal figures, warlike in appearance though mysteriously and wrongly called Adam and Eve, which emerged from the clock whenever the hour struck. He was almost too far away to hear it under other noises. But he had still an hour's time, as well as another appointment close by, before he met what was awaiting him at Mrs. Salmon's.

And he might not have cared. He was in too black and bitter a mood.

His day, in one sense, had been more than successful. His visit to Ranelagh, less famous for its gardens than for the great rotunda which bloomed at night with concerts and routs and the masquerades so popular with illicit lovers, yielded little or nothing. He had not imagined it would; this was a device of Justice Fielding to keep him out of the way. It had been different with his quick, secret visit to the Magic Pen on London Bridge. It had required luck as well as planning to go there and escape unnoticed; he could only hope nobody had observed him.

Still more successful was his call at a certain banker-goldsmith's in Leadenhall Street. Being famished, he had eaten a heavy dinner and been careful to use coins only from Justice Fielding's gift of five shillings, two silver crown-pieces, and half a dozen pennies. He should have felt better. But he could not drive away the bitter memory of a scene with Peg Ralston at Justice Fielding's house that morning.

'Why, damn her— No, that's unjust.'

Jeffrey, a man of books somewhat heavy in their contents, also read the romances that had such swooning influence on current taste. He would read these with an eye of levity, reflecting on the difference between the heroines you met in books and the women you met in life.

The heroines in books were inclined towards the vapours;

and so, admittedly, were many women in life. But the heroines
in books remained verbosely lofty of virtue, a quality not quite
so common in life. The heroines in books met all misfortune
or adversity with a patience and long-suffering which was not
common at all.

Well, but what if that were so?

Could you wish any girl you loved to resemble the crafty
prudes so admired by women who read secretly as they drank
secretly? Moralists condemned both habits. Would you like
Pamela or Clarissa if you met either of them? Would you
cherish a woman who rolled up her eyes and moved on her
knees at all times when she was not denouncing your evil in-
tentions? You would not; you knew you would not.

Perhaps the trouble lay elsewhere.

Life was a solemn-faced buffoon. It allowed no consistency,
no reasonableness, not even a sense of the ridiculous to any
persons (women, or men either) when they were caught up
in strong emotion.

You should be enabled to understand this. You should be
enabled to smile at it as you smiled at it in the books of
Henry Fielding, who had drawn people as they really were.
But it seemed impossible. Faced with accusation or inconsistency,
you could only feel guilt inside your wrath and try to avoid
being swept away into words—or even acts—of the same un-
reasoning kind.

" 'Tis a lie," Peg had said, stamping her foot. "You'll not
call me a whore; I am virtuous entirely; I have lost it to none
but you. And it was you procured my arrest; you desired me
to be taken. And if you don't carry me from here this instant . . ."

"Bravely spoken, damn my eyes!" had said the Rev. Laurence
Sterne. "Bravely spoken, my sweet chick. He'll encompass it,
I warrant you. Or, if he can't or won't, he is no man at all."

"Hold your tongue, Mr. Sterne," said Peg. "Hold your
tongue, you odious person. He can encompass whatever he has
a mind to, and against any odds. Did he not carry me from
that other dreadful place? Face down across his shoulder, with
my modesty showing, and a whole company of French dragoons
in pursuit? He could carry me from here too. But he won't.
He wrote to my uncle, and got me taken."

"Peg, will you hear reason?"

"*Did* you not write to my uncle? You said so. And now I
have seen the letter."

"I weep for you," said Mr. Sterne. "And I weep for myself too. For *I* am falsely charged. I would no more have
assaulted the watch than I would have struck that widow across

her chops, being a Christian and a gentleman. If the bishop should hear of this, I am undone. But be of good cheer; *I* shall escape the stone jug; there's one who'll testify before the beak to my good character."

Peg looked at him.

"And now," Jeffrey had intervened, "will you entrust me?"

"I entrusted you before. See where such foolishness has led me. And now it will be Bridewell."

"Peg, I will have you released sooner than you think. And it will not be Bridewell; it will be Newgate."

"Did you scheme this with my uncle too? Newgate? Oh, God, the man speaks as though he were sending me to take the waters at Bath!"

"Are you supplied with money?"

"I am so; I have a purse in the pocket of my petticoat. Why? Would you rob me of that too?"

"Peg, don't be a fool."

"Jeffrey, I can't bear it," the girl whispered. "There are rats; and there are body-louses too, and no servant to pinch 'em dead. I tell you I can't bear it."

"Does—does a day or two mean so much to you?"

"Mr. Wynne," interrupted Brogden, touching Jeffrey's arm, "the time is short. And anyway I think you had best go."

"Yes, go," said Peg. "Go. Go. Go!"

But her eyes melted as he reached the door; he would have turned back again if Brogden had not seized his arm.

They had been in the magistrate's 'study,' a rear room with the sun striking through its window. In the window-ledge were volumes belonging to the magistrate's half-brother, whose family John Fielding supported after Harry died in Portugal. Brogden had drawn Jeffrey out into the passage and closed the door.

"Mr. Wynne," said the clerk, "you must promise me you'll not try to see her until this evening when she is more restored. If you don't promise, I know you'll try. If you do promise, I will go myself with the constable who escorts her to Newgate, and make sure she is not put upon by the keeper. Will you do this?"

"Mr. Brogden—"

"Will you do this?"

"Mr. Brogden, I am grateful."

And so now, tramping westwards along Fleet Street, Jeffrey's mood grew the worse from all sorts of fancies. He kept recalling that scene as over and over a man will press the tip of his tongue against a sore tooth, knowing each time it will hurt.

He was on the north side, within the line of stone posts

which bounded the footway, and on the same side as St. Dunstan's Church. The street could not be called crowded at this hour, though there was the usual crashing of wheels on cobbles and bad language from all the touchy. Jeffrey, going as far as the turning of Chancery Lane, looked across at Mrs. Salmon's premises on the south side of Fleet Street.

It was a very old wooden house. Propped up between a newer brick-built house at either side, it rose to four storeys of black beams and white plaster with tipsily slanted floor-lines and many old-fashioned windows. A wooden fish, presumably a salmon though painted pink, was affixed as its sign to the wall above the door. Also, since Mrs. Salmon aspired to the genteel trade, there was a sign for those who could read. Painted in large black letters on plaster, between the first and the second floor above the other sign, ran a simple legend of THE WAXWORK.

This was a famous establishment, which six years from now would be visited by a Scots lawyer named Boswell. But Jeffrey, like so many London-dwellers, had never been inside.

A smoke-pall obscured the fading sun and Mrs. Salmon's windows too. For a moment Jeffrey stood staring at the house, as though to make sure it was there and couldn't get away. Then he dodged across the kennel to the south side of the street, and entered the Rainbow tavern not far away. In the front room, as he had hoped, he found Dr. George Abel waiting for him.

"Doctor," he began, "it was good of you to come here in response to my letter. In a good cause, Doctor, would you be willing to violate what I take to be the ethic of your profession? Would you even be willing to risk breaking the law?"

"Mr. Wynne," said Dr. Abel, lowering his head, "already I have had occasion to remark on your impetuousness—"

"My impetuousness has gone now; it will not return. I swear this."

Dr. Abel, sitting on a bench behind a long table in the window-embrasure with his back to the street, looked up but did not comment. Jeffrey raised his hand.

"And I forget civility. Will you take a dish of coffee and a pipe of tobacco with me? Last night, at the Grapes, I observed you smoked tobacco."

"You observe much, young sir."

"I must do so to earn my bread. Will you take coffee and tobacco, then? And reserve judgment until I have explained what I am at? This concerns Peg Ralston."

"How is the young lady after last night? How has she fared?"

"Badly, Doctor. They have sent her to Newgate."

"Go on. I will hear you out."

The Rainbow, originally a coffee-house, still made much of this soot-black delicacy. They were served with coffee, with two long clay pipes, and with the tavern's tobacco in a tin canister. A tapster lit their pipes from a glowing coal held in tongs. There were a dozen other guests at tables and benches; Jeffrey kept his voice lowered.

"Last night, when I showed you the portrait of Rebecca Bracegirdle or Grace Delight as she looked in the prime of her beauty, you told me I would not and could not marry Peg because we might be blood-kin. I affected to scoff at this."

"But did not in truth scoff at it? I thought as much."

"Then you are wrong. I scoffed at it and still do. Let's be honest: at the back of each man's mind must ever lurk the words 'what if?' That is all, and it's of scant consequence. It was only one of the reasons which prevented me from wedding Peg long ago if she would have had me."

"Your other reasons, sir, must be uncommonly strong ones."

"Yes. My one other reason was a strong one; but you note I say *was*. It no longer exists. Since last night my circumstances in life have altered completely."

"Since last night, you say? How have they altered?"

"For the moment, no matter."

"Young sir, is this explanation?"

"Doctor, I beg you to have patience. Peg was committed to Newgate for a month. This morning I asked Justice Fielding if he knew of a way I might secure her release before the month had passed. He said she might be released at any time her uncle should withdraw the complaint."

"Well, that is true, surely?"

"Oh, yes. It is the best way and the shortest way, if it can be managed. But it is not the only way, as Justice Fielding must have known very well. If Peg and I become wife and husband, from that moment the sole authority is mine. I can get her released out of Newgate by marrying her tomorrow."

Tobacco-smoke drifted up in the embrasure. Across the room somebody was reading aloud from one of the news-journals provided by every coffee-house and most taverns, and was cursing in admiration for Mr. Pitt. Dr. Abel, a slovenly man but not lacking in his own kind of dignity, took the pipe out of his mouth.

"Is that what you propose? To wed the girl in prison?"

"If need be, though I will avoid it if I can. It is not, let's admit, a way to be preferred—"

"Preferred? It's not to be thought of."

"And yet last night, Doctor, it was you who suggested it."

"I said this foolery of arrest *could* have been prevented if you had been wed long ago. The objections are to any marriage at all. I gave them at length, and imagined you agreed."

"Well, the only objection now is that a woman named Lavinia Cresswell may try in some fashion to strike back at Peg. She must be stopped for good. Do you recall I spoke much of Hamnet Tawnish and of this Mrs. Cresswell, who is his sister?"

"You inveighed against them, yes."

"Now hear the true story," Jeffrey said, "of Peg and my relations with her."

He began to tell it fully from the beginning. If he did not spare Peg, he did not spare his own thin-skinned pride and jealousy. He told of their quarrel and of Peg's flight into France: which her maid, Kitty, had blurted out to her uncle after Peg's departure. He told of his own pursuit at Sir Mortimer's insistence, and of the latter's instructions: that he must keep a worried man informed at all times; and, if he found Peg, he must send a smuggled letter to say when they would return so that they might be met at the Golden Cross Inn. He told of finding Peg, and where he had found her; he told of their flight from Versailles to Paris, and from Paris to London; and, finally, of their arrival at the Golden Cross.

"I see," observed Dr. Abel, putting down a pipe that had gone out. "Once already you had lain with the girl, then? Before ever she fled from home? And so the damage was done?"

"Let's say that Peg and I have been more than friends on more than one occasion. My greatest wish is to wed her. Or do you think me a low fellow for confessing as much?"

"Yes, I think exactly that. But I also think you are not given to speaking scandal of ladies if you can avoid it. Why do you tell me this?"

"Because, without it, the situation would appear to have no rhyme or reason. At the beginning I could scarce understand a word of it myself. And now I have great need of your assistance."

Dr. Abel, under his stolidity as great a moralist as either of the Brothers Wesley, eyed Jeffrey up and down.

"Indeed," he said at length. "I assisted you last night, young sir, in a matter against my conscience. If you think I will aid you again, and this time in the Lord knows what, you suffer from a very rash optimism."

"Perhaps. If you refuse, I can't blame you. I can only swear a great wrong may be done."

"Then it must be done. Are all the world's woes to be piled upon *my* shoulders? And what makes you imagine I can help you?"

"Last night, when you were speaking to Mr. Sterne at the

Grapes, you mentioned a certain name. 'I can't claim to be Hunter of Jermyn Street,' you said. Did you refer to Dr. William Hunter?"

"I did."

"Have you any personal acquaintance with Dr. Hunter?"

"Some slight acquaintance. William Hunter is a brilliant and eminent physician; justly so, from his talents; and I am—what I am. But I daresay he could recall my name."

"Would you be willing to pay a call on one of his patients, passing yourself off as Dr. Hunter's colleague or assistant, and examine that patient to determine the extent of his illness?"

"Now, really!" said Dr. Abel, and struck his fist on the table. "No, really, now. I have heard much in my time, but this goes beyond all bounds. What do you take me for? Have you yourself no conscience?"

"I am a thief-taker, Doctor. In the first twelvemonth at that trade a man will retch at much he is compelled to do. Afterwards he will have as little conscience as I have."

"Yes. So much is plain from your treatment of Miss Ralston. And you are grown old before your time. But you have small knowledge of the human heart, Mr. Wynne, if you fancy that young lady behaved from any motives except affection for your cursed unworthy self."

"I know that now; I don't gainsay it. What I propose is for Peg's help. However, since quite rightly you stand on your dignity and your own purity of motive—"

"Well, go on." Dr. Abel, who had started to get up, sat down again. "This is madness; this is stark mad; I'll meddle no more in the affair. But I will hear you out. You and Miss Ralston, you say, arrived at the Golden Cross. Well? What occurred there to be of such prodigious import?"

Involuntarily he had raised his voice. The reader of the newspaper, engrossed in an account of Mr. Clive's victory at the battle of Plassey in India, glared across at them. Jeffrey looked at the table.

"At the Golden Cross, while Peg scurried away apparently to tidy herself, I went up to a set of chambers called the Antelope, after our innkeepers' taste for putting names to their rooms. And I looked in at the window of the private parlour."

"Well?"

"Up to then I had not considered Lavinia Cresswell as any great menace, though clearly Peg did. If Mrs. Cresswell in a genteel kind of way had become Mortimer Ralston's kept woman, what then? If he appeared to dote on her, what of that either? It is not uncommon among men in their middle or late fifties. But I could not conceive of him as a man who would bear much in the way of nonsense. And I had not even met her brother.

"Now, looking through the window, I commenced to wonder. Sir Mortimer sat eating and drinking at a table. Madam Cresswell paced by the fire and spoke to him. Though I could not hear what was said, this roaring fellow all but cringed. It was as though she held a whip."

"A whip?"

"The term was figurative; but her taste for humilating people is literal. When I entered the parlour, the situation became still more astonishing. Sir Mortimer's first words were a heart-cry about his niece's safety. Mrs. Cresswell would have none of this. She was possessed with the inclination to have Peg thrashed with a strap by Hamnet Tawnish before being jailed on the charge you know of."

And he related the incident.

"I imagined, as no doubt Peg herself imagined, Mrs. Cresswell must have read that angry, ill-advised letter I sent Sir Mortimer from Paris. Yet she did not refer to the *Parc aux Cerfs,* which to her mind would have been unanswerable. She could talk only with a kind of wild malice of 'louts,' 'bumpkins,' 'sluts,' 'cozening eyes,' and suchlike terms. At that time, as I afterwards learned, she had not read the letter or even heard of its existence."

"How do you know this?"

"You shall hear in a moment; it is the vital part of the explanation. For the true riddle here is not with Lavinia Cresswell or Hamnet Tawnish: it is with Mortimer Ralston. He shuffled and wavered before her, this man who should have puffed her away like a dandelion-clock, and agreed to what she proposed for Peg. Then, no sooner was she gone from the room to fetch Peg, his demeanour altered like a conspirator's.

"He begged me to save her from this pair of rogues. He knew Peg and I had been more than friends; he knew how I felt towards her. To 'prove my mettle,' he said, he had sent me on this long pursuit into France when at any time he could have had Peg found by one of his banking agents at Paris. He urged me to wed her now, since she was in danger, and said he had designed such a marriage from the start."

"Upon your honour, young man, is this true?"

"Upon my honour, in so far as I have any, it is sober truth."

"He asked you to marry her. With what response?"

"I said I would cut my throat sooner. You will be greatly in error, Doctor, if you take Mortimer Ralston for the beef-fed country squire he affects to be. He is as cunning as any pawn-broker, and as devious as—as Justice Fielding. Though plainly

Mrs. Cresswell held some threat above him, he denied it. By this time I was become as suspicious of his truthfulness as ever I had been of Peg's."

"What should his truthfulness matter if you cared for the girl?"

"It matters, believe me," Jeffrey said. "They will talk with much complacence of an excellent marriage between a poor man and an heiress, saying he now controls her fortune. So he does, in law. But have you never seen Mr. Hogarth's set of pictures called *Marriage à la Mode?* The woman knows this bondage is only by legal whim. Unless both husband and wife are as insensitive as clods, she will be all too ready to resent it. From the time of the first quarrel she will begin to despise him."

"Even in a love-match?"

"Especially in a love-match. Look at the world about us and deny it."

"Did you tell all this to Sir Mortimer?"

"No. I could not believe Peg was in danger. I could not believe Lavinia Cresswell would dare carry out her scheme, or that Sir Mortimer would not balk her if she tried."

"But again you were vastly wrong?"

"Until this morning it seemed so, yes. Straightway, at the Golden Cross, brother and sister marched in with the news Peg had bolted. They bore themselves like the lords of earth; or at least like the rulers of Mortimer Ralston. And still he did not oppose them. I learned where Peg must have gone, and I followed."

"Why *did* she go to those premises above the Magic Pen?"

"She believed Rebecca Bracegirdle, or Grace Delight, to have been an old servant in my family. Had she met the living woman, she might not have been undeceived."

Jeffrey stared at the window behind Dr. Abel's head.

"Mrs. Anne Bracegirdle and Mrs. Rebecca Bracegirdle, to use the courtesy 'Mrs.' we still employ for actresses, were sisters of very different sort. Rebecca was a dozen years the younger. They trained her early for the stage, but she had no skill in it. At sixteen, to the disgust of her elder sister, she became an orange girl. At seventeen, to Anne's still greater disgust, she married a cabinet-maker in a humble way of life. She found her true talent at nineteen when she caught my Lord Morrmain's eye. Two or three years later she was taken up entirely by Mad Tom Wynne. Yes, if Peg had met the living woman—"

"All this is not to our purpose," said Dr. Abel, and again smote his fist on wood. "I don't question Miss Ralston's conduct. But what of her uncle's? If he is an honest man, how should

he lay information against her and deliver her into these people's hands?"

"He did not do it to deliver Peg into their hands. He did it
to save her."

"To save her? By having her committed to prison?"

"Yes. And it did not cross my dolt's wits until I talked with
Justice Fielding."

Both of them got to their feet, facing each other.

"Early this morning, Doctor, I had another meeting with
Lavinia Cresswell. It was at Sir Mortimer's home in St. James's
Square, where I went to wait on him without being permitted
to go near him."

"Mrs. Cresswell also paid a call there?"

"It was not necessary. The lady lodges there now; she has
lodged there for some time. The meeting need not be described
in full. But overnight her whole demeanour had altered completely. At first it was as though I had met a different woman."

"More tricks and wheedles?"

"No; all sugar and spice. And it was no trick; she was sincere,
in so far as she can be sincere in anything. I looked so closely
for tricks, I sought so hard to entrap her in another matter,
that I failed to see a meaning as plain as any breakfast of
beefsteak with oyster-sauce. She had misjudged me, she intimated. The night before, she declared, she had not yet learned
how I really felt towards Peg."

Momentarily, in this tavern room with the boarded floor and
the red-latticed window, an image of Lavinia Cresswell ob-
truded as vividly as though she were present in flesh and fur-
trimmed robe.

"She made fleeting reference to a letter of mine. Since surely
she must long ago have seen that idiot's note from Paris, I
imagined it must be something new and I wondered what. She
also threw out such impassioned remarks about Peg—'Do *you*
ask this, considering what we have both just learned concerning
her? Would you yourself wed her now?'—that it might mean
some secret of Peg's birth or blood-line."

"Yes," Dr. Abel agreed. "We are forgetting that aspect of the
matter."

"We are not forgetting it, Doctor. Not for one minute. When
I hurried to Justice Fielding in Bow Street I learned the truth.
There was only one letter. But Peg must go to prison, and I
had provided the evidence to send her there.

"Mrs. Cresswell's altered behaviour could be explained now.
After reading that letter, she could not believe Peg would be
married to me or to any other man Sir Mortimer might ap-

prove. Even as fortune-hunters, we were all ruled out. The good Lavinia was free to use her malice as she liked.

"And yet, if she had come by that letter only since we met last night at the inn, how had she come by it? Who showed it to her, and why? The answer is that Sir Mortimer did. It had been sent to him in care of his bankers; he held it in reserve. Deliberately he showed it to Mrs. Cresswell before he took it to Justice Fielding at Bow Street."

"He protected his niece in this fashion? By sending her to Bridewell?—Stop, though!" Dr. Abel added suddenly.

"Not to Bridewell, remember. At Bridewell she would meet indignities he could not bear to have her suffer. Even Justice Fielding hesitated and betrayed the game there."

Dr. Abel sat down slowly, spreading out his hands.

"Mortimer Ralston," Jeffrey said in some admiration, "will gain his ends by any means he must use. He knew I loved Peg; he knew I am not over-concerned with scandal or reputation; he knew I would fetch her out of prison by marriage, beyond reach of two unpleasant conspirators, if he compelled me to do so."

"And Justice Fielding?"

"Justice Fielding, as well aware as I of the character held by Lavinia Cresswell and Hamnet Tawnish, is seldom averse to playing the part of the Almighty if he believes it will serve justice. I venture to think it pleased him when Sir Mortimer came there with the plan. I could not have expected this Roman pontiff of a magistrate to breathe a word to me of it. But Sir Mortimer might have told me! If he is devious, need he have been so devious as this? Could he not have dropped a hint?"

"If memory serves," retorted the doctor, "he more than dropped a hint. He begged you to save the girl. And you said you would cut your throat first."

"Now damme, Doctor, if you too join in the chorus of all the others—"

"Well, what else is true? Whose fault is her plight, if not yours?"

"And if you too refuse your help—"

"Have I said I refuse to help? But how can I help?"

"The old devil is ill and in care of Dr. Hunter. So they say; so I believe. Certainly he is surrounded by servants like jailers. I can't get near him. None but a physician could get near him."

"What's his complaint?"

"I don't know."

"Well, there are ways round that. And of putting all to rights with Billy Hunter. Even supposing I gain his bedside, though, what am I to do?"

"*Was* this his plan, Doctor? If he desires me to take all responsibility, I am ready. My worldly circumstances, as regards marrying Peg, will shortly have changed. But let him say as much! Then I am armed against the enemy. Then at least we can spare Peg the humiliation of being wed in prison."

Jeffrey pointed.

"Furthermore," he added, "you can satisfy your mind in the matter that troubles you most. If Peg and I were truly blood-kin, do you think he would not know it? Do you fancy he would have pressed this marriage? But ask him. Say frankly you have seen the portrait of Grace Delight, and ask him."

"Come, that is better. That is much better." Untidily, wig riding forward, Dr. Abel again rose. "You have not told me all—"

"No, I have not."

"But there are two questions. How have your circumstances changed since last night? What threat can Mrs. Cresswell hold over him? What threat can so much have frightened him that he chose a course like this?"

"My worldly circumstances have not yet changed; but they will. As for the threat, I think I can tell you. It is there for any with the wits to see. The secret, Doctor, is—"

Brisk footsteps rapped across the bare boards of the floor. A black gown billowed round. An eager voice rose up.

"It must be a wicked secret, then. Pray let's hear it.—Come, now," exclaimed the Rev. Laurence Sterne, breaking off in alarm, "but don't start so. Come, now, what's the trouble? Come, now, what a pair of demoniacs you two are!"

# IX

## A Fiddle-Tune at the Waxwork

" 'Demoniacs,' " Jeffrey repeated. " 'Demoniacs.' "

In later years he was well to remember that moment: dead pipes and cold coffee on the table in a window-embrasure, the light thickening outside like the late afternoon roar that had begun along Fleet and under Temple Bar, the clergyman with protruding eyes and hand at breast.

" 'Demoniacs!' " Jeffrey repeated.

"Why, but what's this?" demanded Mr. Sterne. "I spoke in jest, no more. My near friend Hall Stevenson, of Skelton Castle in Yorkshire, presides over a society he is merrily pleased to call the Demoniacs. It does not, I protest, at all resemble the infamous Twelve Monks of Medmenham, who are so given to impiety and devious ways. And don't be misled: I am not truly a Demoniac!"

"We are all demoniacs," said Jeffrey. "Mr. Sterne, who released *you?*"

"From where?"

"From the magistrate's keeping?"

"Why, what's this either? It was my widow released me. Not *my* widow, that's to say, since I am no corp yet. I refer to Mrs. Ellen Vinegar, most excellent young relict of a late pious vestryman of the Church of St. Mary-le-Bow, who attested my character before honest Justice Fielding. And the doctor here, in a manner of speaking, helped too. If he refused to attend the court, being too preoccupied in slaughtering his patients with calomel, he sent a letter to be read when I begged one."

"I did so," confessed Dr. Abel, knuckling his forehead and glowering at Jeffrey. "It troubled me; I am a vestryman of Bow Church too. At least I could say in honesty I had seen no ill act on this gentleman's part since I met him last night, and that I believed him in essentials a man of good heart."

Mr. Sterne fell back a step, like an actor seeing the ghost in *Hamlet.*

"Now, damn my great eyes," he cried, "but both of you seem *sorry* I was released."

"Not sorry, reverend sir. It is only—"

89

"Is this genteel? Is it civil? I am come to express my thanks. Your housekeeper at London Bridge said you were gone for an engagement at the Rainbow. I bespoke a chair all the way, which cost me two shillings, and is now outside with greedy chairmen awaiting more. Is this civility?"

"Mr. Sterne," said Jeffrey, "sit down and hold your tongue."

"I am destined for great things. I can't yet say what, but I am. When I was a boy at Halifax School, I would inform you, we had had the ceiling of the schoolroom new whitewashed—the ladder remained there. I one unlucky day mounted it and wrote with a brush in large letters LAU. STERNE, for which the usher severely whipped me."

"Reverend sir—"

"But my master was very much hurt at this. He said before me that never should this name be effaced, for I was a boy of genius and he was sure I would come to preferment. Is that not an omen?"

"Reverend sir," cried out Dr. Abel, "it is an omen and you are a man of parts. Now why don't you sit down and be silent, as Mr. Wynne suggests? Better still, why don't you return to Yorkshire and write books? Should they prove one half so full of meat as your discourse, then your preferment is gained and so is your name."

"Well, I have thought of so doing. There is a doctor there too, a damned fellow called Burton, I can see already as Dr. Slop. And as for *you*, young man, I was charged with a message for you. Ay, and was resolved to search all London until I found you. And now," said Mr. Sterne, cut to the heart at this ingratitude, "I don't know if I ought to deliver it."

"What message?" Jeffrey demanded. "From whom?"

"Ah! You change your tune, don't you?"

"What message, Mr. Sterne? From whom?"

"Well, I am generous. I take pity. It is from the sweet chick, the delectable morsel of flesh, who shared my unfortunate lot until they took her to Newgate."

"Yes, so I had supposed. What did Peg say?"

"She loathes you," replied Mr. Sterne. "She has bespoke the best room at the keeper's house in Newgate, or will do so. She has sent for great chests and boxes of all her clothes. She says she would not now leave her martyrdom if you begged her on your knees to go free."

"Martyrdom? Has it become martyrdom now? What does the idiot girl think she is at this time?"

"Mr. Wynne," urged Dr. Abel, as Jeffrey began to do a kind of small dance, "I counsel you not to be hasty."

"Martyrdom, for God's sake! Did I consign her to the house

at Versailles? Does she fancy Mortimer Ralston would not have been forced to put her in Newgate, if only for running away as she did? I swear I have all but finished. She deserves to remain where she is."

"Mr. Wynne—"

Even in a tavern, where almost anything except a murder might go unnoticed provided you did not interrupt a newspaper-reader or empty liquor into somebody's lap, they had begun to attract attention. Angry voices shouted out. A tapster stalked across.

And then, from close at hand above a grinding whir of weights as two metal figures emerged from a lofty door, the clock at St. Dunstan's Church banged out the first stroke of four.

Jeffrey halted, emotionally stricken sober. A moment later he turned his usual grave, courteous face.

"Dr. Abel, I ask your pardon. That professional call we spoke of in St. James's Square: would it be convenient for you to go now?"

"Yes, to be sure. And yourself?"

"I have an urgent errand I had all but forgotten. It is close by, but I should have been there before this. Reverend sir, I ask your pardon too. May I assume the responsibility for your sedan-chair on Dr. Abel's behalf?"

"Why, damme, this is downright handsome! But there is two shillings to pay."

"They shall be paid."

It was just as well, he thought a few seconds later at the door of the tavern, that Mr. Sterne had kept the sedan-chair. The afternoon tide, of most who could afford pleasure and many who couldn't, boiled from Strand to Fleet Street in both directions under Temple Bar.

The playhouses opened their doors at four o'clock for a performance that began at six or later. The cockpits—three of them, where steel-spurred fowls tore each other to pieces in a matted arena under tiers of bettors—set off a first bout between four and five. There were those who merely went to stroll in the Park. Yet on foot, or in private chariot or hackney-coach or chair, all struggled like mad to get there. Above Temple Bar the remains of two heads were still stuck on poles from the Jacobite Uprising of '45; but the heads had been there for so long that only a countryman would glance at them now.

Dr. Abel, clutching cane in one hand and wooden box in the other, was jammed back into one of those chairs from which no human being could climb unaided.

"Young sir . . ." The doctor hesitated, lowering his voice. But Mr. Sterne, galvanized when he thought himself winked at by a pretty, high-painted lady in a very small round hat, had already vanished.

"How may I find you if I should have news? Or send you a letter?"

"I am going now to Mrs. Salmon's Waxwork. Afterwards you may find me at the Hummums, in Covent Garden, at any time until I visit Peg this evening."

"At the Hummums?"

"Gently, Doctor! The Hummums is something else besides a place for assignations. It is called a bagnio; you may actually obtain a bath there, hot or cold or of the Oriental sort too; and I have need of one."

"Sir, this attack at Sir Mortimer may prove useless. You are sure you don't mind if I make mention of Grace Delight's portrait?"

"On the contrary. If any person has seen or knows of the portrait, he has and does. And the picture itself will no longer embarrass Peg. I burnt it."

"You burnt it?"

"These chairmen have been paid. After St. James's Square they will carry you where you like. Doctor, it is good of you to undertake this. I would express proper sentiments, as Mr. Sterne so often does, if I could force out the words."

"Pray don't waste them on me. If already you had expressed the proper sentiments towards Miss Ralston . . ."

"Not long ago I could have killed her. I am still inclined towards it. *Au revoir,* Doctor."

"But you still have not answered the question of—"

"Doctor, *au revoir.*"

The front panel closed. The chair lurched away.

Jeffrey, drawing a deep breath, stood back inside the doorway. He looked across the street, and up at two men who lounged on the balcony of the King's Head on the corner of Chancery Lane. Lifting his left arm, he swept it out slowly towards the door of Mrs. Salmon's Waxwork only a short distance away on the left. Unobtrusively the two men nodded. Then, hitching up his sword-belt, Jeffrey strode to Mrs. Salmon's door between its broad small-paned windows. He opened it, and plunged at once into twilight.

"That will be sixpence, sir, if you please."

"Yes, to be sure. Here is a shilling. Are you Mrs. Salmon?"

"Lor', to think you'd ha' mistook me for my aunt!" But the small scrawny girl did not seem ill-pleased. She stood teetering before him in cap and apron, jingling coins in the apron. "It's not often even Kitty is mistook for my aunt."

"Kitty?"

"The other niece. My cousin. Kitty Wilkes. She's a handsome, well-growed creature, Kitty is. And, oh, Lord, how I wish *I* was!"

"I am sure you will be."

Suddenly the small girl flew at the front windows, examined the coin he had given her, and flew back again. "But this is gold! This is a gold guinea."

"Is it so? I—I must have searched in the wrong pocket."

"Now, come! I can't give in exchange for a gold guinea. Not yet. The door is but just open."

"Keep it, then. Pray forget you saw it."

"Well, sir, if you will give yourself the trouble of joining the others . . ."

Jeffrey glanced round. 'The others' he had assumed to be a group of wax figures. They stood patient, unmoving, in a dusky gathering towards the right of the door. Among them were three or four large-eyed children, overawed by the mustiness and menace peculiar to the threshold of such displays. Now he could hear them breathing.

"It will be but a few minutes, I promise," the small girl said reassuringly, "until there's enough of us. Then I will guide all, which my aunt does when not indisposed, and tell you which is which. I am none so skilled as she is at waving the pointer, but I speak the speech pretty well. Still, if you'd choose to go alone?"

"With your permission, madam, the latter."

The small girl, who might have been twelve or thirteen, lifted one shoulder very high.

"A gentleman may buy much liberty for a guinea. Here as elsewhere. Lor', yes."

"Thank you."

"On this floor, as you see," and she gestured behind her, "we have the dwarfs and giants and other monsters, much admired by the nobility and gentry. Above-stairs we have the Kings and Queens of England, equally admired. On the floor above that, highest save the floor where my aunt lodges . . ."

Enraptured to be addressed as 'madam,' she kept an icy dignity. But now he could not miss the conspiratorial look which had been there from the moment he entered.

"Up there we have the curiousest figures and scenes too. I think they will give pleasure. I think, if you should go there, you may find what you seek."

"I think so too. Madam, your most obedient."

"Sir, be pleased to pass."

And she stood aside.

Down the depth of the room behind her, two lengths of dusty

red rope were looped through posts to form an aisle between
displays at either side. Jeffrey could see an enclosed staircase
at the rear. He sauntered towards it, glancing left and right.

The figures were astonishingly well made. If the creatrix of
the waxwork could never have seen a dwarf from Zanzibar or a
Polygar giant with a war-club, then neither had the teller of
travellers' tales who inspired her. Staring glass eyes, bunched
biceps and calf-muscles, carried the reality of a nightmare.
Also, in the way of monsters, there was—

"Stop!" cried the small girl.

Jeffrey, imagining this was for him, swung round. But her
back was turned. Towering above her, outlined against the windows, stood a man also scrawny of figure. He was a street-
fiddler, one of many such entertainers. He wore a battered
round hat; there was a black patch over his left eye, visible as
he turned his head; he carried a battered fiddle to whose neck
was tied a long pink ribbon ending in a bow-knot.

"Be off," said the small girl. "I'll not have your sort here,
and how many times must I say it? I'll not have you Abram-
men forever at these good people, scraping tunes they don't
want for coppers they don't have. Be off!"

"Now, hark'ee, fierce manikin," said the fiddler, bending over
her and speaking in a hoarse, whispery voice. "My money's
as good as another's, look. And also hark'ee . . ."

He bent closer to whisper. The small girl stiffened. One of
the waiting group by the door, hitherto patient, suddenly strode
forward. The small girl raised a hand to check him.

Jeffrey, after studying them for an instant, hurried on into the
enclosed stair-well. Two seconds later found him on the storey
above, where kings and queens stood in rows.

The floor, having a slight slope to the right as you faced
forwards towards the windows, was covered in the same sort of
thick matting used for benches and floor at the cockpits, though
so dirty that its original color could not be determined. A large
arched window, flanked by long windows with oblong panes, admitted tolerable illumination from a thickening sky. Imitation
ermine and glass jewels would have made a braver show by
candlelight, but no doubt they dared not risk fire.

The queens had fared pretty well at Mrs. Salmon's hands,
being for the most part of unearthly beauty. But moral judge-
ment, as usual, was passed on the kings. You could tell any
bad king by his evil leer or a frozen fit of the horrors in which
presumably he had met his end. All effigies seemed a little un-
steady on their legs; they were dominated by an idealized
George the Second, now seventy-five years old but appearing a

red-faced thirty as he threw out his chest beside the late Caroline of Ansbach.

Making no noise on the thick matting, Jeffrey ran up the next flight.

'Then her name,' he was thinking, 'is Kitty Wilkes.'

He had never known the girl's surname or even wondered what it might be. She was dark-haired but of fair complexion; she imitated Peg's mannerisms and the more genteel aspects of Peg's speech; she seemed nervous, rather clinging, for all her stolid appearance. And yet, if she would dare come here to meet him after what had happened in St. James's Square that morning . . .

'*Ware! Take heed!*'

But nobody moved, or seemed to move.

On this floor, with another slope toward the right, they had had built out the so-called grottoes like very wide booths projecting from both sides. You were to look into the grottoes for a vista of some scene in painted wood or canvas, with wax figures against it. Also, since the room was ill-served by its windows and the walls of the grottoes would throw every vista into dusk, they had risked lights of a sort.

On the floor, just inside each wall of each grotto, stood a short candle enclosed by a tin box with a perforated top. Small speckles of light trembled upwards with the effect of a heat haze. And the staircase seemed to end here, though there was another floor above.

Trying to remember what he had heard of the place, Jeffrey thought he recognized Mahomet's tomb with a wax Moslem praying in the foreground. Another vista showed the Lake of Killarney, not very convincing. Since a passion for the Gothic was as current as any craze for the Chinese, he saw a Gothic grotto too.

He moved forward over the grubby matting, glancing left and right. He called Kitty's name loud. Then he went to the Gothic grotto on the right.

A soulful woman in a white gown, who might have been a taller version of Lavinia Cresswell, stared straight back into his eyes. She stood under what appeared to be a stone arch, her back to the prospect of a ruined castle. Faint gleams of light, shifting up from the floor at each side, lent such mimicry of response to her face and eyes that a shock passed before he saw she *was* wax and the eyes were glass.

Yet there had been a stir, a movement, perhaps a rustle of cloth against wood, somewhere in this room.

"Where are you, Kitty?" he called aloud. "Are you here? Is anyone here?"

What he heard may or may not have been an answer. But
it came, very faintly, from the direction of the stairs and from
the room below.

> *London Bridge is falling down,*
> *Falling down, falling down,*
> *London Bridge is falling down,*
> *My fair lady.*

Jeffrey, standing motionless, turned his head round towards
stairs that were well behind him and on his right.

It could hardly be called a tune, that faint scraping of an
ill-made bow across the strings of an ill-made fiddle. It could
hardly even be called a voice, hoarse and little above a whisper.
But someone, standing below-stairs in the gloom amid the
kings and queens, scraped and sang at that chant of dialogue
which has haunted childhood for centuries.

> *Build it up with bars of iron,*
> *Bars of iron, bars of iron,*
> *Build it up with bars of iron,*
> *My fair lady.*

Back, in the same whispery voice, came the response and
denial:

> *Bars of iron will bend and break,*
> *Bend and break, bend and break,*
> *Bars of iron will bend and break*
> *My fair lady.*

Still it did not falter or even hesitate:

> *Build it up with pins and needles,*
> *Pins and needles, pins and needles,*
> *Build it up with pins and needles,*
> *My fair lady.*

> *Pins and needles rust and bend,*
> *Rust and bend, rust and bend,*
> *Pins and needles rust and bend . . .*

Jeffrey Wynne did not remember hearing the last three words.
On went suggestion and answer, first with gold and silver and
then with penny loaves. He did not hear this either. It seemed
to him that his wits opened, though to any person who saw

him it might have seemed he had lost them. He looked back into the eyes of the wax figure.

'That's it!' he whispered to himself. 'That's the answer to it. There can be nothing else, since . . . *Ware!*'

The sense of danger, tapping a warning to the muscles even before it reached the brain, was no mere instinct. There was a movement, perhaps only a noise of breathing, close behind him.

Jeffrey fell flat on his face, kicked out savagely as he rolled sideways, and bounced to his feet like an India-rubber cat.

The sword-blade in the hand of the man behind him, driving out at full-length lunge for Jeffrey's back, flashed silver in the lights underneath. But the attacker, though off-balance when his thrust missed, almost managed to check the lunge. The sword-point stabbed at the white gown on the wax figure; but it only just pierced satin, rocking the dummy without upsetting it, before the attacker had gathered his muscles for a retreat to guard.

Jeffrey, sword drawn, had little more than a glimpse of a middle-sized man in a blue coat with white waistcoat. Then he went out at full-length lunge for the right side of the attacker's chest.

But he had no chance against this newcomer. Not many swordsmen, caught off-balance at full stretch, could have re-coiled to guard-position and still parried an oblique thrust he must wheel round to meet.

The newcomer parried it—almost with ease.

He was breathing hard, but so was Jeffrey. The parry had thrown the newcomer into an awkward position for a riposte. But he made no riposte; he needed none to show his mastery. Instead he laughed in Jeffrey's face.

"Don't try it," he advised. "You can't touch me, as you see. This small-sword-play of yours, though tolerable enough for a novice, is not what Hamnet Tawnish thinks it is."

"Else you need not have troubled to stab me in the back, if you had thought you could do it fairly?"

" 'Fairly'? What is 'fairly'? Don't talk like a fool!"

The two points, still engaged, circled and ticked against each other. Both men, strung to guard-alertness with knees bent and left hand balanced out, watched each other's eyes through the line of the crossed blades.

Jeffrey saw a flattish, middle-aged face with a snub nose and a contemptuous smile. He saw in it, mysteriously, a personal hatred he had begun to share.

Silver lace glittered on the newcomer's coat. White waist-coat and stockings stood out vividly against blackish matting. Feinting several times, with a dazzle of light on the blade, he

forced his adversary round so that Jeffrey's back was towards
the grotto and his own back towards the stairs. Then he dis-
engaged and moved a little away.

"Don't talk like a fool, I say! Where's the girl?"

"What girl? And to whom do I owe the honour of being
near assassinated?"

"My name is Skelly, Ruthven Skelly, aforetime Major Skelly
of a most worthy regiment. Now where is Kitty Wilkes?"

"I don't know. I should be unlikely to say so if I did."

"Do you want the steel through your guts now?"

"You must try to put it there. I am taking you into custody
for attempted murder."

"Come, that's uncommonly kind of you. How do you propose
to do this?"

"If not in one way, then in another. Put up your sword."

Afterwards Jeffrey could never remember just when the fiddle-
scraping and the whispery voice from below had ceased. He
thought they had stopped abruptly when he fell flat to the floor
in dodging the thrust at his back. But he was never sure.

What he did see now, in the dim light from the front windows, was the burly and blue-chinned man who had just emerged
from the enclosed stairwell a dozen feet behind Major Skelly's
back.

This man, one of those to whom he had made a signal not
long ago on the balcony at the King's Head, was a constable.
He served the same function by day that a watchman served
by night. From a thong at his wrist hung the heavy ironwood
truncheon which was his badge of authority as pole and lanthorn
were the watchman's.

"Major Skelly," Jeffrey said, "will you put up your sword?"

"Where's the wench? She has not taken refuge with her aunt;
that door has been shut to her for years. She is not hiding
below-stairs, or with that thievish girl-cousin who supports her.
She may not even be here. Your life will be the longer if you
tell me. Where is she?"

"Major Skelly, you had better put up your sword. Look behind you."

"Come, have done with this. Do you think I'm to be gulled
with the oldest swordsman's trick that—"

"Lampkin, below the shells. Break it!"

Major Skelly's eyes changed as he saw Jeffrey's. He had
braced himself to turn, but even his incredible speed was not
enough. The ironwood truncheon rose and smote down; it struck
the sword-blade high up, just under the two circular hilt-pieces
called shells; the tempered steel snapped with a crack like an
explosion in this confined space.

Somebody uttered a cry, but not in their group. Briefly Jeffrey looked round, towards the windows at the front and the farthest grotto on the right. When he glanced back again, the constable named Lampkin had gripped a left hand on Major Skelly's shoulder. Major Skelly remained unshaken, still smiling. But his eyes had changed, murderously, and Jeffrey did not meet them.

"Well, my blood," Lampkin said to Jeffrey, with amiable heartiness, "what's to be done now?"

"Did you observe what happened?"

"All of it, my blood! Who was the fiddler?"

"I can't say. He was none of my doing. As for this one, don't trust a round-house. Hale him to Justice Fielding's and lock him up there."

"Now, do you think you can hold me?" enquired Major Skelly. "Do you truly think you can hold me?"

"Stow your whids," said Lampkin, raising the truncheon; "stow your whids, you damned sneaking-budge rascal!"

"I don't blame *him*," said Major Skelly, ignoring Lampkin and looking at Jeffrey. "He knows no better. *You* will see me again, good sir. And sooner than you think. And alone. And you will not like it."

"Take him, Lampkin."

Major Skelly nursed a numbed wrist as he was flung round, but he smiled over his shoulder. The pieces of the broken sword, polished blade and wire-woven grip with engraved knuckle-guard. gleamed against the matting. Fear, hot and unstifled, gripped Jeffrey before he could fight it away.

He walked towards the windows at the front, and looked round the edge of the last grotto on the right. A door was there, in a section of wall projecting almost as far as the grotto. He saw light-coloured eyes and dark hair in a half-open doorway.

"There is no more danger at present, Kitty," he said. "You had better come out now."

# X

## The Bagnio in Covent Garden

On the south-east side of Covent Garden, as the hands of the clock crawled past six, he faced Kitty Wilkes again in another room which also was two storeys above the street-floor like the room at the waxwork.

But all else had changed, including his mood and Kitty's.

Many persons would have been astonished at this room's handsome appointments, no less than its fragrant cleanliness. Against a light-brown wainscot, polished until each panel shone, hung large pictures in gilded frames. But a tester-bed stood in the alcove. Below the dressing-table, draped in silk, you could see projecting the edge of a portable wooden washing-stand with a copper bowl and underneath, like a drawer, a wooden *bidet* which could be drawn out.

Kitty had not failed to observe this.

Stolid and yet timid, even now she would not remove her black cloak with the hood drawn up. She would neither sit down nor touch the tea he had ordered for her together with a sneaker of punch for himself. Her light-grey eyes, set off by dark lashes, regarded him from inside the hood as though from inside a mask.

"I will aid you," she declared with passion. "Indeed and indeed I will tell you what you wish to know. But, oh, sir, pray make allowance for my natural sensibilities! Don't be peery; don't be suspicious; don't press me!"

"Nobody has pressed you, Kitty. Will you allow this?"

"Oh, indeed I do!"

But she lowered her eyes when she said it, after a quick glance at the door.

"You begged to be conveyed away from Mrs. Salmon's—"

"Oh, and I am grateful!"

"You begged to be conveyed from there to a place where we might talk privily. Well, that was two hours ago; and I have allowed time for your natural sensibilities. I went below-stairs; I went through the hot-room and the hot-bath . . ."

"The hot-room?"

"It is in the cellar, and no whit sinister. It is the sweating-room attached to the Oriental baths at this establishment, the only one of its kind in London. I sent a waiter to fetch my good clothes from the other side of the square; and I wear those clothes now, as you see."

"I do indeed. And you locked the door when you left me! You locked me in here!"

"There was no intent to alarm you, be assured. Yet we are both acquainted with another young woman who has a taste for running away at any awkward or inconvenient time. You had some such seeming about you, or so I thought, from the moment we arrived here."

"Pray, sir, where are we?"

"It is a bagnio. It is called the Hummums."

"Yes. I feared as much."

Kitty turned towards the pewter tea-service on a table beside the fireplace. Then, wringing her hands, she turned back again.

"Most fine gentlemen, I know, think it a point of honour that they must seduce or ravish any servant-maid who shall take their fancy. They even think it comical if she should resist. But I had hoped for better behaviour of *you*. Sir, sir, this is not worthy! I am only trying to help Miss Peg and Sir Mortimer!"

"Kitty, one moment!"

"It is not true, as Major Skelly seemed to think, that my aunt's door is forever closed to me. We quarrelled; I own it. Aunt Gabrielle gave me something of education, and hoped I should take upon myself the conduct of the waxwork. She was much incensed when I thought to find an easier life as a lady's maid.

"Well, she was right; I was the fool and dupe. After what has happened I can't return to St. James's Square, even if I should desire it: which I don't. But how shall I return to my aunt either," and again Kitty glanced at the tea-service, "if I am to be drugged and ravished in a common bagnio? Because there is so little virtue among fine ladies, is there no virtue at all in this world? Is it even comical that there should be?"

"I don't think it comical, Kitty."

"In your heart you do. They all do."

"Whatever I think or once thought, I am well paid out for it. Now, will you listen to me?"

"Sir—"

"There is no drug in the tea and no design against your virtue. I brought you here because I await a message from a certain Dr. Abel; it is the only place he knows to find me.

But he is not here; he has sent no message; I can't say what
may have happened.—Wait!"

The clock at St. Paul's Church, Covent Garden, rang the
half-hour after six. Once more Jeffrey went to the window and
looked out.

The light was fading into dusk. Some drunk soldiers reeled
out from under the eastern piazza, with prostitutes running beside them as though at football. Otherwise Covent Garden lay in
somnolence until it should awake with the uproar of gaming-
houses and night-cellars.

From here on the south-east side, fairly high up, he had a
good view out over the square. At both Covent Garden and
Drury Lane Theatres, whose shapes he could see ahead of him
and on the right, the play would have begun. Pit and boxes
would be filled to watch wigged actors declaiming under chandeliers bright with candles; Mr. Garrick himself was appearing
in *King Lear*.

But the light was fading here, and hope with it. On Jeffrey's
left, as he glanced down towards the turning where Southampton
Street mounted to Covent Garden from the Strand, he could
see an undertaker's sign, a tavern sign, the red-and-white striped
pole which marked a barber's. But nobody moved on the cobblestones; there was no sign of Dr. Abel.

"Sir—!"

"Well, have it as you please." Jeffrey turned back. "Yet my
sole design, like yours, is to aid Miss Peg and fetch her out of
Newgate before the doors are locked this night. Are you aware
she has been sent to Newgate?"

"Yes, I am aware. Madam said it would be Bridewell—oh,
most gleeful! Since last night there has been little talk in that
house save of London Bridge and Bridewell, London Bridge
and Bridewell, London Bridge and Bridewell. But at scarce
noon today Miss Peg sent a message for much of her clothes
to be delivered to the keeper's lodging at Newgate. I chose
them; a footman took them. And almost I decided not to aid
her."

"*Not* to aid her?"

"As though she took joy at being imprisoned! As though she
would mock and taunt at us all! It was hateful."

"Have you ever been inside Newgate Prison? Even as one of
the visitors, that's to say, who throng there in droves from eight
in the morning until nine at night?"

"Visit Newgate? No, never! It would terrify me."

"Then do you fancy she is not more terrified as a prisoner?
Peg is frightened out of her wits and strikes these attitudes
to keep up courage. It may drive her to some greater act of

folly if she is not released. Do you dislike her so very much?"

"Dislike her? Dislike her? Oh, God help me, I am more attracted to her than is seemly or than befits my place. I—I own at times I have been envious of her; she has so much in this world that others don't have. But I have tried to atone for this. Have my actions not atoned?"

"They have. Now look at me, Kitty."

"Sir—!"

"It grows darker, but look at me! Do you still believe, can you possibly believe, I have any intent to seduce or ravish you?"

"No. No, not now." Kitty spoke after a pause, and with something like a sob. "I am not clever; I am sometimes stupid; I am always fearful. Well, what *would* you have of me?"

"I must learn what you desired to tell me in St. James's Square this morning. I must learn all you know or even suspect. All!"

Shadows thickened in corners of the room; shadows blurred the paintings in gilded frames; shadows crept out across polished boards to where Kitty stood at the fire-place. She whipped off her cloak, folded it with care, and draped it across a chair. Then, breathing quickly, she stood there in a gown that was of coarse green serge but greatly became her and had a frill of lace round the square opening of the bodice.

"All I am sure of," she said, "is that I was resolved to hazard it when I listened outside the door and overheard what you and madam were saying in madam's dressing-room. Yes, I listened; we all listen. And again it was London Bridge and Bridewell, London Bridge and Bridewell, with the other things in madam's wicked mind. Yet I was sore afraid. When I detained you below-stairs in the foyer, and Hughes pounced upon us ..."

"Hughes?"

"That is the knavish steward whose skull you near cracked against the cabinet; and, oh, I am so glad you did! I hoped and prayed he had not heard what I said to you. If he had not, I thought, I might still meet you at the waxwork. Each week, if it should be convenient to madam, I am permitted an afternoon free to go and visit my aunt Gabrielle."

"To visit your aunt?"

"Aunt Gabrielle, I tell you, will have me back at any time I so desire it. But I do not truly go to visit her; I have been too foolishly proud, since I said I could fend for myself. I go only to meet my cousin Denise at the door of the waxwork, when Denise is free too. We walk in the Park, and eat cream buns, and dream of what our lives might be."

"Denise is the small scrawny girl, very precocious, who behaved this day like a great mistress of intrigue?"

"Yes; and so she is. She envies me; I envy her; it is ever the same."

"Well? Go on."

"Well!" Kitty wrung her hands. "The afternoon I am permitted to go abroad is always a different day. This week's was to be a Saturday, today. Because it was arranged aforetime, I hoped I might go from the house unsuspected. And I ran to take counsel with Denise. 'But what,' said I, 'if Hughes overheard? What if they be peery of me? What if madam should send someone to follow when I speak with Mr. Wynne?' 'Lord, lord,' cried Denise, 'but that is not easy.'"

"Yes. I can hear her saying it."

"My aunt *is* ill; that is truth; she can't leave her bed. We could act unbeknownst to her, Denise said. There—there is a street-fiddler we know well. He calls himself Luigi, as so many musicians take foreign names, though he is no foreigner at all."

"*You* sent that fiddler?"

"Well, Denise did. 'Twas she who thought of it."

"What was the fiddler to do?"

"Luigi (oh, or so we thought!) would follow and warn you or me if anything went wrong."

"How?"

Kitty lifted her shoulders.

"If you arrived soon after four o'clock, as I thought you must, Denise could hold back the first group of visitors; this is always done. She would know you from my describing; she could send you ahead of the others, with a broad hint to seek me on the floor of the tableaux. And *I*, I should be waiting where you found me: on the enclosed stairs up to my aunt's lodgings, with the door to the stairs half open so that I might run either way without being surprised."

"But the fiddler?"

"Luigi would wait in the street. When you should arrive, Denise should make a sign at him through the window to enter after you. She would pretend she desired to turn him away, but yield and allow him to go with the first group. Then, while Denise took long at the business of showing our visitors the parcel of dwarfs and giants on the street-floor, Luigi could leave the group and creep upstairs to make sure no person had followed to do us harm.

"Don't you perceive it? By that time, Denise swore, Luigi would know whether a trap had been set. If no person followed you, I would come out and meet you. If some person did follow, Luigi would play and sing a tune that would warn me."

*"London Bridge Is Falling Down?"*

"What else? What else was suitable? Denise said. And who is peery of a street-fiddler, sawing away either without-doors or within? If I heard that tune, I could remain hid with the door locked. Luigi could whisper to you that you must go away. Oh, I thought it so clever and so crafty! Were we to blame if the plan miscarried?"

"Nobody blames you, Kitty."

"You—you mean that truly?"

"I mean it truly. But how, in exactness, did the plan miscarry?"

"Why, we had not thought any would try to stab you in the back! We had thought any follower must be among the visitors through the front door, and not hid in the waxwork since the morning opening as Major Skelly must have been. I can't in exactness say what occurred, but it can be guessed. When Luigi saw him creep after you with sword drawn, Luigi's poor courage came as unstuck as mine. He played only a stave or two about London Bridge, and then, as afterwards you heard Denise cry in the uproar, he ran away as though from the devil."

Kitty writhed. Suddenly, as though in impatience or disgust, she stamped her heel on the hearthstone.

"But I am a fraud too!" she cried. "Denise and I were not to blame, did I say? That's a lie; you know it. Without the best of good fortune, you would now be lying dead at the Gothic grotto. Yet I could think only of how incensed Aunt Gabrielle might be at a brawl in the waxwork, and must beg and scream to be carried from there that instant. It was all a waste. It was all for nothing."

"It was not a waste, Kitty."

"Sir?"

"It was not a waste; be comforted. This tune of London Bridge and of the knitting-needle, as I apprehend it, had no meaning to your mind save as a warning. But to me it conveyed the right clue by the wrong means. This tune of London Bridge and of the knitting-needle—"

"Knitting-needle? What knitting-needle? In the song of *London Bridge Is Falling Down,* as I have ever heard it, there are no words of a knitting-needle."

He had stopped abruptly. They stared at each other, now little more than outlines to be seen in the thickening dark.

"True," he answered. "True; I had not collected my wits; pray forget I said this. And why do we stand here so? Lights! There must be lights!"

He turned away, not meeting the wide eyes. On the dressing-table, against the wall by the window and just underneath a

large painting, stood two candles in polished pewter holders
with a tinder-box between them.

Jeffrey blundered over to the dressing-table. A flint snapped
against an oiled wick; yellow light pushed back goblins.

It ran up over brown panels, restoring reality. It caught Kitty's
fair complexion and her green gown; it touched the suit of plum-
coloured velvet, coat threaded with silver, which Jeffrey had
been wearing the night before. He swung round from the
dressing-table, white wig in silhouette and a monstrous shadow
of him across the ceiling. But that light did more than strike
glints or bring back reality; it was as though, in some subtle
sense, both his mood and Kitty's had altered.

On the wall behind him, above the dressing-table, hung an
oil painting in imitation of Rubens: in full-flesh detail it showed
Venus in the arms of Mars. Kitty, who blushed easily, might
have been expected to avert her eyes. She did not do this. Instead she stood with her back pressed to the ledge of the
chimney-piece, looking past him at the painting.

"Sir, sir, you are not open with me!"

"Am I not? Why?"

"What is it you would hide from me?"

"No, Kitty; what is it you would hide from *me?* What is the
secret?"

"Secret?"

"With that mummery at the waxwork you risked my life and
your own. You did this, as I understand, to impart news of such
great significance that Major Ruthvern Skelly might have done
murder because of it. Well, what is the secret? Or is this
news of no great significance at all?"

"Oh, but indeed it is." Kitty's eyes returned to his face. "God
He knows it is! Sir, it concerns Madam Cresswell and Hamnet
Tawnish."

"You would not tell me, I hope, that those two are not really
brother and sister? That they are no blood-kin at all? That in
fact they are husband and wife and have been husband and
wife for some time? Surely this is not all?"

*"All?"*

"That was what I said. Any person who studies those two
must see there is little true resemblance between them. Mrs.
Cresswell is short; Hamnet Tawnish is very tall. Her hair is
fair; I have not seen him without his wig, but his long blue chin
suggests hair very dark. Any fancied similarity is in carriage,
in demeanour, in bloodless cast of countenance; in their features they have no resemblance whatever."

The girl stood motionless.

And Jeffrey's shadow bent crookedly across the ceiling as he moved forward.

"Come! If you were listening outside the door when I spoke with Mrs. Cresswell, sure you must have known I guessed this? You must have heard her fly into a rage when I suggested a secret husband, and intimated it might be this so-called 'brother'?"

"In very truth madam was enraged," Kitty cried, "as I saw through the keyhole before I fled away." Here Kitty's face flamed. "Yes; why should I not? Considering the wicked things which occur in that house, what with Mr. Tawnish going to her bedchamber by night when Sir Mortimer is not there, I am most grateful to escape the house and return to my aunt. But madam is *married* to Mr. Tawnish. Her marriage-lines, writ on parchment, she keeps in the drawer of her dressing-table; I have seen them. If Sir Mortimer should ever learn she is married . . ."

"I greatly fear he may know it already. We must have a better answer than that."

Kitty sprang away from the fire-place and ran from him. But she could not run far. She turned in terror, gripping her fingers together, with the brown-and-gold bed-curtains at her back.

"Sir, what's the matter? What have *I* done? Why do you use me as if you thought me a liar, and mistrust every word I speak?"

"Have I said I mistrusted you? Yet you seem most incredibly innocent. And also ignorant as to what kind of secret may be dangerous. If Sir Mortimer's mistress is another man's wife, she has done nothing for which we could put her behind bars or even balk her malice against Peg. Certainly she would not have committed murder to keep it dark. There is something else besides all this, something else behind Mrs. Cresswell's slyness or malice. What is it?"

"I don't know. Pray believe me: I don't know!"

"You watch and listen, as handmaids do. What can it possibly be? Think!"

"Well—there are other men. Or there have been. Madam has a great fondness for younger men, as indeed you must have seen when she made a set at *you?* One night, I recall . . ."

"Yes?"

"One night"—Kitty moistened her lips—"there was a most cold and whispery quarrel when Mr. Tawnish was in her room. 'Is it so?' sneers Mr. Tawnish. 'Would you have fared better if you had remained with him? Would your lot have been more enviable with the cupper?' "

"With the—"

Again she shrank back. Jeffrey halted his advance towards her as though he had been struck in the face. His left hand dropped to the pommel of his sword. Then his shadow stayed motionless on a white ceiling.

"Kitty, are you sure of those words? Those exact words?"

"I am sure."

"What did you understand him to mean by the term *cupper?*"

"I can't tell. How can I? I heard no more words that were clear. And it may have meant nothing."

"Or it may have meant much."

"Sir, have I leave to go from here now? May I go back home to Aunt Gabrielle?"

"Young men!" said Jeffrey, unheeding. "Young men!" He glanced round at the table by the fire-place, and then back again. "Mrs. Cresswell's marriage-lines, you tell me, are kept in the drawer of the dressing-table there. Are there any other documents or papers in the same drawer or elsewhere among her possessions? Any other documents, that's to say, which are also writ on parchment?"

"There is one other in the drawer."

"Have you looked at it?"

"No, I have not. Because you believe there is no such thing as virtue, you must not think me sly or without pride either. The drawer is unlocked; madam is mighty bold and careless; any who opens the drawer may find these documents for all to see. Oh, heaven pity me, but this is poor thanks or reward when I have only tried to aid Miss Peg."

"On the contrary, you have earned the highest possible reward. Mrs. Cresswell, it seems, has grown a trifle too bold. If we act with despatch enough, we may catch this elusive lady and hold her fast."

"Through what *I* said?"

"Through what you said. There are parchments in a clumsy wooden chest above a print-seller's shop. There are parchments in a fine lady's dressing-room many miles away. It is only fitting that there should be a connection between these. For together they may supply the motive for a murder last night on London Bridge."

"London Bridge?" Kitty screamed.

That was where he and Kitty both heard the knocking at the door.

They would have heard sounds before that if they had not been so preoccupied. First there had been a light scratching of fingernails outside. Then someone coughed faintly. Next, when this failed, knuckles tapped at the panel.

"Mr. Wynne! Mr. Wynne! My Wynne!"

"Yes?"

Jeffrey knew the voice. It was Mr. Septimus Frolic, the proprietor of the Hummums, in a kind of discreet agony. From his tone you could imagine him both attempting to bow and stand on tiptoe at the same time.

"Not for worlds, gad's-my-body, would I disturb any gentleman when he is taking his pleasure. But I can't help it."

"You are not disturbing me. Open the door."

"Open the door?"

"Nor am I taking my pleasure, as you so tactfully put it. Did I not tell you I was expecting a visitor?"

"Mr. Wynne, sir, you were not expecting *this* visitor. He is from the magistrate-in-chief across at Bow Street. He is the law. That's why I can't help it"

"Leave off!" said another voice, thin and elderly but so hoarse Jeffrey hardly recognized it.

And the door was thrown open.

"That will do," Joshua Brogden snapped at the proprietor. "I will tell His Worship how you tried to impede me. Now go."

Few had ever seen Justice Fielding's clerk either ruffled or upset. But he was badly upset at this moment. All good nature, all sympathy had dropped away. His mild spectacles and sober black clothes seemed charged with a demoniac quality foreign to him at other times. He entered and closed the door. Even then he did not reveal his full state of mind.

"Baths!" he said, cocking an ear as though for the benefit of a listening proprietor. "Rooms where gentlemen may sleep off a carouse! Rooms where heads may be mended and blood let after a brawl or a duel! Rooms where . . . well, we'll say no more of *that!*"

"Shall we not?" Jeffrey demanded. "Mr. Brogden, may I make you known to Miss Katherine Wilkes?"

"Your servant, madam." Grudgingly Brogden ducked his head. He opened the door, peered out as though satisfied, and closed it again. "I hope, Mr. Wynne, that your present air of comfort and even smugness belies your state of mind."

"It does not. There is reason to feel smug."

"I am sorry you think so. You are in great trouble, Mr. Wynne. You are in greater trouble than you imagine." Suddenly Brogden squeezed his eyes shut and inhaled a breath as though it hurt him. "She is mad! She is moonstruck! She should be locked up perpetually for her own good, and no doubt His Worship will see she is."

"Who is to be locked up? Or whom do you speak?"

"Of whom *should* I speak but your friend Peg Ralston? This lunatic girl has escaped from Newgate Prison."

# XI

## The Way Back to Newgate

"Mad!" repeated Brogden, shaking a skinny arm and fist. "Mad, mad, mad! What's to be done now?"

"Pray, sir—" Kitty began timidly.

Brogden stamped across to the dressing-table. He snatched up a candlestick and held the light high. First he looked round at the paintings, which were all of the imitation-Rubens sort like that of Venus and Mars; then he looked up narrowly at Kitty, several inches taller than he.

"Young woman," he said, "are you known as 'Kitty' Wilkes? Are you here as a witness and for no other purpose?"

"Oh, indeed I am!"

"H'm. I was deceived once before; I'll not be put upon again. Don't think to cozen me by a good and modest seeming."

"Oh, I will not! Pray, sir, is it difficult to escape from Newgate?"

This was unfortunate.

"Young woman, are you familiar with the procedure governing that prison?"

"Nay, I know nothing!"

"Why, then: any person not locked in a cell or laden with fetters may walk out of Newgate at any time he chooses, with none to say 'Boh!' to him or even observe him among the visitors. But felons condemned to hang or be transported overseas are locked up in irons and too well guarded. Lesser offenders never even try it. Those without money must wear fetters: they can't escape. Those with money may usually buy their freedom: they don't want to escape. All, that is, except this zany girl who must change her gown and run from there with a handkerchief at her eyes as though weeping! Such an excess of stupidity is not in nature."

"Gently," said Jeffrey, and seized his arm. "Gently, now."

Brogden faltered. After that outburst he became what clearly he was: an old, somewhat confused man, with natural kindliness and anxiety welling up through his sense of duty. The light of the candle, still held high, began to tremble. Jeffrey took the candlestick from him and set it back on the dressing-table. Then the clerk passed a hand across his eyes.

"You are right," he confessed. "I am not wont to fall into tantrums. They must be resisted. At the same time . . ."

"Brogden, this is not good for you. Sit down. Let me order you a negus or even a brandy."

"I can't take my ease. I must not. You don't seem to envisage what may be the consequence of this escape."

"It is bad enough, though far from hopeless. What a fool! Good God, what a fool!"

"Yes; she is foolish enough in all conscience."

"I don't mean Peg. I was referring to myself. I should have known her well enough to foresee it."

"Where is Miss Ralston now? Where can she have gone?"

"I don't know."

From the corner of his eyes he was watching Kitty Wilkes. Kitty, after that brief flare of fascination concerning the ways of Newgate, had become stolid again. Jeffrey paced back and forth at the fire-place.

"Mr. Wynne, Mr. Wynne, this is entirely between ourselves! Where is she gone?"

"I don't know, I tell you. *I* did not contrive this escape."

"Well, you had better find her. I like this young lady. She can be as exasperating as one of my own daughters. Yet she thinks herself much abused, and she is desperately fond of you. Let us hope Justice Fielding will take a lenient view. For you still don't seem persuaded of the danger."

"What danger?"

"Sir Mortimer Ralston, we hear, is gravely ill."

"Yes, he is ill. I have sent a physician, a friend of mine, to discover—" Jeffrey stopped pacing. "How do you know he is ill? And how came you to find me here at the Hummums this evening?"

"No matter. It would be disloyalty to His Worship if I said more. But what if Sir Mortimer should be dying?"

"*Dying?*"

"According to news received not long ago, he has been struck down by what some are pleased to call a choleric fit; it is more accurately known as apoplexy. Has he ever before suffered a seizure of this nature?"

"Well, yes. Now you mention it, he—he had some such attack when he first heard Peg was determined to become a playactress."

"It is a dangerous malady of the brain, I have heard. It has carried off men more robust than he. On his information (and yours, by the way) his niece has been committed to prison from a month. If Sir Mortimer should die, can he withdraw the charge?"

"No, admittedly not. But—"

"Hear me!" Brogden insisted, wrinkling up his face. "After being given a light sentence for a light offence, this girl deliberately flouts the law by escaping from jail. That is no small matter; that is serious. Do you begin to understand?"

"I . . ."

"You can't help her now: as by marrying her, for instance. If Sir Mortimer should die, and Mrs. Cresswell should care to charge her with being incorrigible, Justice Fielding might have no choice but to commit her for trial before a jury at the sessions-house. If she were convicted at that trial of being incorrigible, she could be sent back to Newgate for an indefinite time."

There was a silence.

"Brogden," Jeffrey said in a voice he very seldom used, "what damned hypocrisy is this?"

Kitty shrank still farther back, this time into the alcove beside the bed, looking out with a strange set expression. But Brogden had drawn himself up with no little dignity.

"Young man," he replied, "you are advised to guard your tongue before speaking so. I have done you no harm. And I am not a hypocrite."

"Nor is Justice Fielding, I suppose?"

"No, nor is Justice Fielding."

"His motives were good, let's allow. He desired to save her from Lavinia Cresswell and Hamnet Tawnish, to say nothing of a murderous knave named Ruthven Skelly, who will not meet justice until they are nubbed at Tyburn. He and Sir Mortimer devised this plot to safeguard Peg in prison. But she was innocent of harlotry; he knew it, and I think his conscience now troubles him."

"Even if the original charge were false—"

"Yet he would utter pious cant of returning Peg to Newgate as incorrigible? On the word of Mrs. Cresswell, whom he knows to be a rogue? When Peg was innocent to begin with?"

"Well, she has broken the law now! And that is the law, if an enemy should care to invoke it against her. His Worship, I may say, is prepared to be more lenient than she deserves. To be frank, I am come here with a message from him."

"I see. He offers me the chance to save his face. What is it?"

"If you speak in this vein, young man, I have no more to say to you. Good evening."

"Stop! Hold!" Jeffrey blundered against the table which held the untouched tea-service and the untouched sneaker of punch. He looked down at the sneaker of punch, a glass vessel like a very small bowl with a tin lid, as though it gave him a sharp reminder. "I ask your pardon," he added. "I was carried away."

"So was I, and I ask yours. But you don't make it easy for those who would aid you."

"How true that is," breathed Kitty. "Oh, indeed, how true!"

"Be silent, you," Jeffrey snapped at her. "What is this offer?"

Brogden touched his spectacles.

"First, you shall find this girl and hale her back to Newgate whether she likes it or no."

"A delirious prospect, good sir. What else?"

"Our danger is that one of the three rogues you mention, Mrs. Cresswell in particular, may force Justice Fielding to act against Miss Ralston. Therefore, as a second condition, you shall find him evidence to put all three behind bars. Do this, and His Worship will overlook the matter of the escape."

"Gad's life, he does not want much!"

"Come, it is not so bad! I may now tell you a part of your work has been done. Justice Fielding prophesied, or so he informs me, that Hamnet Tawnish would soon be denounced by a victim he had cheated at cards. He was denounced this afternoon. And so we hold one of them at Bow Street already."

"Brogden, you are right." Jeffrey smote his fist on the ledge of the chimney-piece. "This cursed devious magistrate sets no impossible task. For we hold two of them already, and now I think I can snare you the third."

"*Two* of them, did you say?"

"The second is Major Skelly. Sure you have heard of Major Skelly, since you are so deep in Justice Fielding's counsels?"

"Yes; who has not heard of him? And I included him in the three. What of that?"

"From Justice Fielding I had borrowed two constables, Deering and Lampkin, to await me where and when I should direct. Deering, the more intelligent, was designed for an errand which is not yet finished. Lampkin, the brawnier, I had told to follow me into Mrs. Salmon's Waxwork."

"Yes?"

"It was as well he did. Major Skelly tried assassination with a stab in the back, but missed. Lampkin was witness to this. He then saved my life from a swordsman I could never have touched, smashed the blade with his truncheon, and took Major Skelly into custody to be locked up at Bow Street. When you see him there, our second trophy of the chase—" Jeffrey broke off. "What's wrong? What ails you?"

"Mr. Wynne," cried Brogden, with a shaky hand at his spectacles, "is this some unhumorous jest to strike back at His Worship? Lampkin locked up nobody at Bow Street. I have been there all this afternoon, and I know."

Again there was a silence.

The clock at St. Paul's Church whirred in its throat before tolling out the first stroke of seven. All Covent Garden, save for church and poorhouse on the west side, had begun to awaken with the whoops of night. But Jeffrey set his mind on those clock-strokes, counting them as he counted to keep his temper, before looking up again.

"Lampkin?" he asked. "Bribery again?"

"If you were fool enough to trust him, and not take the prisoner yourself."

"Yes. I trusted him."

"When will you learn from His Worship's warnings? Until he shall stamp it out, there is scarce a man below the rank of the high court—thieftakers, watchmen, constables, prison officials; ay, and many magistrates too—will not take a bribe at the right time. And then swear they didn't, and who's to prove it? Major Skelly? We have lost him."

"We have not lost him, curse it! There is my own evidence."

"Not if Lampkin has been bribed to swear against you. A court at the sessions-house may believe you; it may not."

"Nor am I the only person who saw all this."

"That's better. Who else saw it?"

"She is *there*. Speak plain, Kitty!"

"Oh, I am happy to do so." Wringing her hands, Kitty emerged from the alcove. "What would you have me say?"

"I would have you say the truth. You saw this happen?"

"To be precise," Brogden intervened, "you saw an attempted murder?"

It seemed as impossible to doubt her sincerity, Jeffrey thought, as to doubt her passionate meekness. She dropped a curtsy at Brogden. Her eyes were all candour under the dark hair. She approached as the perfect picture of the virtuous servant-maid, Pamela Andrews out of Mr. Richardson's novel.

"I was on an enclosed pair of stairs," she answered, "and looked out but once. I saw these two gentlemen at fencing beside the Gothic grotto. But I heard all that was said. I heard the sword smashed; I heard another voice, which I took to be the constable's; I heard Major Skelly accused and taken."

"It is no crime," Brogden retorted, "if two men should be fencing and neither is hurt. Nor is it more than contributory evidence if one of them should be accused. I speak of a stab in the back, which is the only matter before us. Did you see this?"

"Nay, sir, how could I? But Mr. Wynne told me it was so."

"Now, by God, Kitty—!"

"Young man," said Brogden, "it will do little good to lose your temper or intimidate this deponent."

"Oh, indeed, it will not," Kitty wailed. "What I say is true;

Mr. Wynne knows it is. I am a wretched creature, if you like.
But I am a girl of good repute. Please, please may I go now?
May I return to the shelter of my aunt's home?"

About to ask another question, Jeffrey controlled himself. He
glanced first at Kitty and next at Brogden. Then he picked up
Kitty's cloak from the chair by the fire-place.

"Yes, Kitty, you may go. Here is your cloak; put it on."

"Is that all?"

"For the moment, at least, that is all. Turn round, pray; let
me set the cloak across your shoulders. There, that is better!
And now, with your permission, I will escort you below-stairs and
see you to a chair or a coach."

"A chair or a coach? Have I the money to lay out on such
luxuries?"

"Or has Mr. Wynne the money?" asked Brogden, looking
sideways. "A room at a bagnio, I believe, costs half a guinea
for two persons."

"Sir, sir," Kitty cried, "this is most kind of you. But it is not
far. It will be easy to walk in short-cut to the Strand and
Temple Bar."

"It will also be easy," said Jeffrey, "for one who would catch
you there in the dark. I am not the only person against whom
Major Skelly uttered threats. You shall have a chair or a
coach."

Kitty hesitated, fingers at her lips. Again Brogden glanced
sideways. Suddenly it was as though doubts, fears, rages all
boiled up at once in that panelled room with the flesh-coloured
paintings on the walls.

"Indeed?" said Brogden. "Well, escort the girl if you must.
But be sure you return here instantly. I desire a word in private
with you."

"Have no fear for my return," Jeffrey snapped. "I desire more
than a word in private with *you*. Come, Kitty."

In silence they went down through matted corridors and stair-
cases dimly lighted. From behind one door issued a sound of
drunken snoring. Outside another door was a tray with empty
bottles and a woman's broken garter. Kitty shied away from
these. But they were on the landing above the foyer before she
seized his arm and spoke.

"Sir, I have told you the truth!"

"I don't doubt it, Kitty."

"You say nothing. But you are furious; you would strangle
me; I am sensible of it. How can I convince you?"

"By answering me a question beyond earshot of Brogden.
No, it does not concern the waxwork! It concerns Miss Peg."

Here on this landing there was no sign either of the hot-room in the cellar or of its adjoining surgical chamber where wounds could be dressed and blood let with a suction-bowl. But a hollow echo in the quiet suggested big rooms below the street.

Again Kitty turned an apprehensive face. He quietened her.

"At noon today, you said, Miss Peg sent a message for clothes to be delivered at Newgate. What clothes did she call for? Don't look so startled. Answer!"

"Why, sir, the choice was left to me. Save, she said, that she must have a fine gown to be worn at evening, and also a sober cloak (like this one, I suppose), and also a mask."

"A mask?"

"A vizard-mask. I can't imagine why she should wish a mask at Newgate, or a gown for evening either. But I sent them."

"Describe this gown. No women's details; they would be gibberish. Tell me distinguishing colours alone."

"It was cream-coloured, then, overlaid by a sacque of flame-and-blue, and sewn with pearls. The other clothes—"

"They don't signify. Was the message sent word-of-mouth, or in a note by street-porter?"

"In a note, to be sure! The other way is not genteel."

"You destroyed the note, I hope?"

"No; why should I destroy it? I left it in Miss Peg's room."

"That is unfortunate. I must make great haste; I can't delay now. Stop; don't tremble; you have done well. Come along."

They descended to the dim light of the foyer, which was warm with hint rather than a tang of steam. A buff-and-scarlet uniform loomed up. And unexpectedly they came face to face with Captain Tobias Beresford, sauntering up from the cellar after the refreshment of an Oriental bath.

Tubby did his best to turn away and pretend he had not seen them, which was the unwritten law if you met an acquaintance here in female company. But he met a different reception.

"My dear Tubby," said a cordial voice, "how are you? This is well met!"

"Hey?"

"May I make you acquainted with a friend of mine, Kitty Wilkes? Kitty, this is Captain Beresford of the Guards. He is a brisk fellow, as you see."

Clearly Tubby had tried to estimate her place in life; and then, after one close look at her, was stunned by her appearance. Sweeping off his black three-cornered hat, much larger and heavier than Jeffrey's ordinary tricorne, he made so deep an obeisance that his hat touched the floor.

"M'dear," he breathed, "m'dear! Your most obedient."

"Let us hope you are, Tubby. Business, regrettably, detains me here. Miss Wilkes is the niece of Mrs. Salmon, who keeps that admirable waxwork between the Temple gates; and she has a most natural fear of footpads in dark streets. It will be better than a chair if you engage to lend her your arm on the way home."

"Oh, sir," begged Kitty, clasping her hands together, "would you be so good?"

"Why, split my bottom—your pardon, m'dear!—why, sink me, that's to say, I should be proud and honoured. Also, Jeff, this is downright handsome of *you*. After the unpleasantness last night, I mean. No offence, hey?"

"None whatever, if you remember her fear of thieves."

"Ho!" said the other, and tapped a heavy sword-pommel. "I'll remember it, I promise you."

"Then a fond good-evening to you both."

They went out together, looking at each other, towards a street-door propped open to the fine September night. A linkboy with a streaming torch ran past outside, illuminating faces. For a few seconds Jeffrey stared after them. Then, no longer amiable, he hastened back up to the room three floors above.

Brogden, hands on knees, sat wizened in an elbow-chair that had been turned round from the hearth. The change of mood was abrupt; Jeffrey slammed the door when he closed it. The candlelight jumped.

"Well?" said Brogden. "You desired several words with me?"

"If I am to receive an answer, yes."

"Speak, then."

"Have you one half as much evidence against Hamnet Tawnish, now imprisoned at Bow Street, as you have against the more dangerous Major Skelly?"

"No."

"Yet you say there is little case against him. Why? What devious plot is being spun this time?"

"There is no plot, devious or otherwise, unless it should be yours. Perhaps Justice Fielding would teach you a stricter observance of your duty. Perhaps Justice Fielding—"

"Justice Fielding, Justice Fielding. In candour, I grow weary of the man's name."

"And, no doubt, will not remain much longer in his service?"

"It may be."

"Yes," said Brogden, looking up over his spectacles, "we thought it might be so. That is the one word I want with you. Take care, Mr. Wynne. Take care you are honest with His Worship the next time he questions you."

"I shall take care. Meanwhile, did you escort Peg to Newgate this morning, as you promised you would?"

"Yes, I did. I was trying to render you both a service. I wish now I had not."

"Did she speak to you of any matters on the way?"

"One might say so. She railed at you and used intemperate language because you were not at her side to press her hand and speak encouraging words. I defended you, telling her quite truthfully you had been ordered away on an errand by His Worship, and explaining this."

"Did she make comment?"

"Yes. It was also intemperate. But she looked very thoughtful, it seemed to me."

"What happened when you arrived at Newgate?"

"Young man, does this matter?"

"Yes. I swear it matters, if I am to find her. What happened at Newgate?"

"What usually happens? We were greeted by Mr. Goodbody, the governor or keeper, with his customary request for 'garnish.' If Miss Ralston had not paid this, as I told her, her outer clothes would have been stripped off by other prisoners and sold to buy drink. When I advised her to draw her purse, and she displayed many sovereigns, Mr. Goodbody became mightily affable. He said she might have a private room in his own house for half a guinea a day."

Brogden rose from the chair. He bustled across to the window, his sense of grievance struggling against some other emotion, and turned round with his head outlined against the candle-lit panes.

"*I* served her in this," he said.

"Mr. Brogden, you must not think me ungrateful for your assistance."

"Indeed?" The clerk lifted his fist. "*I* made Goodbody yield much in the price he had demanded for a room, no less than what was to be the cost of her food at his table. *I* fended off a horde of fighting Viragos who jeered her, and a horde of diseased ruffians who would have pawed her. When they make so pretty a tale of Newgate in the *Beggars' Opera,* with thieves dancing to music, they should go and see the reality."

"They should. Peg would be the first to agree."

"She begged if she might send a note to her former maid, one Kitty Wilkes, for clothes to be fetched. She begged if she might have hot water and a wooden tub for a bath. Both these favours were granted."

"At a price, no doubt?"

"At an exorbitant price, to be sure. But what would you have? Such is the custom; we can no more change the custom than we can change the law."

Here Brogden pointed at Jeffrey.

"Yet all this time, as I now see, she was scheming a plot for escape. I left the prison at not much past eleven of the morning. By midafternoon, to my shock and Justice Fielding's, comes a messenger from Mr. Goodbody to say she was found missing when they sat down at two-o'clock dinner."

"And afterwards?"

"Afterwards comes Goodbody himself to Bow Street, damning and blasting as I have seldom heard him. On the floor of her room was found the grey travelling-cloak in which she arrived there. Enquiry among the turnkeys recalled observation of a woman, apparently young and pretty, who had left by the main gate among the visitors—"

"How dressed? In what sort of gown?"

"They can't be sure. She wore a black cloak with the hood drawn up, and had a handkerchief at her eyes as though weeping for someone condemned to death. 'Tis a common enough occurrence."

"But that is not all you have to tell me, I think. What else?"

"Well!" answered the clerk, hunching up one shoulder. "It was necessary to apprise Sir Mortimer of this escape. How could we know he had been taken ill last night? And so I sent a letter above Justice Fielding's signature. There was no reply by porter until a short time ago."

"Still, why should there be this talk of dying? If he could reply at all, he can't be in such grave condition."

"It was not a note from Sir Mortimer himself. It was from his physician, Dr. William Hunter. Nor was he in dangerous condition until—" Brogden paused. "When my letter was put into Sir Mortimer's hands, he fell down in an apoplectic seizure from which he has not yet recovered."

Jeffrey smote his own hands together.

"This was no one's fault except the girl's," Brogden said.

"No doubt. It never is. What happened?"

"Another physician, for some reason, had called at the house about that time: half-past four. Mrs. Cresswell and the servants, not knowing him, refused to admit him."

"Was he named Dr. George Abel?"

"The note did not say. When Sir Mortimer collapsed, however, Mrs. Cresswell shouted that this other physician must go up and attend the patient until they should fetch Dr. Hunter. Both physicians have been at his bedside ever since; they are not hopeful."

"Then Mrs. Cresswell read your letter too?"

"It was she who gave it to Sir Mortimer. We have all a score to settle with the lady." Brogden moved out from the window.

"Well, you are acquainted with the situation now. If you swear this girl did not tell you where she was going—"

"She did not tell me, no. But I may have some notion of where she is gone."

"In that case, you had better bring her back."

"My notion is only the wildest guess; it may be all moonshine. Besides, even if I should find her, how shall I return her to Newgate this night? The doors are locked at nine. They would not be opened afterwards for the King himself."

"I am going to St. James's Square now," Brogden retorted, "to do what I can. It will suffice for His Worship's purpose if you take the girl there and let her uncle see her. If Sir Mortimer should not die, which seems unlikely, it may be possible to drop the charges against her. In either event . . ."

The flames of the candles, caught in a draught, threw broad and fluttery light up across the painting of Venus and Mars. Brogden advanced still farther, fists clenched at his sides and eyes fixed on Jeffrey.

"You had better find her," he said. "You had better find her. You had better find her."

# XII

## Pistols above a Lake

FAR up-river, opposite trees and fields along the Chelsea bank, the wherryman pulled steadily at his oars.

Ripples shimmered past under the white eye of the moon. The damp breeze caught at Jeffrey's hat and wig as he sat in the stern of the boat. A very faint sound of music, intensified by loneliness, began to steal out across water from beyond those trees. At first Jeffrey scarcely heard it above the creaking of the rowlocks; then it grew louder at every stroke.

'Give me one turn of good fortune,' he was praying to himself. 'Give me one cast of dice that are not cogged. If I am mistaken in this, as I probably am, Peg has lost her chance and I have failed her again.'

The wherryman grunted. Glancing over his shoulder, he steadied the left-hand oar in its rowlock; the right-hand one dipped and feathered for a turn towards the Chelsea bank.

"Easy-ho!" growled the wherryman. "Was it Hospital Steps or Ranelagh Steps you wanted?"

"Ranelagh Steps, I said."

"Ar; I thought yer did. And there's a masquerade at the rotunda tonight, which there is most nights when there's no concert. But it's an odd sort o' cove, ain't it, as goes to Ranelagh by water in the night-time?"

"This odd sort of cove has his reasons."

"I bet yer have. Easy, me hearty!"

Jeffrey, on a wire of nerves, had stood up facing a wherryman whose back was now towards the bank. And he looked left and right.

In that loneliness, with Chelsea village little more than a few houses straggling farther west, only two buildings loomed up high against a pallor of moonlight. On the left was the dark-brick bulk of the Royal Hospital, where pensioners from old wars lay sealed up in poverty and sleep. On the right rose the rotunda of Ranelagh Pleasure Gardens, unmatched for splendour inside its shell.

Each was set well back from the river behind deep gardens and formal rows of trees. The Royal Hospital was dark. Even the rotunda, for all its blaze inside and its immense band of music thumping out a grand march, showed only chinks and glimmers at velvet-masked windows.

The waterman, digging oars deeper, looked up under a distortion of moonlight.

"In the day-time, ay! When they visits the gardens, ay! But for a masquerade at night, when the gentlemen is mostly drunk and the ladies don't wear much clothes, nobody goes by water that I've ever heard. They goes by land to the Ranelagh Road side, and straight in to the rotunda. The back gate o' the gardens ain't even attended."

"Quite true."

"I know," the wherryman said darkly. "*I* know."

He had shipped oars. The boat slid in sideways and bumped against stone water-stairs. The wherryman gripped the iron ring in the steps and held it there.

"Now get out." His voice went shrill. "That's a pistol stuck in the slip-pocket inside your coat, ain't it? You're on the pad, ain't yer? Your mate's here already, ain't he?"

"My mate?"

"Military-seeming cove in a blue coat and white waistcoat. Nimble as a cat for all he looked thick-built. *Ah!* Recognize him, don't yer?"

"I think I have met Major Skelly, yes."

"Well, you rob who yer please. But I'll touch nobody as does. Now pay the fare from Mill Bank Steps and be off."

Jeffrey jumped out on the landing-stairs. Then, at a cry from the wherryman, he turned round.

"Here is your money," he said, extending his hand with closed palm upwards. "Will you wait here for my return?"

"Not me! We talk o' Tyburn, don't we, as if 'twas the only gibbet? And yet everybody knows you can't go in or out of town in near any direction without seeing the deaders hung up in rows for a warning; and half of 'em is footpads or highwaymen. Wait? Not me!"

"Not even," and Jeffrey opened his palm, "for this much again?"

The wherryman began to curse with frantic greed.

"Quiet! Lower your voice!"

The cursing died to a whisper under cold river-wind.

"Whether you believe it or you don't, I am no footpad or highwayman. I came by water from Mill Bank Steps, only a very short distance away, because I have no card of admission for the rotunda-side. Nor do I attend the masquerade in any case. My business is with one Charles Pilbeam and his wife, who dwell in a cottage in the gardens; and I shall be short."

"Old Charley Pilbeam? Cove as keeps the grounds? What's the lay with *him?*"

"No matter. Will you wait?"

"Ay, I'll wait. But if I hears shooting—"

"This 'mate' of mine: how was he armed?"

"Like you. Sword and pistol."

"Then there may be shooting. And it will mean your life if you should leave before I return. Do you apprehend this?"

The moon-distorted face cursed and cowered. Jeffrey threw a coin into the boat. He ran up the water-stairs and hurried along a lane past the side of the hospital gardens to the gate in the stone wall at the rear of Ranelagh.

The gate, by which day-time visitors paid half a crown to enter the gardens, was fast locked. Impeded by the sword and by the firearm inside his coat, Jeffrey climbed the wall and dropped into shadows at the other side.

There he waited, peering round.

On either side of a central greensward, at the back of which stood the open-air stage for juggling and conjuring, a double line of poplars enclosed a sanded walk stretching towards the rotunda some two hundred yards ahead.

'Military-seeming cove in a blue coat and white waistcoat. Nimble as a cat for all he looked thick-built.'

Jeffrey took the left-hand path.

A wind went rustling and whispering, sinuously, through the tops of trees. Its noise should have been lost under the gaiety of music swelling from the rotunda. But you heard the branches' sibilance; you saw shadows moving; you walked lightly even on sand.

Inside that rotunda, as his imagination pictured, two tiers of private boxes were set in a circle of crimson-velvet curtains round a matted floor. Mirrors and flower-stalk lamps flashed back from its central pillar, and fiddles sang under a roof of twenty-three chandeliers. The doors of each private box on the ground floor opened out into the gardens, which were kept dark for the convenience of masqueraders at romping. There had been satires written, of course, on guests who did but parade endlessly round and round the central pillar to see or be seen.

> *A thousand feet rustled on mats,*
> *Over carpet that once had been green;*
> *Men bowed in their three-cornered hats*
> *With the corners so fearfully keen.*
> *Fair maids, who at home in their haste*
> *Had left all clothing else save a train,*

*Swept the floor clean as slowly they paced,*
*And then—walked round and swept it again.*

And yet Jeffrey, remembering those recent verses, could be thankful the gardens were not invaded by a throng. If you sensed the pulse of heat and life inside, you saw nothing here except shadow-dapplings in an avenue of trees.

The music soared up and stopped. Jeffrey stopped too. Someone else was moving as stealthily as he.

On his right, past an opening in the poplars, he saw the long and narrow artificial lake they called 'the canal.' A footbridge led out to an open pavilion, with a Chinese-style roof, in the middle of the lake. Day-time visitors could sit at tables to eat cakes and drink tea there, or ride in a gondola now moored to the footbridge.

He could have sworn he heard a chair scrape inside the pavilion; and then he could have sworn he hadn't. On his left, down another path past an opening in the poplars, stood a rustic cottage so embowered in bushes that he might not have observed it if he had not known whose cottage it was.

And then he saw.

A woman, moving in his direction down the sanded walk from the rotunda, had stopped dead too.

"Mrs. Pilbeam!" he called softly. "Mrs. Pilbeam!"

Her eyesight was bad or she was confused by the sound of his voice. She ran straight towards him, making for the path that would lead to the rustic cottage. She was a short, stout, middle-aged woman, wearing a mob-cap and carrying a covered tray. When Jeffrey loomed up in front of her, the woman flinched and gulped back a scream.

"Mrs. Pilbeam! Look up! Look up at me! Don't you recognize me? I was sent here this morning."

His urgent whisper coiled round her in reassurance. Startled eyes, against the sort of face called comfortable, made an upturned shining under the moon.

"Bow Street," she whispered back. "Bow Street!"

"Yes. Now where is she?"

"Where is who?"

There was no guilt in the voice, only fright and fierce resentment. Jeffrey drew her to one side into shadow.

"May I repeat, Mrs. Pilbeam, that I was here this morning?"

"And may *I* repeat," the well-spoken words whispered back, "that we told you? If my husband keeps the grounds, and has the hire of gardeners and cleaners, does that mean he knows which of them may have been picking pockets?"

"No, it does not. We were agreed upon it."

"My husband is seventy-five. He served with Duke Marl-borough's self at Oudenarde in '08 and Malplaquet in '09. Every poor pensioner next door bows deeply in passing him. Hath any man ever impugned—?"

"None has or does," Jeffrey interrupted. "But I speak of a girl named Peg Ralston."

"Do you so?"

"She heard all this tale from Brogden, Justice Fielding's clerk. She arrived here early this afternoon, with a cloak hiding a formal gown. If she could persuade you to hide her in the cottage by day (and not by money either, I think), then she could show herself at night when there are three or four masquerades a week. She could even go abroad in the town, masquerades being so popular in London, and none suspect her from the very paradox that she hid her face. Thus she could bide until the time she hoped I would prove her innocence and set her free."

Jeffrey leaned forward, twitching the white damask cloth off the tray. On it was the kind of refreshment they provided at the rotunda: slices of chicken-breast, bread-and-butter cut thin, and a glass of champagne.

"I beg you, Mrs. Pilbeam, to tell me where she is."

Mrs. Pilbeam snatched back the cloth and retreated a step.

"Lawk-o'-mercy, but haven't Bow Street enough to do without this?"

"Without what?"

"A poor girl is locked up in her room by her uncle, and can't get out to marry the man she loves—"

"Is this what Peg informed you?"

"She is a sweet creature!"

"Some might declare it. She is also a very unwise girl and a romantical liar. She was locked up at Newgate Prison."

The glass of champagne spilled over. Again a vast wind went rustling, whispering as though searching, through leaves as yet hardly coloured with the tinge of autumn. Yet a scent of autumn blew with it.

"Mrs. Pilbeam," Jeffrey pleaded, "I won't threaten you. I need not. Your honesty, and your husband's, is unquestioned. But you are the more open of heart to the tales of a silly if admittedly ill-used girl, whose headstrong behaviour has put herself again in hazard. Therefore . . ."

Another voice spoke, in a furious whisper that carried clearly.

"Leave off!" it cried. "Stop tormenting the woman, can't you? I'll not have it."

Jeffrey whirled round. He had not been mistaken about the scrape of a chair inside the pavilion on the canal.

Rhinestones glittered on a black vizard-mask, and the mouth below it was contorted. The wearer of the mask stood on the footbridge at the entrance to the pavilion. White shoulders rose above a white gown enclosed in colours that might have been flame-and-blue drained to grey by the moon.

"I am a fool, am I? I am a liar, am I?" Then the shoulders were contorted. Eyelids winked inside the mask, and tears shone against it. "But, O God, I am so grateful you are come!"

And thus he found Peg.

Jeffrey ran out across the footbridge. He saw her arms open. From the direction of the rotunda, much closer now, the orchestra had soared into a dreaming melody of horns and strings. That was when the pistol-shot exploded ten yards behind his back.

Something like a fist whacked the rustic support just above their heads. Peg, crying out, was borne backwards into shadow and to the floor. Jeffrey scarcely heard the crash as Mrs. Pilbeam dropped tray and plates and glass. His sword-scabbard rattled against the floor; so did the pistol he was trying to disentangle from inside his coat. He rolled over and scrambled to his knees.

Then silence, except for Peg's breathing. Nothing moved outside. Nobody spoke.

The moon was almost overhead; it threw dense shadow inside. The breeze blew through a pavilion entirely open, under the supports to its Chinese roof, except for a zigzag of oak panel enclosing it from the floor to a little below waist-height. Jeffrey stood up straight, looking round and round across silvery water on every side.

Still the quiet held. Mrs. Pilbeam had fled away up the path to her cottage. There was no more clamour, even, from birds disturbed in trees. The next conversation, in whispers, he would remember for all time.

"Jeffrey—"

"Don't try to get up!"

Life, still the buffoon at moments of the sincerest emotion, had left Peg on the floor in a position half sitting, half reclining with her back against a chair. Her legs were sprawled out under a disarranged hoop. Tears of sheer indignity shone through the eyes of the mask. When she would have scrambled up, his left hand clamped round her shoulder.

"Stay where you are. The oak should be proof against a pistol-bullet at this distance. Did you see who fired at us?"

"No, no, no! I—I saw a flash beside a tree in the poplar-walk. Who could have done that? Who would have done it?"

"I believe it was a certain Major Skelly, Hamnet Tawnish's friend—and Madam Cresswell's."

"Well, why does he wait? Why can't he show himself or call out?"

"The good major thinks to terrify or goad us. Let him wonder, Peg; let *him* be the first to act."

"Can't we run from here?"

"Only across the footbridge or wading deep in water as targets. He has had time to reload the pistol."

"But you yourself have a—"

This time the hand clamped round her mouth.

"May I remind you, madam, that sound travels across water?" Then again he gripped the bare shoulder. "And stay where you are, I say!"

"I'll *not* stay where I am. My gown is filthy! This floor is filthy! There are tea-stains, and wine-stains, and blotches of cake too."

"Most distressing, no doubt. Still, better a grubby backside than a bullet through the head."

"Oh, dear God—" whisperingly Peg appealed to the roof— "but how loving-sweet this man is! I had as lief be enamoured of a bargee on the Thames."

"No gestures; draw your arm down! It is like—like Venus's in the painting; it may be seen. And remove that mask; the rhinestones catch any light. Have you your cloak here?"

"It is on the table here beside me."

"Pull it across you. The most part of your gown is white."

Peg touched neither mask nor cloak. But her voice began to tremble as she watched him look round, his right hand with the pistol going behind his back.

"Jeffrey! What would you do?"

"I can't meet him with the sword. But he may not know I am otherwise armed. If I could draw his fire, so that he missed a second time . . ."

"Foh! You'd not shoot him dead from cover?"

"Most willingly, if I could. But we can't hit anything in such a light and at this range. *He* could not. It must be done at close quarters."

"Come back from that doorway! Not on the bridge; not in the moonlight. O God, these fools who have no caution . . ."

Jeffrey recoiled. The fury of whispers, striking at his back when he had expected a shot from behind a tree, brought the sweat out on his body. But the trees remained quiet; the music sang from the rotunda; the gondola swayed at its mooring. He slipped back into shadow, a stifled volcano of curses.

"Not that *I* care, Mr. Jeffrey Wynne. And don't pretend it's for *me*. When was *I* ever helped when I had need of it?"

"Now, damn your eyes, which are the loveliest I ever saw—!"

Peg, snatching off the mask, looked up at him. With eyes grown accustomed to the dark, he had never been so conscious of her face and body. "You had better hear this now, my vessel of stupidity. The trouble is that I have loved you far too much, and still do."

"Could you not say so?"

"I do say so. Hold your tongue and listen. Last night I was resolved to rob and to do murder if need be, save that you intervened at the old woman's rooms. This morning I did rob, or thought I did, so that I might have you in the role of wife that will so ill become you."

"You robbed? Who?"

"I said I thought I did, until I examined the carved chest with the parchments in it. And whom should I rob but a dead woman, Grace Delight?"

Now, never ceasing to peer round and round, never ceasing to watch the banks of the canal, he flung the whispered words above her head.

"You did not see the painting that showed her in youth, with a great web of diamonds round the throat. You did not know her husband had been a cabinet-maker. You could not have guessed how truly and completely she had been a miser all the days of her life, though you sensed it.

"Other matters I told you or demonstrated before you. My grandfather spent all our fortune on her, and decked her with half the jewels of Golconda. If a treasure of jewels had been concealed anywhere in those rooms, I thought, it must be in a false compartment in the bottom of the chest beneath those parchments."

"Jeffrey, what have *I* done? Please, please, what have *I* done?"

"Hold your tongue, will you?"

"But . . ."

"Someone, as we saw, could easily have climbed up to the Thames-side window from the footway on London Bridge to murder and rob Grace Delight. And, shortly before you and I entered together, this is what the murderer did. Having killed her—"

"How?"

"Having killed her, I say, the murderer either was interrupted or else could not find the jewels and determined to try another time. The chest, as I showed you by the dust on the under-side of the lid, had not been opened or disturbed.

"Now, Peg, we return to your case.

"You were taken into custody by the watchmen. Last night and this morning, be assured, I tried in several ways to effect your release. A last plea at Justice Fielding's house, when he and I were in the front parlour and you and Mr. Sterne were detained at the back, made evident that I might free you only by wedding you."

"By . . . what did you say?"

"I said: by wedding you. Don't question or argue this; such is the fact. By a marriage at Newgate, I could have made null your uncle's guardianship and taken you into mine."

"Jeffrey, Jeffrey, if only you had told me this."

"When should I have told you? During our talk at Justice Fielding's, when you were in such a taking that even Mr. Sterne grew uneasy and Brogden intervened because he thought you half crazed?"

"*I hate you.*"

"Peg, we have no time for tears or vapours now. Leave off. Major Skelly is too close."

Peg, about to hammer her fists on the floor, checked herself in fear and looked up at him through weeping.

"Well, I was resolved to wed you if you would have me. But not as a pauper. I would hazard much, Peg, but with your humours and vapours, I would not hazard *that.* If a great store of jewels had been hid in that chest, as I believed, I must do robbery after all to be independent of you."

"Fool! Fool! Fool!"

"Perhaps so. In any event, this afternoon, I returned to the old woman's lodgings on London Bridge. Tubby Beresford had caused the street-door to be locked and the key removed. There was a guard on the bridge. But these obstacles were none so formidable. They set watch only on the entrance-arch between the watch-towers. They don't trouble to guard the footway on the west side of the bridge. And in general they are right. With vehicles gone from the carriage-road, nobody thinks of using this other path, as you and I did not think of using it last night. You recall?"

"Yes!"

"In fact, I deemed it ideal for my purpose. The footway may be reached through any alley or the back of any house on the west side of Fish Street Hill. I could go there, I thought, unseen or at least unremarked.

"That is what I did, Peg. I climbed up to the window as the murderer had done. I found what I hoped for, near as great a store as any pirate's hoard, under the parchments in the false bottom of the chest. But there was one danger I foresaw and did not heed."

"Danger?"

"Justice Fielding."

The night was alive with whispers beyond the banks of the canal; water lapped whisperingly at the pavilion. But still nothing moved. Jeffrey heard small noises with such clearness, he suddenly realized, because the music from the rotunda had stopped.

"This blind man, Peg, is too formidably intelligent. He sees too much; he learns too much without telling where he has learned it. He makes you feel a child before a parent against whom you would rebel. This morning, in that cursed spider-parlour of his, he suspected what I meant to do before I was quite determined to do it."

"He is frightening, I allow. Still—!"

"Justice Fielding will never speak plain; that is not in his nature. Yet his hints and warnings grew so pointed I could not miss them. I even thanked him for his warning. In my folly I thought it only a general warning. I did not believe they would set close watch on me."

"And they have set close watch on you?"

"Undoubtedly, from what Brogden said tonight."

"Jeffrey, did you take the jewels?"

"Some part of them, yes."

"And that horrible man suspects it?"

"More: he knows it. I have been spending more money than he gave me, and Brogden indicated that too."

"And you have done a hanging offence, and they know it? And you are in far worse danger than I ever was?"

"Oh, no," Jeffrey said. "Though I did not know it when I opened the chest, what I did was quite legal. The law at least can't touch me."

"Then what do you mean?" Peg cried. "Dear God, will you *say* what you mean?"

Her voice went shrilling up, uncontrolled. And a man stepped out from behind a tree in the poplar-walk.

Though Peg could not see this, she saw her companion stiffen. This time Jeffrey had forgotten to hold her, and she scrambled to her feet. A voice, resonant and jeering, rang across from someone on the path to the footbridge across the canal.

"Come out, Wynne," it called. "You're a brave fellow, we all know, when there's a six-foot constable to do your work. What d'ye dare when there's only a woman?"

Jeffrey did not answer.

From the doorway of the pavilion to the bank of the canal was twenty feet. The narrow wooden bridge, without handrail, spanned it a little distance above-water. From the opposite bank the sanded path ran another five feet through grass to the opening between the poplars.

Major Skelly must have fired his first shot at Jeffrey from behind a tree at greater range. Now he was narrowing the gap, walking slowly in a straight line. Stockings, waistcoat, wig, even white face distorted with malice, stood out like a cameo in a nightmare. But dark-blue coat and breeches were invisible save for a flicker of silver lace that made the figure blur and sway against its background.

"I know you're there. You can see me, though I can't see you. D'ye fear *this?*"

Stopping within a pace of the bridge, he held up the pistol in his right hand.

"It's empty. There was but one charge of powder and ball."

And he flung the pistol high towards the canal, his right hand darting across to draw the sword.

The pistol splashed into water, sending out ripples round a moored gondola. And at the same moment music smote at them like a physical force of sound.

Cymbals began it; drums took it up under a thickening note of horns. Major Skelly, with the moonlight on the sword-blade, stepped out onto the bridge.

Jeffrey stood motionless, a little to the right of the open doorway, looking out across a waist-high panel. Peg, frantic, clutched at his left shoulder with both arms and spoke almost against his ear.

"*Jeffrey, now.*"

But there was no move or response. Major Skelly's catlike tread carried him closer. With his right hand he held the sword to reflect moonlight. His left hand stole back round inside his coat and up towards the back of the waistcoat too.

"*Jeffrey, fire. For God's sake, fire.*"

Whereupon she screamed out as he flung her away from him, towards the left, so that she staggered against chairs and fell across a table.

Major Skelly stopped short, eyes shifting. His left hand, closing round the butt of a second pistol, slipped out from inside his coat.

Jeffrey did not wait. He ran out through the doorway, on the bridge and in the moonlight, his arm rising to fire. The other man's mouth fell open in the shock of the unexpected at seeing this, but Major Skelly was still the first to pull the trigger. And they fired almost point-blank in each other's faces.

Blinded and deafened, Jeffrey could not seize back wits or eyesight. He knew his legs were shaking. He knew the bullet must have missed him, though the right side of his face began to throb raw from the burn of powder-grains.

But he had not heard the cloud of birds go whirring up from the trees, or even the heavy splash beside the bridge. He did not understand until he looked down vaguely amid smoke that had begun to blow away.

A tricorne hat floated against heaving water. A man floated there too: face upwards and arms out, drifting farther from the bridge. The water washed across that face, momentarily to clear away blood and show Major Skelly, mouth still open, shot through the brain between the eyes.

# XIII

## Midnight in St. James's Square

THE light-of-weight chaise, drawn by fast horses and hired for that reason at the King of Prussia Inn at the water-stairs not far from the Horse Ferry, clattered through empty streets with its horses at a gallop.

Once more Peg and Jeffrey occupied opposite corners of a carriage similar to last night's. This time she sat on the left-hand side facing forward, and he on the right. But the jolting was much the same as they smashed along the Mill Bank into Abingdon Street, across Old Palace Yard, up Margaret Street and Parliament Street towards Whitehall and Charing Cross.

Peg, still white and shaky after the events in Ranelagh Gardens, voiced a last protest.

"Jeffrey, I beg! We have no need for such haste."

"We have great need. It is late; I must learn what has passed in St. James's Square."

"I shall be sick again, and humiliate myself again. Why, why? And why must you have held so long in shooting at that odious man? Had you such awful scruples of firing when he could not see you?"

"Scruples, madam? I could not take the risk of missing him. If I had missed, even without the second pistol he was hiding, he would have had me helpless at the sword's point."

"Foh! You could have disarmed him with the sword at any time you chose!"

"Madam, shut up."

"And I am sensible of what to expect"—Peg bit back tears—"whenever you are pleased to address me as 'madam.' Jeffrey, Jeffrey! Is it so impossible to say 'darling' or even 'dear heart?' Must the closest of most intimate speeches forever begin with 'damn you'?"

"It—it is regrettable, no doubt. But it can't be helped. That is the effect you have."

"Oh, fie! And yet one night, when you were drunk, you held me down and recited lovely things writ by somebody called Herrick and somebody else called Donne."

"Well, I was drunk. I was not myself."

"You *were* yourself. Can't you be drunk more often?"

"At some less harried time, Peg, I shall be happy to oblige. Meanwhile, let us think ourselves fortunate this night."

"Fortunate, upon my soul!"

"More than that. Music or no, it was a miracle none heard those shots or saw what happened save old Charles Pilbeam. We could have been delayed at best or held in custody at worst. It was a miracle the wherryman awaited us, though he expected gold and got it. As for the garden wall . . ."

"I knew this," Peg said with the breathlessness of a pounce. "I knew you would say it. And you will never cease to remind me."

"I will never cease to admire you. Few women would be willing to climb headlong in hoop and petticoats over a garden wall five feet high, or possess the agility to do so if they would. Now for God's sake spare me more references to your modesty, which in any case is at one with Prester John and the snakes of Ireland. We have serious matters ahead of us."

The cobblestones in Whitehall, among the town's worst-paved surfaces, sent their carriage slewing round as the horses stretched again at a gallop. Peg, about to arise in outrage, was flung back.

"We have serious matters ahead. But it is none so bad as it might be. Two of them are disposed of."

"What gibberish is this? What do you speak of?"

"Two out of three are gone. Hamnet Tawnish is locked up at Bow Street, and Major Skelly is dead. Let Mrs. Cresswell be accounted for, as may perhaps be done now, and I need not return you to Newgate tomorrow morning."

Beyond their right-hand carriage-lamp the equestrian statue of King Charles the First loomed in the middle of Charing Cross. They swung left up Cockspur Street towards the turning to Pall Mall. But Peg would not have noticed if they had been driving towards an abyss.

"Newgate?" She shrank against cushions. "Return to Newgate?"

"Did you fancy I carried a safe-conduct? Did you not hear what I told Mrs. Pilbeam?" Jeffrey looked round. "Well, I don't relish telling you. But the fact may not be necessary."

"I'll not go to Newgate! *You* will. You are the one in danger."

"No, Peg."

"*I* say you will. You robbed that old woman of a great hoard of diamonds, and now they will hang you, and I shall never see you again."

"Peg, stop this! The shocks have addled your wits. I took various items of jewellery, in the main diamonds, valued by Messrs. Hookson of Leadenhall Street at the estimate of thirty thousand pounds. And there are more still there. But these were mine to take. What did you yourself see in that chest?"

"Faugh! I saw astrological charts. I saw old, useless parchments writ in old ink."

"Yes. But there were also, for your observation, one or two new parchments in fresh ink. What other writings are always done in parchment, so that they may be preserved for all time? Legal documents, Peg: marriage-lines, deeds, and—wills."

He looked away, closing his eyes, after which he looked back again.

"And what went on in the heart of Grace Delight, who once was called Rebecca Bracegirdle? She never knew me, or my father either. Yet I owe apology to her memory. I should not have burnt the painting that showed her resemblance to . . . well, no matter. I should not have wondered if her murderer ought to be punished."

His hand hovered to the right side of his face, which throbbed painfully, and he turned back to the window.

"One of those documents was a will, executed in full legality, leaving all of which she died possessed to Thomas Wynne's heir or heirs. How should I have got jewels in one minute and be spending gold almost in the next? Mad Tom Wynne was more than well known to Hookson's. On the evidence of that will, before it is admitted to probate, they were quick to offer whatever moneys might be needed."

"Oh, I am glad! And I am no lady of quality either; I am a most ungrateful bitch and you know it. But—Newgate! Oh, save us, *Newgate!*"

"You shall not be taken. Or, at least, not if I can prevent it. If Justice Fielding has been spinning no more plots in his spider-parlour . . ."

"Jeffrey, why should he spin plots?"

There was no answer. The carriage rattled along Pall Mall for the right-hand turning through John Street into St. James's Square.

"Why should he?" Peg persisted. "At the King of Prussia, when I was at you and at you before we entered this carriage, you said he and my uncle had—had schemed to put me there because they would protect me. No doubt I should be grateful for that too; but I am not, rot me, and I'll not say I am! I could kill both of them."

"You may not be obliged to kill your uncle."

"No. I . . . I had forgot what else you told me. I did not mean it of him; truly I did not. Why, why should all things be so unfair and unkind and most horrid vexatious?"

"That is ever the cry, Peg. It is not new. It will go up from those stones when you and I are dead and gone."

"Who cares what shall happen when we are dead and gone? It is new to *me*; I hate it. Also, if this odious Justice Fielding meant well towards me, why should he ever seem like a bogleman pursuing *you?*"

"I can't say. Mrs. Cresswell—"

He paused. And Peg, as though suddenly remembering, fell silent too.

They jumped through the narrowness of John Street, past Norfolk House at the south-east corner of the square. From the belfry of St. James's Church in Piccadilly, its spire clearly seen by moonlight on higher ground to the north, the clock had begun to strike twelve. Now only the setting moon poured its light into St. James's Square.

The Trustees kept this square better illuminated than most. A lamp was affixed to each side of the octagonal iron railings enclosing the circular pond or basin in the centre. And tonight Mr. Pitt, who had received good news from India which took three months to reach him by sea, was holding a modest rout at his temporary house on the west. It being Saturday, with chariots to be called at midnight, footmen had just thrust lighted flambeaux into link-brackets on either side of the street-door.

The watchman with his lanthorn went bawling the hour as soon as the church-clock finished striking. Magically, a crowd of pinch-faced idlers appeared to see the guests leave Mr. Pitt's. The coachman from the King of Prusia, cutting a way through these idlers with his whip, made a flourish of whirling the carriage round to the door of the house rented by Sir Mortimer Ralston near York Street.

And Peg shrank back again as Jeffrey jumped out to hold open the carriage-door.

"You are at home, Peg, if it can be called that. Give me your hand."

"I'll not get down. Not yet, that's to say. I am filthy, do you see?" She opened her cloak to show a gown in disrepair from climbing across a wall. "I will await you."

"No, you will not. This is much what you said last night. And there must be no running away again."

"I'll not run away. I swear it."

"You shall have no opportunity. Will you come into the house with me, at my side as you should, or must I carry you across my shoulder?"

It was not necessary to drag her. Once she had made up her mind to enter, Peg almost ran up the steps. Jeffrey had hardly struck at the knocker before the street-door was flung open.

"Sir, sir, pray give yourself the trouble of entering."

Every candle had been lighted in the carved and gilded chandelier of a marble foyer. Soft light shone on its Ionic columns with scrolled and gilded capitals, on the staircase of black-and-white wood, on the Chinese cabinet at its foot.

Hughes, the same major-domo, held open the door. But now Hughes almost cringed. So did a footman in flame-and-blue livery, who had just moved out from under the archway to the room on the left. It was as though someone had cracked a whip here as the coachman had cracked a whip in the square. In the middle of the foyer, eyes on the street-door, stood Brogden.

"The young lady is here, I see," Brogden said. A little breath of relief escaped him, and he glanced round nervously. "You have done well, Mr. Wynne. I may say you have done very well."

"Thank you. How is Sir Mortimer?"

"He is in much the same condition. Perhaps a little better, Dr. Hunter thinks, though still insensible."

"Where is Mrs. Cresswell?"

"She is gone."

"*Gone?*"

"Tut! The lady is not gone for good, though I wish I could say that too. She is gone abroad for the evening, or so I apprehend; no more. —Mr. Wynne, where are *you* going?"

Now, why had everyone here become so uneasy? Was it the presence of death, or near-death? Hughes closed the door with a soft and echoing slam. Each tick of the grandfather clock on the landing tapped its beat against a hollow of silence. Jeffrey, hurrying towards the stairs, glanced back over his shoulder.

"There is a matter which must be investigated in Mrs. Cresswell's dressing-room. Peg, will you be good enough to remain with Mr. Brogden?"

"The young lady will remain," Brogden answered. "You have nothing else to tell me, I daresay? Concerning Major Skelly for instance?"

"Yes. He is dead. I shot him."

Brogden's hand quivered at the side of his spectacles. Without looking back again, Jeffrey took the stairs three treads at a time.

In the upstairs corridor, with its marble floor and its arched roof where gods and goddesses were painted on plaster, waxlights again burned in wall-sconces. He glanced at the closed door of Sir Mortimer's room; to his imagination, at least, even the doorway breathed of drugs and death. He hurried on to Lavinia Cresswell's room at the front overlooking the square.

It was empty. The yellow-brocade curtains on the two windows facing forward, like the yellow-brocade curtains of the immense bed in the alcove at the left, were tightly drawn over closed shutters. But good illumination came from five tapers burning in a candelabrum on the dresssing-table against the wall to the right.

The place remained as stuffy as it had been that morning, underlain by a scent of rice-powder. Outwardly Lavinia Cresswell's room seemed as neat as Lavina Cresswell's person; her image seemed to walk there.

Jeffrey stood just inside the door, staring across at the dressing-table, with its mirror hooded in pale-blue silk and more of the same material draping it in folds to the floor. Now that he had made such haste to get here, he half-dreaded testing what he hoped was true.

Every piece of furniture, made by Mr. Chippendale, stood out in polished wood against white walls or a Savonnerie carpet. Jeffrey went across to the dressing-table and opened the silk-masked drawer below the ledge. The drawer, which should have contained two documents written on parchment, was empty.

"This does not matter!" He realized he was speaking aloud. "There will be a record at Doctors' Commons. This does not matter!"

But he yanked the drawer almost completely out to make sure he had overlooked nothing. It remained empty.

A ripple went up across the candle-flames. Outside, from far across the square, a stentorian voice seemed to be speaking between pauses and shuffling movements. It was only a footman calling coaches on the steps outside Mr. Pitt's. But it was so thin and distant, with no words distinguishable, that it might have been summoning the dead from their narrow houses at past midnight.

The private coaches, called chariots, commenced to gather and rumble away. Jeffrey looked back from the windows, and down again at the dressing-table.

The yellow-cushioned dressing-stool, its surface heavily pressed down, had been pushed round at right angles to the table. Across the surface of the table itself a dusting of rice-powder had drifted or had been spilled.

And Jeffrey, attention arrested, bent to study it.

Boxes and jars of unguents had been pushed back against the mirror, together with a hare's foot for applying powder. Against this spilled powder there was a mark as though some rectangular object, such as a large and heavy jewel-box, had rested there before it was picked up. There were several smaller marks, blurred, which seemed to indicate someone might have brushed the surface with the underside of a closed hand.

"And the blurred mark on the edge of the table: was it a broom leaning there? Or, instead ..."

He was speaking aloud again. Though not conscious of this, he had the unmistakable eerie sensation of eyes fixed upon him. He straightened up, looking round past the candelabrum. It was only Peg, who had slipped in unnoticed, but she wore such a look that fear struck him again.

"Peg, what is it? What's amiss?"

"Your face!"

"My what?"

"The right side of your face! I had not seen it in a good light."

Fear collapsed in exasperation at the trivial. Jeffrey caught sight of his own image in the dressing-table mirror.

"My beauty, madam, is neither remarkable nor indeed observable. It may not be improved by a speckling of burnt powder-grains driven into the skin when a firelock is discharged too close, and it hurts like the devil. So much is true, but . . ."

"Oh, I am so sorry!"

"Why? The powder-grains may work themselves out as the grime will wash off. If not, there is no harm done. It would be idle to complain of disfigurement when initials are carved in a mud fence."

"I'll not have you say that. I'll not!"

"Curse it, madam, must there be a quarrel even concerning my phiz?"

"You are an ill-mannered villain; you will accept *no* sympathy. And the true reason you curse me is that you had thought to find evidence against That Woman, and you have not, and you are furious, and now I must be catched back to Newgate? Is it not so?"

"If you are reading my thoughts again . . ."

"*Is it not so?*"

"No. Or, at the worst, only temporarily so. There is evidence; it exists."

"Jeffrey, what were you seeking?"

"Marriage-lines. I told you at the King of Prussia that she and her 'brother' have been dwelling here since you fled to France. I told you they are not brother and sister, but husband and wife."

"Well, and what of that? You also said it would be no weapon against her in the law."

"You misunderstand, Peg. I referred to a second set of marriage-lines. If already she possessed a husband when she blushed as the bride of Hamnet Tawnish—and not necessarily a defunct or non-existent Mr. Cresswell—it would explain much in the fury of her conduct. She could be transported overseas for bigamy. She would look lightly on the death of anyone she believed could prove the truth."

"That woman?" breathed Peg, lifting her hands from inside the cloak and pressing them against her cheeks. *"That Woman?* Oh, I would dance for joy to see all her pretences struck through! But I don't believe it. She is too filthily prudent."

"Are you sure?"

"I—I am not sure of anything!"

"The good Lavinia can be astonishingly imprudent at times, as I discovered from an episode in this room that need not be described. She is a mingling of caution and rashness, of craft and stupidity, of prodigality and avarice; she has shown it in her other acts. There is more than one indication of another husband, and more than one indication of a different kind of guilt too."

Jeffrey broke off.

"I had almost forgotten," he added abruptly. "Other evidence, to be sure. Courage, Peg! If Justice Fielding does not prevent me again, we may have you clear of this business tonight and not tomorrow. Where is Brogden?"

"He was below-stairs when I left him."

But Brogden was rather closer than this, as Jeffrey discovered on throwing open the door to the upstairs corridor. Brogden stood at the head of the big staircase, to be seen in right profile as though on his way down rather than on his way up.

Jeffrey shouted his name and ran towards him. Brogden stopped; the spectacles swung round.

"Deering!" Jeffrey called.

"I beg your pardon?"

"Deering! One of the two constables I borrowed this morning for special errands. The other was Lampkin, and failed me when he took Major Skelly's bribe."

"I am aware," Brogden said a little testily, "who Deering is. What do you wish of him?"

"Has he returned to Bow Street? Has he enquired for me since I saw you last at the Hummums?"

Jeffrey, reaching Brogden, just refrained from seizing him by the coat. The little clerk looked up.

"Yes, Deering returned to Bow Street. But he is not now on the roster to serve at night."

"He will do so. This one I paid well to serve me, and hope I made no mistake. If our cursed magistrate-in-chief does not prevent me again, Deering may account for much."

"Stay a moment, Mr. Wynne," struck in a cold, harsh, poised voice from beyond Jeffrey's shoulder. "You go over-fast, as usual.

Let us put first things first. It is you, I think, who should
account for much."

The door to Sir Mortimer Ralston's room now stood wide
open. From the head of the stairs Jeffrey could look diagonally
into it.

Two tall folding screens, one of stamped Spanish leather and
the other of French tapestry-work, had been set in such fashion
as almost to enclose from sight the foot of the alcove with its
bed. Near these screens, in a chair facing the doorway—chin
raised, stately of presence—sat Justice Fielding himself.

# XIV

## A Challenge from Bow Street

CLEARLY Mr. Fielding had been here for some time. Clearly he minded the sick-room smell and atmosphere as little as he minded other unpleasant aspects of his duty. Clearly he was prepared to wait for as long a time as might be needed.

The folding screens enclosing the foot of the bed in the alcove might have been rich with colour under a good light. Now they were as sombre as the magistrate-in-chief's clothes. A single candle burned on a chest-o'-drawers against the left-hand wall, silhouetting him rather than illuminating him. And so John Fielding sat in an elbow-chair, gently waving the switch in front of him. Under a hat pulled down on his own hair rather than a wig, the blind face was terrifying from its very placidity.

Brogden, transformed back from a human being into the magistrate's faithful Dog Towser, hastened across to stand beside him. Jeffrey followed slowly across the Aubusson carpet. If Brogden expected storm-signals, he got them from both the other two.

"Good evening, Jeffrey," said the magistrate.

"Good evening, sir."

"You don't sound surprised to find me here."

"No, sir; I am enlightened. *You* are the bogle-man. *You* have brought the disquiet to this house."

"Then let us hope," and Justice Fielding spoke not without complacence, "that my presence will ever strike fear to evil-doers. Or are you minded to disagree?"

"The principle is well enough, sir, when they are in fact evil-doers and not people who have tried to serve you with small assistance on your part."

"Indeed!" said Justice Fielding, and cut at the air with his switch.

Light footsteps ran along the corridor outside. Justice Fielding cocked his head. The footsteps stopped, and Peg entered.

Inside the folding screens there was a sharp sound as someone struck flint and steel. The gleam of a second candle sprang up. Through the narrow opening between the screens Jeffrey could see only closed bed-curtains at the foot. He could not tell who might be beyond those screens except, presumably, Sir Mortimer

143

Ralston in the bed itself. But he heard someone move round into the alcove between bed and wall, and a sound as of a candle-holder put down on a table.

Peg looked in that direction too. She had thrown off her cloak, which was hung across her arm. The bare shoulders rose from a gown of white and flame and blue more clearly soiled and tattered, with pearls missing from the edges of the sacque. Fear breathed from her; when Justice Fielding turned his face, she shied back as though the eyes watched her face.

"Is he there?" she asked, extending an arm towards the alcove. "Is my uncle there? May I have leave to see him?"

"He is there. But none may speak with him until I do, and even that may not be possible."

"I—I meant no harm."

There was a brief hesitation before the magistrate answered.

"Nor did any of us," he said harshly. His thoughts seemed to turn inwards. "This is no excuse."

"For whom?" said Jeffrey.

"Least of all for you. Yet I will not judge too soon, lest again I judge too hastily."

"You say 'again,' sir?"

"I do. What is this tale Brogden tells me, having got it from the young lady here? That you met Major Skelly with pistols on the bridge above the canal at Ranelagh, and shot him there? Can you demonstrate it was not deliberate murder?"

"Yes," said Jeffrey, controlling himself. "Peg, speak out and bear witness. Did I try to murder him?"

"Why, 'twas t'other way of it!" Peg cried at Justice Fielding. "Jeffrey was challenged and threatened and then tricked by Major Skelly, who said he had no other pistol save the one he threw away."

She poured out the story. At times it was a little incoherent, but it was accurate enough. Several times Brogden almost intervened, but each time he hesitated.

"This seems straightforward," snapped Justice Fielding, "and wears the semblance of truth. Notwithstanding, this young lady can scarcely be called an unprejudiced witness. It would be better if there were another."

"There is another," said Jeffrey.

"Yourself?"

"No. Former Sergeant-Major Charles Pilbeam, Royal North-umberland Fusiliers. You are acquainted with the name, sir; you sent me to his house this morning. He is of excellent repute. Should you care to take his deposition, he can swear to all that passed."

"Then we are on ground somewhat safer." Justice Fielding

drew in a deep breath; the switch moved more slowly as he waved it. "Did you go to Ranelagh with the intent to kill this man?"

"No; how could I have done that? But I feared he might be there; and, if he were there, that I might be obliged to meet him on his own terms."

"By which you would say, in plain words, Major Skelly's death might become necessary?"

"In effect, yes."

"Why should it have been necessary?"

"Because you wished him laid by the heels, as a condition of keeping Peg from Newgate. Is that true, sir?"

"It is."

"Yet you were not prepared to accept the clearest evidence of his guilt in a felony. This afternoon, at Mrs. Salmon's, Major Skelly made his first determined attempt to kill *me* by any means which came to hand. According to Brogden here, presumably speaking on your behalf, it was not enough evidence if Major Skelly should stab me in the back with no witness except myself. Sir, how much evidence must you have? How many witnesses do you want? How far must you cog the dice against your own servants? Finally, good Magistrate, in what remote era were you yourself ever accustomed to use plain words?"

"Pray believe me," said Justice Fielding, rising slowly to his feet, "that I will use plain words now."

"And so," interrupted another voice, "and so, with your permission, will I."

The folding screens which closed off the alcove were pushed a little way apart. In the aperture, one hand on each screen, stood a slender man so poised of manner and elegant of dress that you might have guessed his profession to be any except what it was.

This newcomer's age might have been just on forty. His wrist-ruffles had been tucked up into the sleeves of a black-satin coat elaborate with silver lacework against a black-and-white waistcoat. The cleanliness of his hands seemed almost shining as he held the screens apart. His voice, beautifully modulated, carried authority too.

"Justice Fielding," he said.

"Dr. Hunter?"

"The crisis is past, or so we believe," said Dr. William Hunter, nodding behind him. "Sir Mortimer should recover."

He pushed the screens wider apart. It was still not possible to see past the closely drawn patterned-damask curtains at the foot of the bed. But Jeffrey could now look into the alcove. Dr. George Abel, as slovenly as the other physician was fastidious, stood at the head of the bed beside a candle burning on a table there. He stood motionless, chin in fist, looking down at a patient who moved and moaned in the bed.

Peg let out a little cry. Dr. Hunter motioned her back and again addressed Justice Fielding.

"It was most urgent, you said, that you should obtain some statement or deposition from this patient?"

"It was and is," the magistrate answered grimly. His shuttered face turned towards Jeffrey.

"Well! If Dr. Abel and I continue to watch through the night, that may be possible. But I must beg you, with all good will, not to use a sick-room as a court-room too. Whatever thunderbolts you may have to launch at that young man there, let them be launched elsewhere."

"It shall be done. However, Doctor, you warrant this gentleman will make recovery? You give guarantee of it?"

"Good sir, I am not God Almighty. But I think he will recover. And therefore . . ."

Dr. Hunter paused.

Through the open doorway, calling John Fielding's name, hurried none other than Hughes, the major-domo with the iron-shod staff. It was as plain that he had been listening outside as that he had been caught into what Hughes might have called a fit of conscience.

His obsequiousness made him writhe, and the queue of his wig flew out behind. He hurried head down, as though he would run straight into the blind magistrate. Brogden, scandalized, stepped in front of Hughes and held out a hand.

"What's this?" said Brogden, with a very passable imitation of Justice Fielding's own manner. "What's this, sirrah, that you intrude here?"

"Pray, sir," and Hughes made an imploring gesture with the staff, "you must not impede me. You shall not impede me! I have matters of great moment to impart to this gentleman. For justice' sake, for honesty's sake—!"

Still little Brogden fended him off.

"Your Worship," he said, "I am loath to have you disturbed. Yet I would wish you could set eyes on this fellow here."

"His identity is not unknown to me," said John Fielding, who resented any allusion to blindness. "Well, let the fellow speak. I am accessible to all men, else I am nothing." Rather grandly he drew himself up; you would have sworn he looked straight into Hughes's eyes. "What is it, fellow?"

"For justice's sake—!"

"Stop," interrupted the other, swinging round toward Jeffrey and Peg. "Miss Ralston! Mr. Wynne! There is a drawing-room below us, I think? To the left of the foyer as one enters? Go to that drawing-room, both of you. I will wait upon you very shortly.

"Go, I say!" he repeated, as Jeffrey made a movement of protest. "We are all become mightily concerned with justice and honesty on a sudden. Let us hope, Mr. Wynne, you will profit by this example."

"And you too, sir," said Jeffrey.

He seized Peg's arm. In silence, under a pressure of unasked questions, he hauled her out into the corridor and down the staircase to a marble foyer bright with candles.

The drawing-room, beyond an arch supported by double Ionic columns in the architectural style of William Kent, also had a marble floor and a roof as lofty as the foyer's. More wax-lights in a chandelier shone on a harp and a harpsichord under double lines of portraits on the walls. If the new Chinese furniture clashed with the room's older decoration, this seemed to afford Jeffrey some satisfaction. He eyed it before pacing up and down.

"My uncle will get well," Peg said at him. "He will recover; you heard Dr. Hunter say so, did you not?"

"Yes."

"Then what is the matter? What are you thinking of?"

"Peg, I don't dare tell you."

"Dear God, why? Because the news is so bad?"

"No; because for once the news may be good."

"I don't understand!"

"For the moment, in case I should be wrong, that may be better. But all are now mightily concerned with justice and honesty, as you heard. Also, Mr. Fielding's godlike composure shows a sign of faltering. He has not at all liked the things he has heard or guessed here this night."

"But what does it mean?"

"Listen!"

In a house whose walls were too much like a sounding-board, it was not easy to catch distinct speech. Though they could hear loud voices from upstairs, with Justice Fielding's tones dominating, echoes rolled back and confused the words.

A silence followed. Presently, while Jeffrey tapped his fingers on the closed case of the harpsichord, footsteps began to descend the stairs to the foyer. There were two sets of footfalls: one ponderous, the other lighter but keeping time with the first.

Justice Fielding, his face brightly lighted and his hat pulled farther down, appeared under the arch of the drawing-room. Though he moved the switch in front of him, he was guided by Brogden leaning unobtrusively against his left shoulder as though Brogden were not there at all.

"They await you, Your Worship," the clerk whispered.

"Am I unaware of this? Can I not hear them breathing? —Leave off!"

"As Your Worship pleases."

Brogden stepped back. The magistrate, after lowering his head for a moment, lifted it in no little pride.

"Jeffrey," he said, "are you and this girl both in hopes of escaping just punishment for what you have done?"

"Sir," answered Jeffrey, crushing down the temptation to retort in a very different manner, "sir, we are in hopes of it."

"Good. Will you then be frank with me and confess your errors? Will you do this without further evasion or attempt to justify yourself?"

"Sir, I will try."

"For honesty's sake, as Hughes might say?"

"No. For Peg's sake."

"Well, that is something. It is not much, but it is something. When you left my house this morning, and went this afternoon to London Bridge, it was with deliberate intent to rob the woman Rebecca Bracegirdle, who chose to be known as Grace Delight?"

Here Justice Fielding held up his hand.

"Yes," he added, forestalling objection, "I know *now* a legal will was drawn to the favour of Thomas Wynne's heir or heirs. I know this because Mr. Gervaise Finch of Hookson's, who somewhat imprudently advanced you funds in anticipation of probate, called upon me this night to put questions. But I did not learn it until past seven o'clock, when I had despatched Brogden to you with an ultimatum. Nor does it alter the ethic of the matter. Did you yourself know of this will before you found it?"

"No."

"Though you knew of, or at least suspected, the existence of a fortune in jewels?"

"Yes; I suspected it."

"Yes; so did I."

And Justice Fielding pointed with the switch.

"Many persons, Jeffrey, have heard the tale of Mad Tom Wynne and his legendary mistress. Some few persons, not least of all the magistrate-in-chief whose business it is to learn such things, are acquainted with the fact that Grace Delight was that woman. This morning, when I questioned the girl Ralston here—who told me, as I informed you, more than she believed she was telling me and more than she believed she knew—it became clear your intent was still to rob."

"And so," Peg cried, "the trap was set for him? Because of what *I* said?"

"It was indeed." Justice Fielding swung back towards Jeffrey. "I gave you opportunity to tell me of the jewels; you did not do so. I gave you warning; you did not heed it. I even sent you on a futile errand to Chelsea, so that you might have time to reconsider. Still you remained heedless. Have you thought on the appearance of this?"

"Appearance?"

"Yes. You, who prated so glibly of snaring two rogues in Hamnet Tawnish and Lavinia Cresswell, were prepared to act as they themselves might have acted. Do you dare complain I have not treated you fairly? Can you wonder I was inclined to be suspicious of any testimony you might produce?"

"I—"

"Well, can you wonder?"

"No." Jeffrey spoke after a pause. "No, I don't wonder. Anger makes us fly to intemperance. But I am puzzled."

"As to what?"

"There is reason not to trust me. None the less, to judge by your tone as you judge by mine, it is as though you were making an appeal, or offering me something, or professing once more to believe in my honesty."

" 'Professing' to believe in it?" the other exclaimed. "Despite myself, I do believe in it."

"Why?"

"You might have sworn you knew all the time of that will's existence, and none could have proved you a liar. Now tell me this: could you have killed the old woman to take her jewels from her?"

"I don't know; I don't think so."

"Unless you had discovered by the will that these jewels were already yours to take, could you have carried through your plan of taking them at all?"

"I—"

"No," Justice Fielding said sharply; "no, you could not even have done that. Yet some person did kill her. This is a matter of murder, as you and I have both known from the beginning."

"Sir, this morning you declared it was a natural death."

"Did I so? Come!" snapped the magistrate. He was leaning forward, his face wrinkled in its intensity. "I am a blind man in only one sense. Pay no heed to what I say when I attempt to draw you out. Grace Delight was murdered. Do you know who killed her?"

"Yes." Jeffrey moistened his lips. "Yes, I think I do."

"Could you prove how she was killed?"

"If need be, perhaps I could."

"Ah! It seemed evident you could. Then you shall find me her murderer, Jeffrey; I give you twenty-four hours to do so."

Silence.

Nobody spoke inside that marble sounding-board. Justice Fielding stood under the archway, pointing with his switch. Jeffrey, studying him, had drawn back beside the harpsichord.

"I see," Jeffrey said at length. "You set one more task for me to prove my honesty, and then we_are quits. Is that it?"

"In effect, that is it."

"What of your threats that Peg may be returned to Newgate?"

"The girl shall not be returned to Newgate in any case. Here is my word upon it."

"Sir, what if you can't prevent the law from taking her? I had hoped to drive Lavinia Cresswell into a-corner. But I have failed in this. Mrs. Cresswell is still unbroken, still dangerous. What if she should demand Peg's return to prison, which has been the great danger?"

"She will not demand this. Matters have altered since Hughes spoke to me."

"Altered? How?"

"Mrs. Cresswell is no longer with us. Mrs. Cresswell has packed her boxes and taken flight."

Now it was Jeffrey who uttered an exclamation.

"That is what Hughes had to tell you, was it?"

"Yes."

"She did not merely go out for the evening, as Hughes and the other servants swore to you at first? Something drove or persuaded her into leaving the field for good? Hughes, one of her hired jailers, either did not understand or did not care at the time she fled? But afterwards, finding the law at dangerous questions and hearing Sir Mortimer will recover, he hastens to confess all and swear no evil was of *his* doing? Is this a fair summary?"

"It is an over-excited summary. But I daresay it is fair."

"Justice Fielding, when you connived with Sir Mortimer Ralston to put Peg in prison, did Sir Mortimer tell you Mrs. Cresswell held a threat above his head or the exact nature of that threat? I doubt he did; I think Sir Mortimer duped you as he has duped others, and only now are you commencing to guess how much. Justice Fielding, have you yourself used the best judgment in this affair?"

"It may be . . . Well! It may be I was ill informed. What of that? It is hardly to our purpose."

"But it *is* to our purpose," Peg burst out. "Foh, you villain!"

"Young woman—"

Peg, hitherto in such awe of him, had heard words which stung her to tears of fury. She stamped her foot.

"Villain, I say! You would lay all blame upon Jeffrey, then? You would pretend to be an all-knowing bogle-man, would you? Whereas in fact you have floundered beyond your depth, and can't get back, and won't admit it; but you will appear a great fool, rot me, unless my Jeffrey shall come to your aid!"

"Your Worship," cried the scandalized Brogden, hurrying forward, "this is intolerable!"

"Brogden," retorted Justice Fielding, turning his head, "hold your tongue. There may be much in what the girl tells us."

He turned back towards Peg.

"I am not omniscient, young woman, though it were wise for a magistrate to seem so if he would hold his authority. I am a human soul like yourself, prone at times to behaviour I can't justify."

"Yes," Jeffrey said. "We are all demoniacs."

"Yet I have pardoned much, Miss Ralston, which another man would have punished severely. And I will abide neither pertness in woman nor insubordination in man. Jeffrey, you shall find me this murderer. Don't think to trick or outwit me; you can't do it. Above all, ask no questions as to what may go in my mind."

Brogden subsided. Peg, in a little dance of tears and rage, was quietened by Jeffrey's hand on her shoulder.

"Such pronouncements, sir, have a noble sound. They are not practical. How can I be sure of the murderer if I may ask you no questions at all?"

"Are these questions to be long?"

"No; they are very short."

"Then you may put them."

"Sir, Mrs. Cresswell was driven or persuaded into flight. When did she leave?"

"Some hours ago, Hughes says."

"Where did she go?"

"Hughes does not know, or swears he does not. She must be found."

"What impelled her to go?"

"Come, how shall *I* say? Still, if the woman Cresswell, like Hughes, saw that her game was ended and her course run . . ."

"Under favour, sir: that is true, but only part of the truth. She has shifted her interests, not yielded. Did she receive a note or a message from outside the house? Did she speak at any length to someone inside the house?"

"No. She received no note or message, Hughes says; I think

him too frightened for lies. To each of the physicians, they tell me, she spoke only briefly when each arrived. And there is no other person to whom she could have spoken."

Jeffrey struck his fist on the top of the harpsichord.

"Sir, are you sure there is no other person?" he asked. "Someone was in her dressing-room this night, and spoke with her for at least a little while. Who was it?"

"That, young man, is the problem for you and not for me. Are there many more of these questions?"

"No; there is only one." Jeffrey's glance wandered round the drawing-room. "This morning, Justice Fielding, you reminded me I had wished to remain alone with Grace Delight's dead body in the rooms above the print-seller's shop. Who told you I had expressed this wish?"

"Nobody. It was an anonymous letter."

Jeffrey stared at him.

"I repeat, young man," said the magistrate, "it was an anonymous note writ in capitals. Brogden shall show you the letter. But does this tell you so much?"

"Sir, it does. It makes me sure of the murderer."

"Then find him," said Justice Fielding. He drew himself up. "I don't threaten you; I ask you to prove yourself an honest man. Find him, though there should be a last and bitter fight. And I give you twenty-four hours."

## XV

### The Demoniacs Begin to Assemble

"I give you twenty-four hours."

Twenty-four hours; that was what John Fielding had said.

Well, Jeffrey reflected as the sedan-chair bearers brought him swinging along Great Eastcheap to the meeting of Grace-church Street with the top of Fish Street Hill, it must now be well over twenty hours.

A deathly quiet lay within the liberties of the City on Sunday night. He had heard no clocks, but he had heard a watchman go bawling the hour of ten in Cannon Street a little distance back.

The same ghostly moon stood above river and London Bridge as when he had pelted here on Friday night in search of a runaway Peg. It was chillier now, though; as it should be, considering what he had in mind.

'Gently!' he thought.

He climbed out of the sedan-chair, steadying himself for balance when he pushed open its flap. He paid the chairmen, with their eager eyes and their over-developed calves. He waited until they had gone. Then he ran down the slope of Fish Street Hill, looking for a sign in the shadows on the right.

The thump of his footsteps roused a dog's barking. Jeffrey ran more quietly; the noise died. He was almost opposite the Monument when somebody made a hissing sound for attention, and he stopped.

"Deering?"

"Ay, lad?" a voice called back, from beyond the stone posts which marked the footway. "Not a smell of 'em so far. But—"

"Wait there," Jeffrey said. "There is something else first. Wait there."

"Ay, lad."

And he ran on.

Just ahead loomed the entrance-arch with the two watch-towers of London Bridge. Already audible was the *thump-thump* churning of paddle-wheels for the water-works underneath. Jeffrey approached the guard-room of the tower on the left, and knocked at its door.

"Captain Courtland?" he said enquiringly, to the guardsman

153

in grenadier cap who opened the door. "Captain Michael Court-land? Is he here?"

"Not tonight, sir."

Across the whitewashed room two more rankers of the 1st Foot Guards, caps put aside, sat at a table playing at spoil-five. They sprang to attention when another door opened. Captain Tobias Beresford, glass in hand, gulped down the contents and then lifted eyebrows in astonishment.

"Hey?" Tubby demanded. "You again, Jeff? Mike Courtland has leave to be at some rout or other; he's there and I ain't, curse him. I'm on duty for both of us; these people in the Guards have too much freedom. What d'ye want of Mike?"

"I don't want him in especial. You will do as well. There are no sentries on duty, I observe."

"No need for 'em now, my boy. This is our last night here, thank God; tomorrow they commence demolishing all the houses. If anybody wants to creep back home for a damnation few hours—why, good luck!"

Bulky in his uniform, rolling amiable pouched eyes, Tubby broke off to study his visitor.

"What's this, Jeff? There's a devilish official look to you."

"There is. Here," and Jeffrey took a folded paper from his inside coat pocket, "here is a magistrate's writ signed by John Fielding. It gives me all authority on the bridge tonight. Do you understand?"

"Well, I can read." Tubby handed back the paper. "But what's afoot? D'ye complain if I don't post sentries?"

"On the contrary, that is what I desire. See that there are none. And remain within-doors, your men and you too. Whatever you may see or hear on the bridge, don't stir out or interfere."

"Hey?"

"One last order, Tubby. On Friday night you found a key to the street-door of the premises above the Magic Pen. You locked that door and took the key. If you still have it, give it to me."

"Damme, Jeff, is there such need of the key? Why d'ye return there? And how'd you get those powder-burns on your phiz?"

Jeffrey ignored most of this.

"No, I have no strict need of the key," he said truthfully. "But I had better take it. Do you still keep it?"

"Ay; 'twas left with Mike Courtland."

"Then fetch it. You have seen Justice Fielding's writ."

Tubby, darting back to the inner chamber of the guard-room, deposited his empty glass there and returned with a large half-rusted key.

"Writ or no, Jeff, I like this no better than I did. And you're not honest either, sink me. Ghosts! There's no ghosts on London Bridge. I've talked to a dozen people since Friday, and they swear there's none."

"Ghosts? Who spoke of ghosts?"

"You did."

"I was not the only one. Good-night, Tubby."

He dropped the key into his inside coat pocket. There was one other object in that pocket tonight: an object so very thin that it took up little space, but long and fashioned of steel for all its slenderness, so that the key made a clinking noise against it. One of the guardsmen at the table, perhaps from hearing more talk of the supernatural, suddenly looked round. Tubby Beresford threw out his hands.

"Hark'ee, Jeff—"

"Good-night, I said! Mind you stay within-doors, and don't see the ghosts which have no existence."

Jeffrey left the guard-room without hurry, closing the door with care. Once outside, he hurried under the tunnel of the entrance-arch and out across the wooden carriageway over London Bridge.

The moon shed such murky light that he could remain unseen unless he ran straight into someone. Nor would his footsteps be heard under a boiling roar of water beneath the piers. If he could not help a feeling that eyes were watching him, yet he knew this must be sheer fancy.

He reached the Magic Pen, and the street-door to the rooms where Grace Delight had died. With his left hand he touched the keyhole and found the dried soap he had been told was there. With his right hand he unlocked the door, pushed it open very briefly, then closed it and locked it again.

Afterwards, the errand done, he ran back to the City side of the bridge and up Fish Street Hill as far as the Monument.

'I was slow-witted,' Jeffrey thought, with inner rage.

For it caught his eye, that Monument, as he had failed to remark it on Friday night. They had built it to commemorate the Great Fire, within a stone's throw of Pudding Lane where the fire started. The great Doric column towered dark against a moonlit sky, with steps inside the column so that you could mount to an open platform nearly two hundred feet above Monument Yard. By day, when a press of wagons went shaking along Gracechurch Street, visitors could feel the platform sway and vibrate underneath them.

'Slow-witted!' Jeffrey raved to himself. 'Considering what can be seen from there . . .'

"*S-ss-t!*" hissed the voice from across the road. "Lad!"

The officer named Deering, an elderly man with patched clothes and a shrewd, vigorous face, edged out into faint light from the lattice of the Grapes Inn near which he stood.

Jeffrey, waking up, went over to join him. Deering carried a dark-lanthorn; its shutter was closed, but you could smell heated metal through the other odours of the street.

"Lad, what were you at? The Magic Pen?"

"Yes. No sign as yet."

"Christ Jesus, I *said* there wasn't!"

"How long were you there? Watching on the bridge, I mean?"

"All the time." Deering spoke querulously. "All this perishing day and the night too, up to ten o' the clock when you said to meet you here. Bread and cheese in my pocket but no drop o' gin for the guts. Course, I can't say who might ha' gone by way of the back window."

"Nobody could have gone in or out that window since I was there yesterday. Now open the shutter of your lanthorn: just a little. Here!"

The quick mutters flew back and forth. A dim ray shone as Jeffrey extended the little finger of his left hand.

"Soap," he said. "It was undisturbed in its outline. Observe also: it's quite clean too. No key has been inside the lock until I used *this* key to try it a few minutes ago."

He extended the key Tubby Beresford had given him.

"Our quarry used soap to get a mould for a skeleton key. But nobody has touched the lock since then. We're still in time."

"I could ha' told you that too. The locksmith in Cheapside—" Abruptly Deering's light went out. "Oh, ay," he growled in understanding. "If you don't trust what I tell you—"

"By this time I trust nobody."

"Well, that's the right thing. That's what your noddle's for, lad. Where are we bound now?"

"If you're spent, Deering, you will need strong waters against what is ahead. Into the Grapes, then."

"Ay? But what if the pretty 'un should come a-raiding while we're in the taproom?"

"In that case, the pretty 'un will linger. Since you've not lied to me, we can risk it now."

"Easy, lad! I'm not a young man; you'll break me arm!"

"I can endure to break somebody's neck, which may be the best course tonight. Into the Grapes!"

A drop of rain stung and hissed against the closed dark-lanthorn. On Friday night, when Jeffrey entered the sanded passage beside the taproom, the place had been at least tolerably well lighted. Now only a floating wick burned blue in a bowl suspended at the rear of the passage.

A handbill in smeary type, pasted against one wall, announced the arrival or departure of coaches with grandiose names. But the passage was too dark to read any type. It seemed drained of all life; the shadows gave this commonplace inn an air faintly foreign and more than a little sinister.

And Jeffrey came face to face with the same fat, suspicious landlord he had met two nights ago.

"Yes?" said the landlord. "What do you want?"

"I desire—"

"Whatever it is, begone! There's none to serve you in my taproom on a Sunday night."

"Now this, mine host," Jeffrey said, "is the fine English hospitality we meet so often. Have we some law an innkeeper must close his taproom on Sundays?"

"There is no law. But there is my convenience."

Then the landlord went from fret to elaborate sarcasm.

"This house of mine, like the Bull and Mouth in St. Martin's-le-Grand, is the coaching-station for the north of England. You don't know that, of course?"

"I know it."

"By the law you're so fond of, I must serve hot food to passengers. You don't know that either, I suppose? You think this easy, don't you, for a man with his wife in the megrims and his tapsters drunk?"

"At least, mine host, their reasons are observable."

The landlord began to yell, and then controlled himself.

"I'll give you more than reasons. The Rolling Thunder for York leaves here at midnight. If you would bespeak a place in the coach, or a room at my house either, come in and be welcome. If you wish only to swill in my taproom, you'll go elsewhere and be quick at it."

"Stop!" said another voice in tragic tones. "Stop!"

Out from the taproom, with a lofty and spiritual air which was not assumed but deeply felt, sallied the Rev. Laurence Sterne.

"Good man," he addressed the landlord, "let me teach you Christian duty towards your wife and all mankind. *I* am a passenger by that coach. I don't know the ragged fellow, but that gentleman there," and he nodded towards Jeffrey, "is a near and dear friend. They shall drink in your taproom if they wish, and I engage they shall drink with moderation. You'll serve them, surely?"

"Why, sir . . ."

"Wine is a mocker," said Mr. Sterne, "and strong drink is raging. They shall be sober men, as I live. Fellow and gentleman, pray enter."

"Upon consideration," Jeffrey began, "I scarcely think—"

"Enter! D'ye hear me? Enter!"

In the taproom, with its black beams and sweating walls, a candle was stuck in the neck of a bottle on the table by the chimney-piece. Here, before a very small fire, Mr. Sterne's loftiness became tinged with emotion.

"No, no," he continued, as though they had plied him with questions, "I had not intended to return to York so soon as this. But my pastoral duties call, and so does my poor wife. Besides, in strictness between ourselves, I am not sure I have carried myself altogether as befits my cloth and station. A small lapse; it shall not occur again. And certes I shall be sorry to go."

"We shall be sorry to lose you, Mr. Sterne," Jeffrey said politely. "At the same time, this is a long and arduous journey; and the more so when it begins at night. Don't you think it advisable to take an hour or two's rest first?"

"Arduous?" said Mr. Sterne, who was whistle-drunk but carrying it pretty well. His scorn reached into corners. "Arduous, pish! 'Tis a matter of but two days, barring mishap. And there are compensations. Do you like fair hair?"

"I beg your pardon?"

"Fair hair and blue eyes?" asked Mr. Sterne. "There is a lady engaged to travel by the same coach. Not too young, but who likes 'em too young? Not too tall; but who likes 'em too tall? She is handsome, divinely shaped, and of the true *bon ton*. I am not yet acquainted with her; she won't speak to me; nor could I see her last name when she wrote it for the way-bill. But I know her first name, which is Lavinia. Good sir, what will you drink?"

Deering, about to put down the dark-lanthorn on the table, nearly dropped it.

Jeffrey looked round from the fire. "Lavinia?" he said. "Does the lady stay here at the inn, then?"

"No. Oh, by great ill fortune, no! The dear creature crept in with all but furtiveness, and so crept out again."

"Does she travel alone?"

"Alas, no. She wrote a second name, though I could not see whose. Still! Even if it should be a husband, much may be accomplished on a night journey when husbands doze."

"Mr. Sterne, surely you asked the landlord for the name of the other passenger?"

Lean and cadaverous, Mr. Sterne turned his head in much dignity and some astonishment.

"Asked the landlord? Asked the— Come, I have it!" Enlightened, he tapped the side of his nose. "You fancy it was *here* she bespoke passage?"

"Well?"

"Not so, damme! It was at the coach office at Green Man Cellar in the Strand, where I betook myself this morning after my devotions at St. Clement's. Afterwards, it is true, I did ask our surly host of the Grapes. His own way-bill may not arrive until near the time of the coach's departure at midnight; he don't know.

"But I will tell you what, fellow and gentleman!" added Mr. Sterne, beginning to bristle. "We will deal a shrewd blow at this knavish landlord who won't tell me news and won't serve you drink. We'll deprive him of profit, God damme! In my bedchamber above-stairs is a bottle of brandy, I vow, only half drained this night. I will fetch it; you shall join me; we'll show him. Eh?"

"Mr. Sterne—"

"Nay, don't move! It is good of you to offer to accompany me, but I'll not hear of it. Call for glasses; cock a snook at the rogue; I will return in an instant, I do assure you!"

Stately, pushing his hands out as though he would push them away, he marched under full sail out of the taproom.

Jeffrey looked round. No drop of rain had fallen since that first spatter on the dark-lanthorn. But the wind was rising, as it had risen on Friday when rain threatened; he could hear it sing at the eaves and growl in the chimney.

"Lad," Deering said in a fierce whisper, nodding towards the door, "did you expect this?"

"No, of course not! And we don't know it's the same woman. But I can see now the odds were in favour of it."

"Then you can see more than me, which you can anyway. York?" Deering rapped his knuckles on the table. "Mr. Fielding's People might ha' put questions at all the coaching houses from here to Finchley before anybody thought o' York. Why York?"

"I don't know; there may be many reasons. Yet it is not far from Hull—which is a seaport."

"Seaport! Seaport! Oh, ay. Well, we have something. Part o' the quarry at least should be here well before midnight."

"What is the good of that, if the main quarry shall not go near the bait in the trap?"

"Well, what if neither of 'em goes near the trap? Had you thought o' that?"

"Believe me, I had. We are not finished, but it would be a damned unsure close-run thing. Deering!"

"Ay, lad?"

"Much as I mislike depriving you of brandy or even of gin after a whole day on watch . . ."

"We go back to the bridge on watch? Is that it?"

This was the point at which they heard the street-door of the inn open and close. A voice, startling Jeffrey far more than it startled Deering, boomed with hoarse and hollow effect along the passage.

"Hey, now!" called the voice. Then, after a hard-breathing pause: "Hey, now, lackaday! Landlord! Who's here?"

Jeffrey, enjoining silence with finger at lip, seized Deering's arm with his other hand and dragged him towards the door of a smaller room. Here he pointed through it to still another door at the back of the inn.

"*You* return to watch," he whispered. "I will meet you as soon as I may. *You* return to watch."

"How? That's only the way to the jakes, ain't it?"

"No. It will lead you to a lane, and by any alley from there to Fish Street Hill. Make haste!"

Deering yanked loose his arm and darted back into the tap-room. But it was only to pick up the dark-lanthorn from the table. Afterwards he saluted his companion, tiptoed through the smaller room, and was gone.

Jeffrey himself went to the table. Drawing out a chair, letting it rattle against bare floor-boards, he sat down diagonally facing towards the broad doorway to the passage.

Footsteps, at first a little uncertain, lumbered down that passage. Whereupon uncertainty seemed to vanish. Somebody struck a heavy stick against the wall outside. The footsteps hurried.

In the doorway, breathing stertorously, stood Sir Mortimer Ralston.

# XVI

## Life-in-Death

"Hey, now—!" Sir Mortimer blurted.

He wore an ill-fitting wig and the sort of narrow tricorne hat known as a Kevenhuller. He was wrapped in a cloak, and leaned on a thick cane underneath it. His great height and breadth and paunch gave an illusion of filling the doorway. Though he looked little less haggard than when Jeffrey had last seen him, he had recovered some of his old fire and bluster.

"You wonder, I'll warrant," he roared after a slight pause, "at the reason I am come here. Why, to find you as Peg said I might! Is that what you wonder?"

"Perhaps."

"What's this 'perhaps'?"

"Perhaps I wonder," Jeffrey said, "you were mad enough to venture out at all. Are you so earnest in intent to kill yourself? Did the doctors permit this?"

"Doctors! Fiddle-faddle!"

"Did they permit it?"

"Fiddle-faddle, I say! I'll receive no commands from a parcel of quacks."

"And receive commands only from Lavinia Cresswell?"

"Boy," said Sir Mortimer, "you forget the respect due your elders."

"Sir, we have gone beyond showing respect or feeling it either."

"God's death, we have! You are in the right of it there, at least. That's more reason for me to seek you."

Sir Mortimer's face was of an ugly mottled colour above the heavy jowls.

"Who pitied *my* condition?" he asked. "Who told me one word of what was passing, from the time I was took but partly ill on Friday night to the time I was struck in a fit nearly twenty-four hours later? This woman of London Bridge, this Grace Delight . . ."

"Whose true name," Jeffrey interrupted, "was Rebecca Bracegirdle."

"Whose true name was Rebecca Bracegirdle. I'll not deny it

now; I'll not deny anything. None told me she was dead, even, still less she was done to death by violence."

"Sir, who told you she died by violence?"

"Peg did, and swears you said it. Peg told me this morning, when I waked from a swound and drove away Dr. Elegant Hunter and found Peg a-weeping at my bedside. She's a good-hearted wench; there is none better. Therefore—"

He looked round over his shoulder. The landlord of the Grapes, bounding up in slippers, went unheard until he burst into a tirade that his house would be no more invaded by outsiders with no business there.

"*Get out,*" snarled Sir Mortimer.

The old breed of his age behaved as such. Groping inside the cloak, he produced a bulging purse and flung it on the floor of the passage with such force that the catch burst and coins rolled.

"Take it; eat it; use it as you please. But be off and hide."

Jeffrey had jumped up to support his arm as he tottered. Help was not needed. That whole incident, with the landlord scooping up coins and flying, went past like an explosion in a dream. Jeffrey sat down again. Sir Mortimer advanced towards the table.

"Next, as touches Peg. You are pledged to wed her, she tells me. Is this true?"

"It is."

"You'll not disavow it, no matter what you may hear?"

"No."

"That's better. That's sense." Sir Mortimer breathed relief with a vast puff of cheeks. "You should have seen her this morning, I tell you. At my side and a-begging my pardon. *She* ask *my* pardon, ecod! I ask hers, with all my heart. And it like to have broke my heart, too, though you think I have none to break."

"This concern for your niece, sir—"

"Niece?" said Sir Mortimer. "*Niece,* you young dolt? Peg is my daughter."

"Yes," Jeffrey agreed without inflection. "She is your daughter."

The other man, in the act of removing his cloak to show a soiled finery of flowered-satin clothes, flung down the cloak on the floor as he had flung down the purse.

"You did not guess that? Don't tell me so: you lie! Other things you may have suspected, as that I had the wench clapped into prison for—for her own sake. Or Peg says you suspected. But my daughter? You did not guess *that?*"

"No, I did not guess it. Few thief-takers could have been more mistaken."

"Come, that's better!"

"Is it? At least it is comical I should have told Peg, mainly in jeer, she was more like your daughter than your niece. It is comical that none save Lavinia Cresswell should have found the secret you strove so hard to keep. For the truths and the dates were strung like beads on an abacus for any person to count with. Perhaps some other person did count."

"Liar!"

"Yes; be comforted; no other person has guessed."

Wind prowled at the eaves. Sir Mortimer, about to raise the heavy cane high in the air, lowered it again.

"We were befooled, as others would be," Jeffrey said, "by thinking of Rebecca Bracegirdle as much older than she actually was. And because women's gowns and hair-styles in portraits were the same sixty years ago as they were forty years ago. And also because . . ."

He looked up at his companion.

"Rebecca Bracegirdle, a dozen years younger than her sister Anne, was born about 1688. She became Mad Tom Wynne's kept woman in the full dazzle of her beauty at twenty-two or twenty-three, say in 1711 or 1712. When her beauty had begun badly to fade, twenty years later, she became violently enamoured of a much younger man."

"I don't deny—"

"*He* deserted her, this younger man, some four years after that. She was become miserly and unpleasant. Or did her mental strangeness only begin then? For I hardly need tell you that this woman, as a circumstance most uncommon but far from unheard-of, was not past childbearing in her late forties. And Peg was born towards the end of '36."

"Hush, for God's sake! Hush!"

"It shall be said once, and not again. But it must be said."

"How did you learn this if you did not even suspect it? When did you learn it?"

"I learned only yesterday afternoon. In a wooden treasure-chest she kept two fresh parchments writ in fresh ink. One, as Peg may or may not have told you, was a will. With the other, as Peg can't have told you because she does not know, an old and mad woman poured out her story. Rebecca Bracegirdle, now Grace Delight, had little reason to feel kindliness towards you or even towards the child you had fathered and taken from her—"

"What could the cursed woman have done for the child? What could she ever have done for Peg?"

"What did *you* do for Peg?"

"I took her into my own home, that's what. I passed her off

as the child of my younger brother and his wife. My brother's wife was no heiress, as we gave out; they agreed right readily for ready money, and so will all people for the rhino. But the money I settled on Peg was mine. If you doubt how fond I am of this wench . . ."

"Oh, you are fond of her. It was the threat of exposure, wasn't it, that Mrs. Cresswell used to make you cringe?"

"Ecod, it was! What man of good family would have wed the child of a notorious drab? What man, still less, would have wed a daughter who commenced to behave like the mother?"

"Except, of course, a suitor like myself?"

"Not even you, though you love Peg and confess it, unless I had tricked you into it. Or, rot me, I thought you would not!"

"But you know differently now, else you would not have felt so free at stating she was your daughter?"

"I know it now. Peg told me—"

"Of the jewels in the false compartment of the chest?"

"Ay, and it don't please me. You would have stole for her and might have killed for her, like the fool you are! Peg may think that's mighty wonderful; I don't. Still! At least it shows you've got heart."

"Then I might have been trusted with the whole truth, might I not?"

"Ay, but who could be sure of that when you swore you'd not have her in any case? I could no more have told you I was her father than I could have told Justice Fielding when I schemed with him; he'd have been more shocked at my saying she was a by-blow than if I said she was unmanageable. Lad, why d'ye press this? Let be! Or is there something else?"

Jeffrey sprang to his feet.

"Yes. There is something else. With all this talk of 'heart,' you could have saved much heart-burning if you had spoken four words."

Sir Mortimer knew what he meant.

And yet, when he saw the look on the big man's face and the sagging of the mouth as his companion backed away, Jeffrey controlled his own wrath.

"No!" he said. "As you advise me, let be! You are not well. There is no need to speak of it now. But why did you come here tonight from a sickbed you should never have left? Was it only to say, 'I am her father'? In part, perhaps it was. Or—?"

"Lad, need Peg ever know?"

"Not if I can prevent it. She has been called whore too often, and too unjustly, to be forever reminded her mother was one."

"Well, can't it be kept dark?"

"I don't know. Mrs. Cresswell is still at liberty. And there is the matter of Rebecca Bracegirdle's death. And our affairs, yours and mine and everyone else's, rest and resolve and have their origin with that old woman on London Bridge."

"Becky Bracegirdle, Peg says, was frightened to death?"

"Oh, no. If it were a matter of frightening to death, we might never prove murder under the law. She was killed by a human hand, with a human weapon as horribly simple to use as it is difficult to detect. And Lavinia Cresswell—"

"Body o' God!" said Sir Mortimer. "You'd not tell me it was Lavvy Cresswell who killed her?"

He tried to continue, but could not or would not. Wind down the chimney-throat puffed at grey ash on the fire and set the candle-flame to flickering. A stir and a movement beyond shadows made Jeffrey look up. In the doorway of the tap-room, bolt upright and stricken sober with a bottle in his hand, stood the Rev. Laurence Sterne.

"Damme, now!" cried Sir Mortimer, suddenly wheeling round. "Damme, now!—"

"Mr. Sterne," Jeffrey interrupted, "your native wit will have told you that for three days you have walked at the fringes of a murder and of a gallows; and thus far, fortunately, you have observed neither. Don't seek to discover more, I beg. Don't walk further."

"I shall not," Mr. Sterne replied. He was badly frightened; but he carried fright better than he carried liquor, and with some dignity. "Nor am I such a rattle as my nature sometimes makes me. That must be the gentleman with whose—with whose niece I was shut up for some minutes yesterday at Bow Street. No, I shall not intrude. Pray excuse me."

"Stay a moment! There is a service you can render, if you will."

"Or if I am able? What service?"

"This gentleman (Mr. Laurence Sterne, Sir Mortimer Ralston) has been very ill. He must go to his home at once. I can't escort him, even so far as finding a chair or a coach. I am required elsewhere at once; this is vital; I can't delay a minute longer. Will you give him your arm to the top of the hill, and see to the matter?"

Sir Mortimer allowed no chance for a reply.

"Go? *Go,* d'ye say? What foolery are you at? D'ye think I'd go before I had my questions answered and my mind set at rest?"

"You shall go," Jeffrey said, "or you may never have your questions answered and your mind set at rest."

"You're daft! You're moonstruck! I'll not stir!"

"Will you go, sir, while I still ask you as civilly as I can?" And then the atmosphere changed.

"If I do go," retorted Sir Mortimer, beginning in a mighty bluster and ending in a lesser one, "if I do go, I'll go alone. I'll not be escorted by a demnition parson as if I was a babe led by the ear! I walk my own way and I always have."

"Very well." Jeffrey picked up the cloak from the floor and draped it round the other man's shoulders. "Good-night, sir. As a last warning, go nowhere except to your home."

Sir Mortimer, evidently fussed, went lumbering to the door and then turned round.

"Ay, it's well enough for you to talk," he said. "But one day, hark'ee, when *you're* past your best and fallen low, you'll have more feeling than you have now."

"Good-night, sir."

Sir Mortimer banged the ferrule of his cane against the floor. They heard his footsteps, with surprising quickness for one of that bulk and weakness, go down the sanded passage. The outer door slammed.

"And now, reverend sir," Jeffrey said, "will you be good enough to follow him?"

"Follow?"

"Yes. Make sure he . . . he comes to no harm."

"Mr. Wynne, I had not meant to intrude here. I did so but to tell you that a second visitor, another visitor—"

"Yes, yes; perhaps I understand. Will you make sure Sir Mortimer finds a chair or a coach?"

"Mr. Wynne, I have ever been fascinated by the accounts of battles, sieges, fortifications, counterscarps, and what not. Yet I must confess myself a man of peace and not deeds. On the other hand . . ."

"Mr. Sterne, no military strategy is required or indeed desirable. Time presses; for God's sake make haste!"

And then the clergyman's long legs and inquisitive nose had gone.

For one who had been urging so much haste, Jeffrey at first seemed to show a singular lack of it. He stood hesitating beside the table, glancing at the candle and the dead fire. He touched, inside the slip-pocket under the breast of his coat, the very thin steel object concealed there. Afterwards, as though making up his mind, he ran out into the passage, looked left and right, and then ran to the street-door.

Opening this, he snatched at it and held it.

Uneasy wind raked through alleys into Fish Street Hill, amid a dance of shop-signs all acreak. It had grown so dark, under black smoky-looking clouds swelling across the moon, that little was visible except by an occasional rift through cloud. When he looked up to the left, towards Gracechurch Street, he could see neither Sir Mortimer Ralston nor Mr. Laurence Sterne. When he looked down to the right, beyond the intersection of Upper Thames Street with Lower Thames Street, he could not even discern St. Magnus's Church on the east side of the road. London Bridge's towers would have been lost to shadows except for faint light from the guard-room.

No City clock seemed to have been striking the hour, or watchman to shout it.

And yet time *was* going on. Deering . . .

Jeffrey closed the door and turned back to the passage.

Its sanded floor stretched to a rear window giving on the stable yard. Coffee-room and tap-room at his left, passengers' room and dining-room to the right. At the rear, where the little wick burned yellow-blue in a hanging bowl of fish-oil, that passage turned at right angles towards the kitchen.

"Come out!" Jeffrey called. "If you're here at all, come out. They have gone, at least for a while. But I can't search every room, and I can't leave you here. Come out!"

No reply. Jeffrey strode towards the back.

"Did you hear me? I said . . ."

And he stopped.

Peg Ralston, in a grey-silk gown picked out with black and white, ran out from the turning of the passage and towards him. She faltered and stopped in shadow halfway along it, fists down rigidly at her sides. But the pallor of her face, as she ran under the little lamp-flame, had shone in contrast to red lips and wide fixed eyes.

"There is no use to shout," she said. "It needed no shouting before. And why should you shout now or speak to me at all? I *heard*."

# XVII

## Needles and Pins, Needles and Pins

HE COULD see her only in silhouette: the small round hat
tilted on piled hair, the elbow-length jacket above her gown,
the hands clenched at her sides, against a faint flickering light
from the end of the passage. But emotion flowed out as though
he could see every look on her face.

"Oh, I heard," Peg said. She did not speak loudly. "You
might have spared me this, don't you think?"

"How? I told you I would be at the Grapes at ten o'clock,
and warned you not to come. If I guessed too late you might
follow your uncle—"

"It is most monstrous delicate," cried Peg, "to hear him so
gently called my uncle. I did not 'follow' him, except that I
came after him. I am here because I would be with *you*. And
you need not have dragged me out like a taken thief. You
could at least have made believe you did not know I was here;
you could have let me run away and hide my face; and I could
have made believe *I* never knew."

"Made believe? Made believe again?"

"Well, what else have *you* been doing?"

"I thought to conceal the knowledge from you, yes. Now
that you know, and have learned by eavesdropping what you
had no cursed business to learn anyway, try to understand how
little important this is. It matters not one Birmingham groat
who your mother was or what she was."

"It does if *you* think so. And it matters how she *looked*."

"Looked?"

"Yes, looked! We saw her dead in that room: old and gross
and hideous, in a dirty smock and with the sores of snuff-taking
on her nose and lip. And was there not a portrait?"

"Portrait?"

Peg ran forward a little.

"You have not forgot what you told me last night? That
there was a portrait, one I had not seen? That it showed Grace
Delight in her youth and as she once looked, with diamonds
round her neck?"

"Yes; I believe I said so."

"But later, in the carriage to St. James's Square when you

were talking half to yourself, you said you ought not to have burned the painting that showed her resemblance to someone; but you stopped and would say no more. Was the resemblance to me? Don't lie, Jeffrey: was the resemblance to me? Was it a picture of Grace Delight in her youth you kept from my eyes with such care in that bedchamber on Friday night?"

"Yes."

"Was the resemblance so very great?"

"Yes. Yes, it was."

"Yes! And there is the answer for all. That bloated and hideous old woman is what *I* shall look like in *my* old age, or so you think and have always thought. You never look at me without thinking what the mother's daughter may be like even a few years from now."

"Peg, stop! This is lunacy!"

"*You* love me, Mr. Jeffrey Wynne? You even dare *pretend* to love me?"

"For the last time, stop!"

"Dear God, I could die of shame. You have made sport of me at all times; you have lain with me only when you could not avoid me; you—"

She got no further. Jeffrey seized her by the throat with both hands.

Before she could utter even half a cry, he had whirled her sideways and partly off her feet. He shifted his grip to her shoulders and drove her back hard against the wall. There, pinning her upright to face him, he closed his right hand again round her throat.

"That is better," he said. "With your breath mercifully cut off, you will be in a better position to hear truth. And don't struggle, madam. Pray don't struggle, or I will knock that vain and empty head against the wall until you are able to think even less clearly than is your wont. Do you understand this?"

And he looked into eyes grown glazed with terror.

"Do you understand, Peg? If you do, nod once like the ghost I am tempted to make of you."

Now he could feel as well as hear her breathing. She shrank back with a neck-contortion that might have been a nod.

"Then listen. A portrait of Anne Bracegirdle, Rebecca's famous elder sister, hangs in the green-room at Covent Garden Theatre with the dates of her birth and death, 1676–1748, graved below it. You can't have seen this; ladies are not permitted to enter green-rooms unless they become actresses and have ceased to be ladies. This particular portrait resembles Peg Ralston, but not so strongly as to amaze any except one who feels towards you as I do.

"Again, Peg, pray don't struggle!

"I was never acquainted with my grandfather, Mad Tom Wynne; he cut his throat at the Hummums when I was a baby and four years before your birth, because this alluring Rebecca had deserted him for a much younger man. I came to learn her history pretty well. What I did not learn, because nobody could or would tell me, was the name of the younger man. What I did not learn was the woman's age; and I imagined her to be only a year or two younger than her sister. There was rumour of a portrait, painted by Kneller, but nobody had seen it."

Jeffrey paused.

Peg's breathing had grown slower; the fright in her eyes became a look of fascination. He removed his hand from her throat.

"On Friday night, in that upper room, I stumbled on Rebecca Bracegirdle's portrait. It was also your portrait: to the eye, to the mouth, to the life. But to shock was now added utter confusion. The clothes were a court gown of King William's time. This dead woman on the floor might have been your grandmother; she could not possibly have been your mother. Even if she were your grandmother, what in Satan's name was the family connection? By whom? Through whom? In what manner, with overlapping generations? It was more than puzzling; it was nonsense. Do you see?"

"I—"

"Be silent and listen!"

"And I do see," breathed Peg. She did not move her back or shoulders from the wall, but her eyes searched his face. "Sure you were not deceived, I hope?"

"It occurred to me that this woman *might* have been a dozen years younger than I had thought, and the gown of King William's time *might* have been one from Queen Anne's. In this event, it would be possible for the woman to have been your mother; and, as for the man concerned . . ."

"Do you mean my true father? If that is what you mean, say so."

"Yes, that is what I mean. It was possible for your father to be Sir Mortimer Ralston. But I would not be persuaded of this, until yesterday I read the truth in the dead woman's own statement. Like a fool—"

"—which you are—"

"Very well!" Jeffrey's hand hovered again above her throat. "Until then I would not be persuaded. If Mrs. Cresswell held a threat of exposure above his head, I believed it must be of his concern in some Jacobite plot to oust the Hanoverian kings forever and restore Prince Charles Edward of the House of Stuart. There is much loose talk of Jacobitism, which is not serious and goes unheard. Yet Mortimer Ralston would have had the means and the substance and perhaps the will for a serious plot. Mrs. Cresswell, in my presence, had made sly reference to Jacobitism. It must be more than a hanging matter, I imagined, to make him so cringe before her."

"He is not truly involved in such a plot?" Peg cried out.

"No, he is not. I had underestimated his fondness for you. But then, which is the bitterness and the irony, I had underestimated my own."

"Your own?"

"Over everything was the reminder of Mad Tom Wynne. Justice Fielding knew (and said) that my father, Jeffrey Wynne the elder, was irresponsible too. If it was Mad Tom's son who took his mistress, there would have been reason for Mad Tom to commit suicide. If also you were Rebecca Bracegirdle's daughter, you might be my half-sister by a common father. Though I would have denied this, I greatly feared it. And yet —legally or no, half-sister or no—I was resolved to have you despite the devil and the altar. Such clouds were only fancies and phantoms, Peg; they had no existence; you must not be shocked by them. But at least you have the answer about my feelings."

"Shocked?" Peg breathed. "Shocked? Oh, no! I am so very glad!"

*"What's that?"*

"Glad, I said. And I am only sorry, so truly sorry, I said all those spiteful things; and indeed I did not mean them." Peg broke off. "Oh, dear! You are the one to be shocked; you'll be more so if I say I don't care who I am or what I am, or if the whole world should learn. *You* are the one who is shocked; you double your fist as if you could not endure it. Is this so?"

"Well—no." Jeffrey spoke after a pause. "That was only the customary sign in dealing with you. Come and join our club of demoniacs."

The bluish flame swayed in its bowl at the end of the passage. Draughts ran across the floor like rats. Jeffrey addressed the outer door.

"This scheme," he added, "could be altered even yet. But it must not be altered! You are in a humour again. Your humour will be different tomorrow; it will be vastly different. And besides . . ."

It was his turn to stop. Running footsteps pounded up to the inn. Deering, the dark-lanthorn in one hand, flung the door open and showed a wild face in the aperture as though not believing he had found Jeffrey.

"Sir," he said, "what a-God's name's a-keeping you?" He looked again. "Oh, ay! Well! Even if it's the young lady I think it is, don't delay a second longer. The quarry's there."

"Yes. I ask your pardon, I—"

"Lad, lad, bestir yourself or we lose 'em! Do you think they'll be there forever? Or they'll take long a-cleaning the rest of the loot from that chest?"

*"Who* is there?" Peg seized Jeffrey's arm.

"The last two members of our club. But only one of them is the murderer. Only one of them, or so I hope, knows a murder was done at all."

*"Lad, for the last time . . ."*

"Yes; agreed. Deering, escort Miss Ralston to her home and secure her from more mischief. You'll not be required longer."

"Hark'ee, is that wise? If it turns nasty, and you need help?"

"Let's hope it won't. This must be done alone. Have they a light?"

"How should I know? They've locked 'emselves in with the skeleton key. They're sure to have a light, maybe; but how can I tell?"

"Give me the dark-lanthorn, then. That's all."

He had a last glimpse of Peg's eyes, struck to terror again, before he ran down the hill. There was no need to go quietly, with so many street-signs a-creak and the shrewd blowing of the wind. There was no need on London Bridge either.

Nevertheless, once he had gained the entrance-arch and glanced left towards the window of the guard-room, Jeffrey moved at a soft, quick walk. Thirty seconds later, in a lane of half-gale noises above the river, he stood again outside the houses whose patchwork in black beams and discoloured plaster leaned their storeys out above him with the weight of centuries.

He shifted the dark-lanthorn to his left hand. It was blazingly hot, despite the wooden grip to its handle. With a finger-nail he hooked the shutter partway open, and turned its beam on the door he sought.

Locked again, as Deering had said.

Jeffrey moved back, directing the beam outwards and upwards. The front window of the dwelling-premises, on the floor just above the street, had both its casements shut into place. One casement gaped where he had smashed the glass with his fist. But some kind of curtain, apparently like the one he had torn down, again blocked the window from inside.

He put the key into the lock, and turned it slowly. The snap of the lock, the creak from leather hinges, might go unheard under other noises. Still . . .

'Gently!' he thought.

Then he was inside the passage, door closed behind him. He did not trouble to lock it inside, or to put up the wooden bar. On tiptoe, with the shutter of the dark-lanthorn closed to all except a crack, he moved towards those steep ledge-like stone stairs.

Again there was a thin gleam of light through the trap-opening above.

Somebody moved there. The floor above was too solid for him to hear any footfall, but a shadow passed across the light.

Jeffrey stood still, breathing damp mustiness.

With all outside noises closed off, you could hear now. A woman's voice spoke, and a man's voice answered. But they spoke briefly, in short low-voiced syllables, as though not wishing to speak at all.

Again Jeffrey moved forward. The faint thread of light from his dark-lanthorn, playing across the floor ahead of him, found spots of dried blood—Hamnet Tawnish's blood from a skewered wrist—before that light touched the stairs.

He went up softly, lanthorn in left hand, at precarious balance as though walking ledges without a handhold. He had almost reached the trap-opening when betrayal occurred. The nerves he tried to repress, as always, overtook him as he neared an encounter that must be faced. Without warning, without apparent sense or reason, his knees began uncontrollably to shake.

And then it happened.

The metal of the lanthorn clinked audibly against a stone step. His right hand darted across to steady it. Pain from glowing metal burnt him from fingers to wrist; and both hands opened as he clutched at the stone for balance.

The lanthorn fell with a crash to a step a little way below, bounced off that, and struck on the floor in noise which burst like a grenade as its light went out.

From the room just above him the woman's voice cried out. But it was her companion, the man also unseen, who moved and ran. Jeffrey was close enough now to hear incautious footsteps, a man's heavy footsteps, run across the living-quarters to the door of the bedchamber. The woman stood still.

Again infuriatingly, as usual, every trace of nervousness had left Jeffrey Wynne when the time for waiting was past. He sprang up through the trap-opening. He looked at the woman, standing beside a closed window and an open chest, who had turned round to face him.

"My compliments, madam," he said. "This time the crime can be proved."

There was no change in Lavinia Cresswell's lofty, imperturbable look.

"Do you truly think it can be proved?" she asked, and lifted one shoulder.

"Perhaps, madam, we don't speak of the same crime."

Mrs. Cresswell was holding, as though disdainfully, a flamboyant bracelet of gold links set alternately with rubies and emeralds. Again a wax-light burned in the blackened silver dish, which was now placed on a stool drawn near the open chest. It threw glitter and shadow up across the bracelet and across the woman's face.

If she felt emotion at all, it showed only in pinched nostrils and slightly quickened breathing. She seemed almost sombre. Her hat was an old-fashioned bonnet, her black gown severe and widow-like except for the customary low square-cut bodice which pushed her breasts upwards.

"If you mean robbery, dear man, there has been no robbery. Besides, you would need more witnesses than yourself."

"Not necessarily more witnesses, this time. But I don't mean robbery."

"Then what are you thinking of?"

"At the moment I am thinking of how fetching a charmer so many men have found you, from an impressionable clergyman in his forties to a blustering baronet in his middle fifties. And they are right to think so; nobody can blame them."

"La, sir, how exceedingly kind! I must curtsy, must I not? Still! If you don't accuse of robbery . . ."

"No, madam. I accuse of murder."

"*Murder?* I know of no murder!"

"No, I don't think you do. But your husband does."

Nobody moved.

Jeffrey did not turn his head, he did not even turn his eyes, to look sideways towards the doorway of the bedchamber. He was conscious of a man waiting there, little more than a bulky outline with humped shoulders, crouched and waiting just beyond reach of candlelight.

Instead Jeffrey looked into Lavinia Cresswell's eyes.

"It is true," he said, "that the penalty for housebreaking and robbery is the same as the penalty for murder. I venture to correct you: robbery could be proved. A small fortune in jewels still remains in that chest; I left it here yesterday when I baited the trap. Will you look at the window just behind you?"

"Have done with this! I fail to see—"

"If you won't look, I will tell you. The window has two leaves or casements. They are secured by a small metal catch on a hinge, which is upright when the window stands open. When it is closed, the catch falls sideways into two metal slots and holds it locked. This can be done from inside, by twisting the catch. It can also be done from outside, by one who stands on the ladder of beams and jerks both leaves together. When they slam, as is usual with such windows, the catch drops into its sockets and the window is locked.

"Madam, that is what I did yesterday when I left by way of the window. I did so after removing stuffed rags which kept one casement propped open. Any visitor afterwards must enter by the door below-stairs.

"You used bad judgment, madam. If you and some companion crept in here to steal jewels, using a key cut for your companion by a locksmith in Cheapside, and if you were seen to do so by any officer of the law . . ."

Mrs. Cresswell's eyes seemed to have grown paler and shallower.

Candlelight glittered on rubies and emeralds in her hands. She half turned, as if she would throw the bracelet into the open chest; but she swung back again.

"Bad judgment? Steal jewels? As God is my judge, until late yesterday afternoon I had not so much as *heard* of any jewels!"

"Perhaps not," Jeffrey said. "But the murderer had."

There was a short, slight movement from the direction of the doorway on his right. Still he did not look round. His left hand dropped to his sword-hilt and eased it back.

"It is also true," he continued, "that you yourself have few scruples as regards murder. This is so if you can persuade someone else to act for you so that you need not be implicated, when your malice or your fears have been roused too far."

"Malice? Fears?"

"Sometimes one, sometimes both. On Friday night you sent Hamnet Tawnish—"

"My brother?"

"Not your brother. You sent Hamnet Tawnish to follow me when I followed Peg, so that he might fetch her back. He was to disable or kill me in a clean duel if I interfered."

"Come! Can any woman be held accountable for men's duels?"

"No. On Saturday morning, when certain blandishments in your bed-alcove failed and you feared I had guessed of one living husband if not two—"

Mrs. Cresswell drew back her arm as if she would fling the bracelet at his face.

"This time," Jeffrey said, "you sent Major Skelly to the wax-work that afternoon. He was to dispose of me, also by clean swordplay which could not implicate you, and terrify Kitty Wilkes to silence should *she* know too much. But he thought me a better swordsman than I am—Hamnet Tawnish had told him so since Saturday morning—and Major Skelly tried an assassination which failed."

Jeffrey paused.

"These things, madam, show a tolerant attitude towards murder. But I don't stress them. Possibly they can't be proved, certainly they needn't be proved. The murder of Grace Delight, in which you have now entrapped yourself as accessory, is a different matter."

"*Grace Delight?* The old astrologer-woman? She was frightened to death."

"Oh, no."

"I must refuse to hear such absurd—"

"Not absurd. Most persons believe she was frightened to death. At the beginning," Jeffrey said bitterly, "I duped myself into believing this, and so did what the murderer desired. We had better see how he killed her."

Lavinia Cresswell stood with elbow out and arm still back as if to throw. The fair hair and blue eyes, the face grown death-pale under the shadow of a widow's black bonnet, shrank in contrast to the ruby-and-emerald bracelet glittering near her head.

"Now, madam, you shall answer me. There is only one reason, I am told, why fashionable ladies ever come nowadays from St. James's to London Bridge. And this is to buy wares of the pin-and-needle makers, whose shops are as numerous as they are famous."

"I—I have heard so."

"You have heard so? Don't you know so?"

"I know so."

"'Build it up with pins and needles, pins and needles, pins and needles; built it up with pins and needles, my fair lady.' There must be few persons alive who have not heard that verse from the chant concerning London Bridge."

"Rhymes for the nursery, God save us, come with singular inappropriateness at a time of sober earnest!"

"Do you believe this, madam? Have you observed the shop-signs across the road from here? They may be seen easily from the front window of this room."

Ignoring everything else, he turned his back on her and strode to the front window. Across it, on a different rope, had been hung the same rotted sacking he had torn away before. Again he tore it away, revealing a window with one casement gaping in shattered glass. The wind had dropped a little, but a metallic creaking still swayed outside.

"It is too dark for proper observation. But I would show you a shop-sign almost directly across from here, as the lanthorns lighted it on Friday night."

"Shop-signs? I am not in the habit of remarking shop-signs!"

"You should have remarked this one already. It is called the Knitting-Needle."

And he strode back to face her again.

"Now give me your hand, madam. Submit with good grace; give me your hand; and I will show you how the murderer struck her down."

Mrs. Cresswell flung the bracelet at his face.

She threw it awkwardly, elbow out and forearm rigid, so that it flew wide past his head and clattered on the floor. Then, too late, she knew the gesture of spite had freed her right hand. Jeffrey leaned out, seizing that right hand with his left. He pulled her forward and partway round, her back almost towards him and her body between him and the doorway to the bedchamber.

"Let us suppose," he said, "you are not wearing that fine gown of widow's black. Let us suppose you wear only a smock of loose-woven linsey-woolsey, as Grace Delight did, without stays or jupes beneath it."

"Release me! I will not suffer this!"

"You will suffer it. Let us finally suppose this flesh of yours is not the firm flesh it will remain for at least a few years longer, but the flabby hide of a fat old woman I mean to kill. Don't struggle, madam."

The face she had turned across her left shoulder, enraged and yet elusive with a kind of coquetry under the eyelids, held a very different look when she saw what he had taken from inside the breast-pocket of his coat.

"This is a knitting-needle," he told her. "An ordinary steel knitting-needle, save that one end is sharpened to a very fine point and a length has been cut from the other end to make it shorter. Holding it thus like a dagger, if I were minded to do so . . ."

"Let me go, or I shall die! Oh, Christ aid and pity me! I shall die!"

"Holding it thus like a dagger, I could drive it under your left shoulder-blade and strike through to the heart. Don't struggle, madam, or I may be tempted to do this in reckoning for all the harm you have done."

"Harm? Harm? I?"

"And there are worse ways to leave this world. Death would be violent yet near to instantaneous. At my leisure, then, I could push the needle home with my fist or thumb so that the rest of the steel disappeared into flabby flesh.

"The wound, so deep and thin, would be all but invisible. There would be no bleeding on the outside. No mark or cut would be left through the loose-woven fibres of a linsey-woolsey smock. It would bear the appearance, as near as fallible human agency could produce, of accidental death from fright. However, the betraying signs—"

And he released her hand.

Lavinia Cresswell staggered forward towards the wooden chest under the window. Her bonnet and hair were disarranged; her forehead shone blotchy pink above the shallow-looking eyes. Yet lithely she kept her balance and whirled round.

"Who did this?" she screamed. "Who did it?"

"Your husband, dear lady: your first and legal husband. Even if you are surprised, pray don't affect such horror at the deed. He is a poor devil who had to have you, an emotion others have felt for other women, and he could win back your flesh only with the money you called for. In precision, regarding who did it . . ."

Jeffrey strode towards her, but veered and put down the knitting-needle on the stool which held the candle-dish. Picking up the light, he went to the doorway of the bedroom and held the light high so that it fell on the face of the man inside.

"You did," he said. "You did, Dr. Abel."

# XVIII

## The Walker of the Crooked Mile

TOWARDS one o'clock in the morning in that same room, when most of what passed was finished except for some long dying, other faces were there—and other rages as well.

Fully half a dozen wax-lights, unearthed from a store under the hearthstone in the bedchamber, now burned here: two in the black dish on the joint-stool, two in a platter on another stool from the bedroom, two stuck in their own grease to the floor on either side of the trap-opening. The old room was brighter than it had ever been in its history, or than it ever would be until it vanished before workmen's axes into dust.

Justice John Fielding sat with seeming placidness on the closed lid of the chest, switch in hand. Several times, during many repetitions of questions, he had gone so far as to lose his pontifical temper and shout at Jeffrey, who shouted back. His dignity had been regained, but his persistence did not cease.

"Late or no," he said, "you shall answer me. You shall answer me if we are here until daybreak."

"The most part of it," Jeffrey replied, "you already know or guess."

"But I have not heard it from you."

"Not all, it may be."

Brogden could be heard speaking in a low voice to someone in the passage below. Otherwise they were alone with memories in the two rooms.

"Do you mean"—and the magistrate-in-chief's voice grew incredulous—"you would have let these two people go?" He pointed with the switch. "You were mighty secret and evasive as to your plans. If I had not suspected some such matter afoot, and come with two of my people to see what you were about, do you mean you would have suffered these lawbreakers to escape us? To take coach from here to York, to take ship overseas, and perhaps be lost to just punishment forever?"

"Under the circumstances, no. I think not."

"'Under the circumstances'? What manner of answer is that?"

"The truest I can give."

The blind face inclined forwards under its big three-cornered

hat. The switch groped as though finding direction to point at
the trap-opening in the floor.

"Come!" said Justice Fielding. "After there has been so much
confession, why should you hesitate? When the woman Cresswell screamed out her true opinion of this doctor-murderer, *he*
did not hesitate to confess. He asked only that the woman should
not be blamed. In the main, no doubt, it was hypocrisy—"

"Hypocrisy, sir?"

"Can you deny he behaved as Tartuffe might have behaved?"

"So do all of us, at times. But George Abel, for the most
part, is no sham or fraud. His kindliness, his Puritan ways,
his lifelong devotion to work among the poor, when he is of
good family and need not have troubled—these things are real.
His head had been turned until he was half demented."

"Well, and does that excuse him? He broke the law. Can
you deny the wisdom of the law either?"

"No," Jeffrey answered after a pause; "no, I suppose not.
But neither can I preach sermons when I myself might have
done the same thing."

"You are not asked to preach sermons or to defend your own
conduct. I will determine your punishment. Meanwhile . . ."

Justice Fielding pondered for a moment.

"This is a perplexed affair, with many strands now neatly
woven. I touch each thread, I feel the pattern, in all of it
save what directly concerns Dr. Abel, and his murder of Grace
Delight, and his relations with the woman Cresswell.

"Even here, since I know most of the story, I can guess much.
But you shall tell me how you came to suspect him, and step
by step how you were persuaded of his guilt. From the beginning, was it?"

"No, sir."

"Well?"

"On Friday night I had not the least suspicion. We were all
in a state of overwrought feelings. Odd circumstances were
accumulating, including one I felt to be untrue and one I
should have known to be untrue if I had stopped to think.
But very often we don't stop to think of what we already know.
On Saturday morning, however, and in your parlour—"

"Ah! Begin from there."

Through the window behind his companion's head, Jeffrey
could see the stretch of river pale with dying moonlight. But
he did not look at it.

"On that occasion, Justice Fielding, you spoke to me in this
fashion. '*I would draw your attention,*' you said, '*to a circumstance in your behaviour which was remarked as suspicious.*

*Why, last night, did you desire to remain for some time alone in rooms that contained only a dead body?"*

"Now this desire, to be sure, had contained a hidden motive. I wished to open the chest and test my belief that a miser's hoard was there. And so I had asked Dr. Abel if he would take Peg into his house on the bridge, which was not far away, and guard her there while I explored the rooms for ten, fifteen, perhaps twenty minutes.

"But who had informed you of this? And why? I was a thief-taker, confessedly investigating; my request ought to have seemed most natural. Why should anyone—anyone, that is, who did not also know of hidden money or jewels—consider it suspicious at all?

"Only Peg and Dr. Abel had heard me request this. It was not Peg who informed you, you said; and, though you are not widely famed for your candour, you will not tell a lie if you can be pinned in a direct answer to a direct question."

*"You* speak of candour?" enquired the magistrate. "Well, I pardon it. Continue."

"If Peg had not told you, the answer was plain. It was necessary to wake up wits. It left me remembering and much wondering at certain scenes the night before.

"I met Dr. Abel in the tap-room at the Grapes Inn. Peg had been there a little while before, enquiring of a tapster the way to Grace Delight's house. She told the tapster, and told Dr. Abel too, that she was 'taking refuge' there because she had nowhere else to go. Dr. Abel strongly advised her to turn back. Though he did not give her what he said were his reasons, he did state them to me. The house, he declared, had a foolish repute for being haunted; and there was report that men had died there of fright.

"It was the first time I had ever heard such specific report of the place. But I was in a state of mind, at that moment, to accept it; it prepared me when later I found a woman dead apparently without wound. And it was next day that the oddness of this struck me in its full garishness.

"The first suggestion of death by fright came from Dr. Abel; he implanted it, even though he disavowed belief. Furthermore, if truly he had wished to turn back a girl of just under twenty-one, why had he not told *her* this? Why had he waited to tell me?

"Peg and I discovered the body; I had my encounter with Hamnet Tawnish, and presently Tubby Beresford came banging at the door with the military. All this had taken some time. I leaned from the window, shouting that I needed medical counsel; if the old woman had not died of a wound, I said, she had died of fright or the Visitation of God.

"Only then did Dr. Abel—who had promised to follow me immediately—appear in some haste and suddenness as though he had been waiting. He said Mr. Sterne detained him. A man of less confused mind (myself, when this occurred) might have wondered why he had followed at all or what service he thought he could perform there.

"He was struck all of a heap when he saw the blood-spots from Hamnet Tawnish's skewered wrist, and blurted out, 'Whose blood is that?' I asked him to precede me up those ladder-like stairs. Though encumbered by lanthorn, cane, box of instruments and phials, he did this with an agility which showed he could also have climbed without difficulty up ladder-like beams to an outside window. At the top of the stairs he blundered badly, if in fact he knew nothing of what had passed.

"Grace Delight had been his patient; by his own statement, he had visited the house before. A doctor, hearing only that his patient is dead and not asking where she is, will expect to find her in the bedroom. Dr. Abel did not do this. He walked straight towards that chest on which you are sitting now, as though he would seek her on the floor there. I was obliged to turn him and guide him to the bedchamber.

"He is a poor play-actor, in short; his conscience is forever at him; he was as overwrought as Peg or myself. But these were minor indications compared with what he said when he had examined the woman's body. Justice Fielding, if you have ever been of the Army and seen active service in the field—"

Jeffrey, who had been flinging out the words as he paced, stopped abruptly.

"Sir, I ask your pardon! I had forgot—"

"Tush!" John Fielding retorted with lofty composure. "You pay me a compliment by forgetting my blindness. Nor are you so wide of the mark as you imagine. I have been stone-blind only since I was eighteen years old; my father was a general; I might have seen service, though in fact I did not. What was it Dr. Abel said?"

"He said that persons who die by violence, as from a sudden stab-wound, may have their faces contorted and their limbs rigid as Grace Delight's were."

"Well? That is true, surely?"

"Of course it is true. What we call the rigor of death, which ordinarily will occur only some time afterwards, may seize a man at the moment of death from the shock of bayonet or bullet."

"Then wherein did this doctor tell lies?"

"Because he declared, sir, that these were also the symptoms of one who has died of fright without any wound. And I knew they were not."

"How?"

"Once, to my shamed sickness, I was obliged to witness a military execution. The condemned man fell and died before any firelock had been discharged. His limbs and features were limp, not rigid at all."

"You knew this, my good Jeffrey, yet you did not suspect Dr. Abel might be telling lies?"

"No, I did not think it until next day. For I had deluded myself; I had imagined there might still be life in the old woman, and attempted to revive her."

"Was this good sense? If you had been open with me on Saturday morning . . ."

The hour was very late, as a fray to the tempers of tired men. Jeffrey stopped pacing and looked at him.

"Come," struck in John Fielding, before he could answer, "there needs not this tetchiness! But I overlook it. The end of such a case will make a great noise; I must be able to tell people, surely, how *I* divined the truth?"

"By God, sir, this at least is frankness! Very well; I am your man."

"Continue, then. You became suspicious of Dr. Abel. Quite without authority you borrowed two constables for purposes of your own. You went to London Bridge with intent yourself to steal jewels; and you found them. Well?"

"Clearly the old woman had died by some physical violence. Dr. Abel would be in the best possible position to conceal the facts by reporting her death to the parish authorities as caused by accidental fright. In that event, as already I had told Peg, there would be no coroner's quest and no opening of the body. And that is what he did. On the other hand, if he had killed her, how had he done it? I myself could swear there seemed no wound. And what was his motive?"

"Motive?" Up went the blind man's eyebrows. "The jewels; what else? As I could have told you, and later did tell you, there was widespread rumour of such a hoard. Since the woman was his patient, he might well have learned this."

"So he might," Jeffrey agreed, "but why had he not taken them or made no attempt to take them? It was a pressing thing; in two days' time he would be compelled to leave his home on London Bridge. Was it possible he did not know where the jewels were? *I* could not have told, without the knowledge of where to look. Grace Delight had trusted in that chest, disdaining locks and curtaining only front windows so that nobody might espy her.

"As for motive, there was a further consideration. A devoted physician, who has worked long among poor people for slender return—'no quack,' as more persons than the landlord at the Grapes Inn will testify—would seem to be acting entirely out of character, unless he had some overpowering reason not yet revealed to us.

"Therefore I sent him a note, asking him to meet me at the Rainbow Tavern in Fleet Street. If he were a guilty man, he would be sure to come. There I told him a long story, with which you are now familiar ..."

"Vilifying *me?*"

"In part. It was all true."

"And sent him to St. James's Square? Why? Because you had found some link between Dr. Abel and the woman Cresswell?"

"No. I am no reader of minds or possessor of Dr. Dee's black stone. I did not desire him to go to St. James's Square, and was astonished when he agreed.

"The tale I recounted, though it was true and gave me opportunity to set my thoughts in order, was in the main for conveying two pieces of information without seeming to convey them. First: that the youthful Grace Delight's husband had been a cabinet-maker, as indication he might find treasure-trove in the only item of furniture capable of concealing it. Second: that I had stumbled on an unexpected source of wealth and would shortly have my hands on it.

"If he were innocent and this meant nothing to him, no harm was done. If he were guilty, he would try to anticipate me and would walk into a trap. Deering and Lampkin waited across the street at the King's Head: Lampkin to follow me into the waxwork, Deering to follow Dr. Abel wherever he went.

"Whereupon Dr. Abel's conduct at the Rainbow roused fresh speculation. He was much agitated, and kept striking his fist on the table. For some reason he seemed eager to visit Sir Mortimer Ralston's. Though what I proposed would have horrified the Royal College of Physicians, he agreed almost too quickly after his first demur. I might be making too much of this; Dr. Abel liked Peg and was genuinely concerned for her welfare—"

"Or so you fancied?"

"Well, I thought so; I still think so. But there might be more. Kitty was to meet me at the waxwork with information which she said would help Peg, and could do so only if it concerned Mrs. Cresswell. I need not dwell on the circumstance that certain verses of *London Bridge Is Falling Down*, played and sung as I stood before the figure of a wax woman with limbs as rigid as a dead woman's, suggested how Dr. Abel could have killed Grace Delight. But I must dwell briefly on the fact that Major Skelly tried to kill me as well as find and seize Kitty Wilkes.

"There was more here, much more, than my notion that Hamnet Tawnish might well be Lavinia Cresswell's husband. Questioning of Kitty Wilkes, at the Hummums, eventually disclosed it. It was bigamy, another man in her life before she had been wed to Hamnet Tawnish. The Pamela-like Kitty would not confess slyness by admitting that as Mrs. Cresswell's maid she had read a second set of marriage-lines writ on parchment.

"Marriage with whom? Kitty did quote a whispered conversation between Lavinia Cresswell and Hamnet Tawnish. 'Would you have fared better if you had remained with *him?*' sneers Mr. Tawnish. "Would your lot have been more enviable with the cupper?' "

"The cupper!"

"In the vernacular, sir, we sometimes use this term for a physician or a surgeon as we also call him 'leech.' It is derived from the same practice: blood-letting. The cupping glass is applied to inflamed skin; by suction it draws out blood through small punctures previously made with a lancet.

"They are accustomed to employ this practice at the Hummums. Indeed, while I was questioning Kitty, there stood beside her tea-service a small sneaker of punch in size and shape exactly like a cupping-glass. The practice, also—"

"My good young man," Justice Fielding interrupted with some hauteur, "I am acquainted with the practice, and also with the fact that two and two make four. You need not insist upon it. Proceed with matters more relevant."

"It was relevant enough to provide the link between Lavinia Cresswell and George Abel. However, I could not pursue it at once. Brogden arrived with news of Peg's escape from Newgate and your demand that I must find her immediately or she could expect no mercy."

"Could I have done otherwise?"

"Well—"

"You know I could not. Yet one aspect of the events at Ranelagh is not clear. If the woman Cresswell sent Major Skelly for a second attempt on your life, how could she (or he either) have known you would be there?"

"I much doubt she did. She will not speak as to this or anything else; yet I think he was sent there to find Peg and turn her back to the law. A note to Kitty Wilkes, sent by Peg from Newgate, called for the despatch of any clothes Kitty might choose provided these should include a vizard-mask, an evening-gown of fine quality, and a dark cloak. This note was carelessly left by Kitty in Peg's room. When news of Peg's escape arrived in St. James's Square, the good Lavinia could use her wits as well as another regarding where to look for the errant one. It must have been so, I warrant, else Major Skelly would not have arrived at Ranelagh before me. Yet he was not greatly concerned with Peg; he was concerned to have reckoning with me in case I should appear. What happened could not be called pleasant.

"Still, it was Mrs. Cresswell's last fling of malice against Peg. This lady could concern herself with no more, she had time for no more. This became evident when Peg and I hurried back from Ranelagh at midnight on Saturday.

"She had fled from St. James's Square. Though we did not learn at once she had gone for good, I found the drawer of her dressing-table empty. Evidence of her marriage to Hamnet Tawnish had disappeared. So had what I hoped to find as evidence of her marriage to George Abel. There should be a record of this at Doctors' Commons, where all marriages must be recorded. Meanwhile, what was to be discovered?

"Much, fortunately.

"Dr. Abel was still there; circumstances had trapped him into staying. Having called ostensibly to see Sir Mortimer, he could not—and would not—refuse his aid when Sir Mortimer fell down in a fit on receiving that same news of Peg's escape from Newgate. Afterwards he was still detained; Dr. Hunter, an old friend who thought highly of him, arrived and would not let him go.

"He and Mrs. Cresswell had pretended not to be acquainted. You quoted him as saying he had exchanged only the briefest word with her when she asked him to attend Sir Mortimer. And that was a flat lie.

"On the contrary, he had talked for some time with her in her room. If I found no evidence of marriage, I did find evidence of a conference."

"You refer," interposed John Fielding, "to those marks or prints writ in spilled rice-powder on the top of her dressing-table?"

"I do."

"And you interpreted them how?"

"Once we learned from Hughes of Mrs. Cresswell's flight, they told the rest of the story."

"Stay a moment, Jeffrey!" Sharpness, decision, had returned to Justice Fielding's manner. "Before we are come to the end, we must hark back to the beginning. We must consider Dr. Abel's entire conduct and the details of precisely how he encompassed a brutal murder."

"These details, sir, are already known to you from the substance of his own confession!"

"True. That is why I would discuss them. They must be looked upon with eyes less ingenuous than your own, and less tender towards knaves of his sort."

It was as though, hitherto, Justice Fielding had lurked in ambush. He held up a hand for silence.

"Here we have a man, a physician who should have set better example, but who is of violent feelings and strong physical appetite. We will allow he tried to stifle both; what honourable man does not? We will allow he is not affluent; other men are in like case. We will allow he worked hard for the poor; so do others, including myself. We will allow him amiable qualities; many a deservedly hanged knave has given halfpence to children and used kindness towards his dog. What then?

"No, Jeffrey, be pleased not to interrupt!

"This doctor has been wed to a woman of low birth but aristocratic carriage, maiden name Cresswell. She has thought to better herself. She goes on to better herself, or so she thinks, when secretly she marries Hamnet Tawnish in the belief the man Tawnish is both well born *and* rich. She makes no blunder when she becomes the mistress of Sir Mortimer Ralston, but does err again in discovering (as you have been good enough to tell me at last) that this man's pretended niece is his daughter, and uses it as a threat.

"Meanwhile, Dr. Abel must persuade her back to his bed at any cost. You have explained the scheme to rob an old woman after killing her with a knitting-needle in such fashion as to pretend her own spells have frightened her to death. You have not dealt with details quite as bad.

"He is determined to kill her; he carries the sharpened weapon in that box of phials; but he dithers and can't set his mind to it, though he must act soon or both he and this woman will be turned from the bridge. Your case for the defence—"

"I make out no case for the defence."

"No? Well, hear me out."

"As you please."

"On Friday night he is at the Grapes, tippling and bemoaning his lot; when his mind is made up, Miss Ralston enters. He does not guess who she may be; he has not yet seen that famous portrait you tell me of. But she does say she means to take refuge with Grace Delight. If she has come to stay here, he will get no further opportunity for murder and robbery.

"Since Miss Ralston seems determined, he will not truly try to prevent her from going. But he must kill the old woman now, in haste, and rob afterwards. He says he will accompany this girl, if she will wait while he fetches this instrument-phial box from a small adjoining room. It is an empty room; it has a door leading not only to the jakes but to a lane at the back by which he can very quickly reach the footway beside London Bridge and the window to Grace Delight's lodgings.

"*That* was when he killed her, and there was no scream or cry at the time he did.

"It was a brief matter of minutes before he made haste back to the inn, where he met Mr. Sterne. The girl had gone. You appeared; he could weave his tale of ghosts, and in hypocritical sympathy urge you to follow her.

"But the man still could not rest. What was happening? What had happened? Had Miss Ralston perhaps not gone there at all? Observe, Jeffrey, the character of the born criminal; he will not let well alone, as Dr. Abel could not.

"He must learn what went forward. No person at a tavern will question an absence on the excuse of visiting the jakes. By that time Dr. Abel is alone with Mr. Sterne, who assuredly would never mark it and in any case is becoming so drunk that afterwards—as we both know—he does not even recall assaulting the watch in Cheapside. And so this born criminal returns again.

"Miss Ralston, as she informed you, has dallied 'an unconscionable time' on the bridge; so long that you overtook her. When the face of our good doctor is once more pressed through that open window, the body is undiscovered as yet.

"Grace Delight lies where he has struck her down, without pretence of visiting her as kindly physician. But you and Miss Ralston can be heard speaking to each other outside the street-door, both of you crying in loud voices as to what may have occurred inside. The murderer now conceives what he imagines will put the last touch of credence to his prophecy of death by fright.

"He climbs through the window. Miss Ralston shouts the words, 'God, God, do you think I always tell you lies?' and flings open the street-door. The murderer, a figure as grotesque as any conceived by my late half-brother the writer, utters an unearthly cry as though of terror; he lifts and lets fall the shoulders of his victim; and he retreats to the Grapes Tavern for assurance from Mr. Sterne that he has never been absent save at the necessary-house."

Justice Fielding pointed with the switch.

"Since you guessed so much," he added, "did this point occur to you? That it was the murderer uttering a false scream of fear? That it might have been the voice of a man and not a woman?"

"Yes. Or, in exactness, I suspected it long before I knew Dr. Abel must be guilty. Hamnet Tawnish had uttered a noise which sounded precisely like the other—a kind of bubbling shriek—when he fell through the trap-opening after I had wounded him. Sir, why do you so dilate upon facts well known? Why do *you* insist that two and two must make four?"

"I stress it," answered the other, "to put the question with which I began."

"Well, sir?"

"In doing so," said Justice Fielding, "let me conclude with the account you yourself were relating of the events on Saturday night. You and Miss Ralston returned from Ranelagh to St. James's Square. Dr. Abel had been talking long with Mrs. (let us continue to call her that) Mrs. Cresswell in her room? Presumably just after Dr. Hunter arrived?"

"Yes."

"He had sat on the dressing-stool by the dressing-table. In spilled rice-powder on the table-top there was the oblong print where his box of instruments and phials had rested? There were the smudged prints of a fist where repeatedly he had struck it, as though in argument and persuasion? There was even the mark, like that of a broom, to show his cane had been leaning against the edge. Therefore the man was George Abel and no one else?"

"So I read the signs."

"He did not tell her he had killed for her sake? He told her merely that he could lay his hands on a fortune in jewels, and it would be hers for the asking if she fled away with him to a farther clime and a happier sky?"

"It seemed likely they would flee away. I could not say where."

"And she, being in dangerous plight after schemes which might undo her, allowed herself to be persuaded? Deering had been following him on Saturday, and continued watch today? Since the street-door to Grace Delight's lodgings was locked as the rear window was locked on the inside, none could enter these rooms until Dr. Abel got his skeleton key he had bespoke from the locksmith in Cheapside? Therefore one or both of them must walk into a trap you and Deering set?"

"Such proved to be the case."

"It did indeed. Yet you still planned to let these people escape, even after you had trapped them?"

"I—I had thought of it, I confess. But . . ."

"Well, that is my question. It is late, as you say; you may go from here when you have been open with me. The woman had tried to have you killed. The man had hoaxed you as much as you had hoaxed him, and had even written me an anonymous note so as to direct suspicion away from himself and at you. Yet you still could even once have considered letting them go, because you yourself might have behaved as they did?"

"No. It was to keep Peg from learning the truth of her parentage. Mrs. Cresswell will shout this in the dock at her trial; it won't help her, but it will delight Lavinia Cresswell. It is true Peg does know, as I learned only late tonight, and says she does not care. Yet I feared Peg might be of another mind afterwards."

"Then the answer . . . ?"

"The final answer, sir, is no. I could not have let them go. A long look at them, here in this room when the truth was revealed, and even my tolerance found its limits."

Justice Fielding sat back on the chest.

"At long last, my dear Jeffrey," said the magistrate, "I have contrived to teach you. You will leave my service, with so much money to spend, but you will not forget this. There is no more for you to fear from the law; I give you your quittance; go hence without remand. You have learned to observe truth."

Jeffrey Wynne, so tired that he could scarcely stand, turned towards the trap-opening with the candles burning beside it.

"Oh, agreed," he said. "And yet . . ."

"There are reservations?"

"Only, sir, in a sense that neither of us can help. ' "What is truth?" asked jesting Pilate, and would not stay for an answer.' "

# NOTES FOR THE CURIOUS

The characters in this novel sometimes go strange ways to strange places, and view strange sights when they get there. Therefore the following notes are submitted as evidence that the author is not always so bubble-headed a romancer as he must appear.

## 1
### Of London Bridge

It must be remembered that Old London Bridge, which was not demolished until 1832 after the completion of New London Bridge a year earlier, stood about sixty yards to the east of the present one. Nearly all the houses were pulled down during 1757 and 1758; Knight's *London* (Charles Knight & Co., 6 vols., 1841) says that a few remained as late as 1760. Details of the bridge's history and appearance, including a drawing of it as it looked just before the houses were pulled down, will be found in Knight; and also in H. B. Wheatley's *London, Past and Present* (John Murray, 3 vols., 1891). Charles Pennant's *London*, which first appeared in 1790 and was reissued in the heavily illustrated three-volume edition of 1814, contains Pennant's eyewitness description:

"I well remember the street on London Bridge, narrow, darksome, and dangerous to passengers from the multitude of carriages; frequent arches of strong timber crossed the street from the tops of the houses, to keep them together and from falling into the river."

Next, with regard to the idea on which the novel was based:

"Nothing could preserve the rest of the inmates, who grew deaf to the noise of the falling water, the clamour of watermen, or the frequent shrieks of drowning wretches. Most of the houses were tenanted by pin or needle makers, and economical ladies were wont to drive from the St. James's end of the town to make cheap purchases."

## 2
### Of St. James's District

No reader need make incredulous noises at finding a large artificial pond—120 feet in diameter, to be exact—in the middle of St. James's Square. Volume XXIX of the London County Council's admirable 'Survey of London,' *The Parish of St. James Westminster* (Athlone Press, University of London, 1960), tells us that the basin was constructed in 1726 and was not filled in until 1818. Volumes XXIX and XXX, edited by F. H. W. Sheppard, make fascinating reading for anyone who wants to know who lived in what house, and exactly how the whole district looked.

Between 1759 and 1761 William Pitt the elder rented a house on the north side, not far from the one ascribed to a fictitious Sir Mortimer Ralston; but in 1757, according to this 'Survey,' the elder Pitt inhabited a house which is described as unidentified, and so I have taken the liberty of putting him on the west side.

3
*Of Bagnios*

The bagnio, in addition to being bath and medical centre, also formed a unique if disreputable feature of eighteenth-century life. Plate number five of William Hogarth's *Marriage à la Mode* (1745) depicts the murder of the husband by his wife's lover after he has surprised them at a bagnio. In Henry Fielding's novel *Amelia* (1751) the improvident hero, Billy Booth, is lured into an affair with the tempestuous Miss Matthews while they are imprisoned at Newgate; the governor of the prison genially offers them both the use of Miss Matthews's private room for half a guinea a night, and points out that any good bagnio would have cost as much.

London's only Turkish bath at the Hummums—whose name, according to Wheatley, is derived from the Arabic word 'hammam,' or bath—seems to have been held in somewhat higher esteem. It is true that profligate Parson Ford, a riotous figure in Hogarth's *Modern Midnight Conversation*, died at the Hummums and his ghost was said to have appeared twice to a waiter. But many years afterwards so stern a moralist as Dr. Johnson had no hesitation in telling Boswell (*Life of Johnson*. May 12, 1778) of his late wife's curiosity about the ghost, and how she had gone there to ask questions. On the other hand, after Johnson's statement, "My wife went to the Hummums," Boswell makes him add as though in quick explanation: "It is a place where they get themselves cupped."

With one exception, no inn or tavern mentioned in the novel is imaginary. A painting now at the London Museum shows the 'Golden Cross' as it was in 1757. A. E. Richardson's *Georgian England: a Survey of Trades, Industries, and Art from 1700 to 1820* (London: Batsford, 1931) illustrates innkeepers' habit of giving names rather than numbers to rooms or sets of rooms. The 'Rainbow,' in Fleet Street, was established as a coffee-house in 1657 and is later mentioned as such in Number Sixteen of the *Spectator;* it afterwards became a tavern and survives (or did survive) as a pub-restaurant to the present day.

4
## Of the Waxwork—and the 'Gothic'

Mrs. Salmon's Waxwork, between the Temple gates, very much belonged to real life. It was already famous when Boswell visited it on July 4, 1763, as we find from *Boswell's London Journal, 1762–1763,* edited by Professor Pottle (New York: McGraw-Hill; London: William Heinemann, 1950). It had a very long life of popularity. As late as 1785 a lyrical admirer extolled it thus:

> Tall Polygars,
> Dwarf Zanzibars,
> Mahomed's Tomb, Killarney's Lake, the Fane of Ammon,
> With all thy Kings and Queens, ingenious Mrs. Salmon!

And Pennant reproduces a drawing which shows the crazily sloping floors, the many-paned windows, the wooden salmon over the door, the modern brick buildings on either side. Presumably its star dimmed when Madame Tussaud's exhibits were first displayed at the Lyceum in 1802. Since this cannot be proved, and since so little is known of the lady, perhaps apology should be made for giving her a pair of fictitious nieces.

But no apology need be made for the 'Gothic' grotto at Mrs. Salmon's. It is customary to attribute popular interest in the Gothic to Horace Walpole, with whom we shall deal in a moment. In 1757 the elegant Horace had not yet finished bedizening his house at Strawberry Hill with so much Gothic gim-crackery, and published his comically horrendous novel, *The Castle of Otranto,* only in 1764. But the craze for the Gothic, as for the Chinese, long antedated either time. Evidence of this will be found in a very valuable work, John Gloag's *Georgian Grace; a Social History of Design From 1660–1830* (London: A. & C. Black, 1960). What Horace Walpole did was to turn the Gothic into the grotesque, and fill it with spooks whose descendants cause mirth or profanity in horror films even yet.

Still, the mischief he did in this respect is a small price to pay for *The Letters of Horace Walpole, Fourth Earl of Orford,* edited by Peter Cunningham (Edinburgh: John Grant, 9 vols., 1906), a whole pageant from the first letter in 1735 to the last in 1797.

"Fiddles sing all through then," wrote Thackeray in a famous passage: "wax-lights, fine dresses, fine jokes, fine equipages glitter and sparkle there; never was such a brilliant, jigging, smirking Vanity Fair as that through which he leads us."

Jane Austen ridiculed the spooks he inspired. We ourselves dislike him as a person, and enjoy his 'dandified treble' as little as Thackeray or Macaulay did; we can't trust him an inch when he is being malicious or improving on a good story. But few

source materials are so important as this incessant round of high
life throughout two reigns.

5

*Of Ranelagh and Masquerades*

Ranelagh Pleasure Gardens have high testimonials. Goldsmith
and Johnson admired the place; Boswell felt a 'glow of delight'
on entering; Walpole, though not enthusiastic when he saw its
opening in 1742, was soon won over; Fielding thought a masquerade there might be aphrodisiac enough to get a heroine seduced
in a novel, unless the author intervened to prevent it.

Rotunda and gardens were at their best in 1757. Knight quotes
a long description of the rotunda, and reproduces a picture showing rotunda and gardens—including the canal and the pavilion
—from the south side. Though they were closed at the end of the
century because the Company went on spending too much money,
Horwood's *Plan of London, 1792–1899* gives a map of the gardens
and the surrounding streets. In the matter of near-nudity in fine
ladies at masquerades, however, we must be very careful.

The suggestion appears often enough in satires. Most such satires,
when traced back, appear to stem from an escapade of the notorious Elizabeth Chudleigh, who in 1749 appeared at a masquerade in the character of Iphigenia dressed for the sacrifice.

"Miss Chudleigh was Iphigenia," wrote Walpole to Sir Horace
Mann on May 3, "but so naked you would have taken her for
Andromeda."

The trouble is that this masquerade was not held at Ranelagh;
it was held at the Opera House in the Haymarket for the edifica-
tion of the King. Mrs. Montagu, writing to her sister of the same
affair, agrees that "Miss Chudleigh was so naked the high-priest
might easily have inspected the entrails of the victim," but adds:
"The Maids of Honour (not of maids the strictest) were so
offended they would not speak to her."

On the other hand, we must not go too far in the opposite
direction. Portraits of the most virtuous ladies, in mid-eighteenth
century, show them wearing gowns which today would be more
suited to a strip-tease show than to the Court of St. James's.
Let us therefore, like honest historians, accept a pleasant compro-
mise.

6

*Of Rogues and Crime*

Anyone fascinated by this subject is recommended to approach
it by way of Fielding's novels *Jonathan Wild* and *Amelia*. The
first treats satirically of a nightmare half-world and is unsparing
in outspokenness; in the second, even apart from its unsavoury

crew at Newgate, there are few characters who would have been permitted within miles of a Victorian drawing-room.

The reader may be tempted to wonder how far Fielding's love of satire has carried him into exaggeration, both before and after he himself became a magistrate. Granting the grotesquerie of the crooks, could all those who dealt with them—magistrates, prison officials, thief-takers, constables, watchmen—have been equally careless or crooked?

If the student wonders at this, he should next dip into *The Complete Newgate Calendar,* edited by J. L. Rayner and G. T. Crook (London; The Navarre Society, 5 vols., 1926), and read straight through E. Eden Hooper's *History of Newgate and the Old Bailey* (London: Underwood Press, 1935). Supplementary evidence will be found in Alfred Marks's *Tyburn Tree, Its History and Annals* (London: Brown, Langham & Co., 1912) and Horace Blackley's *The Hangmen of England* (London: Chapman and Hall, 1929). It will be seen that Fielding exaggerated little and invented nothing.

In the same way, the paintings and engravings of Hogarth should be examined together with Miss Marjorie Bowen's comprehensive biography, *William Hogarth, the Cockney's Mirror* (London: Methuen, 1936). It may be instructive to compare Hogarth and Fielding as they show themselves in their work and picture the age too.

They had much in common, as Miss Elizabeth Jenkins has pointed out with her brilliant critical study of Fielding. And this is the more striking because at first there seems little temperamental kinship between cantankerous Will Hogarth, the industrious apprentice who did well for himself, and easy-going Harry Fielding, the gentleman's son who was always broke or in trouble.

Hogarth's moral judgements are ferocious. It is difficult not to suspect that secretly he was as drawn towards crime and vice as he was bored by copy-book virtue. His series of *Industry and Idleness* (1747) makes the triumph of the industrious apprentice either lifeless or more dreary than the end of the idle apprentice on the gallows. But he would never have conceded this; perhaps he never guessed it. He paints a frieze of inhumanity and seems almost to gloat. Nor shall we find answers by calling this a typical attitude of his time. *Boswell's London Journal,* in which the the greatest of biographers shows himself also the greatest of diarists, at least once brings a man of decent feelings unexpectedly face to face with what the law means. When curiosity drives Boswell to watch a hanging, he is so horrified that it shakes his nerves and haunts the diary for days afterwards.

Fielding, like Boswell in more than the fact that both were literary artists, was very tolerant of any transgressions he could understand. There was too much in him of Tom Jones and Billy Booth; he knew a young man addicted to drinking, wenching, and extravagance does not necessarily end in a halter at Tyburn. But he could endure the prettification of rogues, as in Gay's *The Beggar's Opera,* even less than he could endure the idealization of the self-righteous prude, as in Richardson's *Pamela.* Above all he hated cruelty and meanness. When he ceased to be young Harry Fielding and became sober Justice Fielding of Bow Street—his health collapsing, his own nerves in rags, with little apparent solution except by tightening the laws—we have the apparent paradox that he could be as merciless as Hogarth sounded. It explains the attitude of his half-brother, and brings us to a final note.

## 7
### The Real-Life Characters

Mr. (later Sir John) Fielding, perhaps the most famous of all Metropolitan magistrates, presided at Bow Street from 1754, the year of his brother's death, until 1779. He took over the plain-clothes detective-force suggested by Henry Fielding and known as 'Mr. Fielding's People' until they became still more widely celebrated as the Bow Street Runners.

It is unnecessary to go into detail here. He has been the subject of a full-length biography, R. Leslie-Melville's *The Life and Work of Sir John Fielding* (L. Williams, 1934), which stamps him under the familiar name of 'the blind beak.' There is a long account of him in Gilbert Armitage's *History of the Bow Street Runners* (Wishart & Co., 1932), and his career is dealt with in Douglas G. Browne's definitive work, *The Rise of Scotland Yard* (Harrap, 1956). Mr. Browne establishes from the Westminster rent-rolls the fact that the house used by Henry, and taken over by John, was on the east side of the street.

Let me hope that no damage has been done to the memory of the Rev. Laurence Sterne, author of *Tristram Shandy* (first part, 1760) and *A Sentimental Journey through France and Italy* (1768). If he proved irresistible as a comic character, it is believed he is made to do or say nothing here which in fact he might not have said or done in life. Percy Fitzgerald's biography, *Laurence Sterne* (The Grolier Society, new ed., 2 vols., 1896), shall bear witness to all this.

Mr. Sterne's attitude towards women was tolerably uninhibited, as he himself was the first to testify. He did belong to the society called 'The Demoniacs'; he did visit London in 1757, pursuing some unstated amorous adventure; his wife, born Elizabeth Lumley, did go out of her mind in 1758; his language may be reconstructed from his books and letters, and one anecdote is quoted in his own words; finally, when he visited London again in 1760, it is gratifying to find him a frequent visitor to Ranelagh. Let us praise his memory; the 'sporting' parson of the eighteenth century did not behave altogether like a vicar in the works of Anthony Trollope, and our lives are made all the brighter thereby. On the other hand, if some admirer of Mr. Sterne should feel he has been done an injustice, no doubt I shall be reminded that in 1760 a fraudulent imitation of *Tristram Shandy*, third part, was published by a miscreant named John Carr.

# FINE MYSTERY AND SUSPENSE
# TITLES FROM CARROLL & GRAF

| | | |
|---|---|---|
| ☐ | Bentley, E.C./TRENT'S OWN CASE | $3.95 |
| ☐ | Blake, Nicholas/A TANGLED WEB | $3.50 |
| ☐ | Boucher, Anthony/THE CASE OF THE BAKER STREET IRREGULARS | $3.95 |
| ☐ | Boucher, Anthony (ed.)/FOUR AND TWENTY BLOODHOUNDS | $3.95 |
| ☐ | Brand, Christianna/DEATH IN HIGH HEELS | $3.95 |
| ☐ | Brand, Christianna/FOG OF DOUBT | $3.50 |
| ☐ | Brand, Christianna/TOUR DE FORCE | $3.95 |
| ☐ | Brown, Fredric/THE LENIENT BEAST | $3.50 |
| ☐ | Brown, Fredric/MURDER CAN BE FUN | $3.95 |
| ☐ | Brown, Fredric/THE SCREAMING MIMI | $3.50 |
| ☐ | Buchan, John/JOHN MACNAB | $3.95 |
| ☐ | Buchan, John/WITCH WOOD | $3.95 |
| ☐ | Burnett, W.R./LITTLE CAESAR | $3.50 |
| ☐ | Butler, Gerald/KISS THE BLOOD OFF MY HANDS | $3.95 |
| ☐ | Carr, John Dickson/THE BRIDE OF NEWGATE | $3.95 |
| ☐ | Carr, John Dickson/CAPTAIN CUT-THROAT | $3.95 |
| ☐ | Carr, John Dickson/DARK OF THE MOON | $3.50 |
| ☐ | Carr, John Dickson/DEADLY HALL | $3.95 |
| ☐ | Carr, John Dickson/DEMONIACS | $3.95 |
| ☐ | Carr, John Dickson/THE DEVIL IN VELVET | $3.95 |
| ☐ | Carr, John Dickson/THE EMPEROR'S SNUFF-BOX | $3.50 |
| ☐ | Carr, John Dickson/IN SPITE OF THUNDER | $3.50 |
| ☐ | Carr, John Dickson/LOST GALLOWS | $3.50 |
| ☐ | Carr, John Dickson/MOST SECRET | $3.95 |
| ☐ | Carr, John Dickson/NINE WRONG ANSWERS | $3.50 |
| ☐ | Carr, John Dickson/PAPA LA-BAS | $3.95 |
| ☐ | Chesterton, G. K./THE MAN WHO KNEW TOO MUCH | $3.95 |
| ☐ | Chesterton, G. K./THE MAN WHO WAS THURSDAY | $3.50 |
| ☐ | Crofts, Freeman Wills/THE CASK | $3.59 |
| ☐ | Coles, Manning/NO ENTRY | $3.50 |
| ☐ | Collins, Michael/WALK A BLACK WIND | $3.95 |
| ☐ | Dickson, Carter/THE CURSE OF THE BRONZE LAMP | $3.50 |
| ☐ | Disch, Thomas M & Sladek, John/BLACK ALICE | $3.95 |
| ☐ | Du Maurier, Daphne/THE SCAPEGOAT | $4.50 |
| ☐ | Eberhart, Mignon/MESSAGE FROM HONG KONG | $3.50 |
| ☐ | Eastlake, William/CASTLE KEEP | $3.50 |
| ☐ | Fennelly, Tony/THE CLOSET HANGING | $3.50 |
| ☐ | Fennelly, Tony/THE GLORY HOLE MURDERS | $2.95 |

| | | |
|---|---|---|
| ☐ Gilbert, Michael/THE DOORS OPEN | | $3.95 |
| ☐ Gilbert, Michael/GAME WITHOUT RULES | | $3.95 |
| ☐ Gilbert, Michael/THE 92nd TIGER | | $3.95 |
| ☐ Gilbert, Michael/OVERDRIVE | | $3.95 |
| ☐ Graham, Winston/MARNIE | | $3.95 |
| ☐ Greeley, Andrew/DEATH IN APRIL | | $3.95 |
| ☐ Hughes, Dorothy B./THE FALLEN SPARROW | | $3.50 |
| ☐ Hughes, Dorothy B./IN A LONELY PLACE | | $3.50 |
| ☐ Hughes, Dorothy B./RIDE THE PINK HORSE | | $3.95 |
| ☐ Hornung, E. W./THE AMATEUR CRACKSMAN | | $3.95 |
| ☐ Kitchin, C. H. B./DEATH OF HIS UNCLE | | $3.95 |
| ☐ Kitchin, C. H. B./DEATH OF MY AUNT | | $3.50 |
| ☐ MacDonald, John D./TWO | | $2.50 |
| ☐ Mason, A.E.W./AT THE VILLA ROSE | | $3.50 |
| ☐ Mason, A.E.W./THE HOUSE OF THE ARROW | | $3.50 |
| ☐ Priestley, J.B./SALT IS LEAVING | | $3.95 |
| ☐ Queen, Ellery/THE FINISHING STROKE | | $3.95 |
| ☐ Rogers, Joel T./THE RED RIGHT HAND | | $3.50 |
| ☐ 'Sapper'/BULLDOG DRUMMOND | | $3.50 |
| ☐ Symons, Julian/BOGUE'S FORTUNE | | $3.95 |
| ☐ Symons, Julian/THE BROKEN PENNY | | $3.95 |
| ☐ Wainwright, John/ALL ON A SUMMER'S DAY | | $3.50 |
| ☐ Wallace, Edgar/THE FOUR JUST MEN | | $2.95 |
| ☐ Waugh, Hillary/SLEEP LONG, MY LOVE | | $3.95 |
| ☐ Willeford, Charles/THE WOMAN CHASER | | $3.95 |

Available from fine bookstores everywhere or use this coupon for ordering.

Carroll & Graf Publishers, Inc., 260 Fifth Avenue, N.Y., N.Y. 10001

Please send me the books I have checked above. I am enclosing $_____ (please add $1.00 per title to cover postage and handling.) Send check or money order—no cash or C.O.D.'s please. N.Y. residents please add 8¼% sales tax.

Mr/Mrs/Ms _____

Address _____

City _____ State/Zip _____

Please allow four to six weeks for delivery.